ALONE ALONG WRITERS' ROADS

ALONE ALONG WRITERS' ROADS

Tom Wood

Book design by Launch My Book, Inc. (www.launchmybook.com) with cover design by Erika Alyana Duran (easduran.myportfolio.com) and interior design by Booknook.biz.

Published in the United States of America by Willow Days Press.

ISBN 979-8-9894397-0-6 (Paperback)
ISBN 979-8-9894397-1-3 (Ebook)
ISBN 979-8-9894397-2-0 (Hard cover)

*To my siblings and friends who provided all that was
wanted during the six years it took to complete my novel;*

*and to my parents, Thomas and Bernice,
and my brother, Phillip,
who sent their guidance from above.*

Contents

Acknowledgments

I began writing this novel in 2017, the year that Catherine left. I planned to finish it in less than a year but learned that, like life itself, events have ways of changing certain plans. One such event, a stage four colon and liver cancer diagnosis, detoured my writing schedule until after the surgeries and chemotherapies stopped having priority. Other delays followed as my story's narrative and characters came alive and required changes, sometimes near complete rewrites. Everything and everyone that arrived later required more edits to accommodate them in the plot and all were exciting for me to allow happen.

My love of stories began before I reached grade school listening to my mother's tales of growing up Irish on Chicago's Southside and to my dad reading the classics or reciting his favorite poems or remembering persons and places from his youth while my siblings and I gathered close to hear his every word. While I was too young to go to grade school, my older sister, Veronica, taught me to love books hearing her read everything from Black Beauty to the Bobbsey Twins stories. When I was old enough to enjoy my own sophisticated choice of novels such as Henry Fielding's, Tom Jones, I discovered that books could provide close friendships.

When illness left me unable to address my daily care needs, these were then provided by my sisters Veronica Wlcek, Mary Palma, and Madonna Fiorelli; and by my brothers, Joseph and Frederick Wood. Each brought me care and comfort, leaving their own homes from Missouri, Georgia, Arizona, and nearby Woodridge, Illinois for this purpose.

My brother, Doctor Joseph Wood personally arranged for me to receive the absolute best surgical and medical care administered by my oncologist Dr. Alex Hantel at the Edwards Hospital Cancer Center in Naperville, Illinois.

To all the writers who encouraged me, particularly Charlene Baumbich, as well as my first readers like my siblings and Sherri Miller and others at RedAdept Editing, I appreciate how much you supported and guided me through this writing journey. I especially want to acknowledge the expert guidance that Joel and Laura Pitney and Sayde Walker gave when I finally got to the finish line.

Alone

by Sara Teasdale

I am alone, in spite of love, in spite of all I take and give—
In spite of all your tenderness, Sometimes I am not glad to live.

Part 1

1

Davis Quigley

THIS LATE IN THE AFTERNOON while turning onto Lockwood Avenue, Davis was surprised to find a parking space in front of his apartment building. After stopping on his way home to enjoy a farewell beer with two of his fellow graduating seniors at Loyola he'd been stuck in heavy traffic. Such good luck reminded him of the old Swedish proverb, *"Luck never gives; it only lends."*

"Looks like someone ought to buy a lottery ticket," Georgia Cobb teased. She met Davis as he went up the stairs to where she stood after delivering mail into the mailboxes on the porch.

"No one gets such a good parking space unless something even better is going on in their life."

Davis smiled as he passed by her. "Okay, Miss post office, I hope you brought me something good that'll make up for my struggle through that traffic on Lake Shore Drive."

"All you got today is something from that college you go to." She sighed. "Maybe your 'something good' is waiting till a bit later tonight, yes?" She aimed a naughty smile in his direction.

Entering his small first-floor apartment, Davis spotted Ellie coming out of the bathroom. She appeared to have just finished showering, probably after completing her three-mile daily run. She was wearing only her short white waffle-weave kimono and seemed surprised to see him. After they greeted each other and kissed, Ellie glanced over where she noticed that the mail he dropped on the nearby kitchen table was from Loyola.

"Did you get the word yet?" she asked.

Davis shrugged. "No news might be good news." Still, her question prompted him to rip open the letter. Ellie moved and stood alongside him, hugging his waist as she pushed him to read the letter aloud.

Davis scanned the letter's contents until he saw the part that would interest him and his fiancée the most. He stopped at the last sentence in the final paragraph. *You are therefore accepted to attend Loyola Law School!* He reread the sentence slowly, quietly emphasizing the words *law* and *school*. Then he looked down at Ellie and gave a loud cheer just as she joined with her own joyful cry.

"We made it, baby!" Davis announced to her and anyone else in Chicago who might be within a city block. "WE MADE IT!"

Ellie laughed and then led an imaginary parade through the kitchen and into the front room and back. Clearly, hearing her lover use the pronoun "we" meant as much to her as anything else he'd said. She was singing a marching song she'd just made up. "We made it, baby," her happy lyrics declared. "We actually, finally, and for sure now and forever have made it… baby!"

Law school was opening a door to their future and Davis was proud of his efforts that earned the key that would unlock that potential. Sharing this moment with Ellie made his love for her seem even more special. What troubled him was a curious suspicion that his choice for becoming a lawyer was lacking something? Why? Wasn't it everything he thought about and strived for even before he met and fell in love with Ellie? Why was her joy prompting this unexpected feeling of envy inside of him? Quick as those uninvited thoughts arrived Davis dismissed them to celebrate their news.

"We made it, baby," he repeated the words in her song while joining her parade "We made it!"

Seconds later, the kitchen, front room, and bathroom were deserted. The parade had proceeded into the bedroom while the letter from Loyola sat on the table, and a short white waffle-weave kimono lay on the floor.

2

Brady Harvey

ABIGAIL KUHN WATCHED AS her court-appointed client was escorted into the office that Connecticut Valley Mental Hospital used when interviewing people awaiting release from confinement. When he sat down across from her, she observed how different he appeared from what she'd expected after reading the Stamford Superior Court's decision to consider his application to be released to home confinement. Except for his hospital-supplied attire, his demeanor, posture, and appearance were that of a young successful businessman. Still, his mere presence brought uneasy feelings inside her.

After greeting him and his attorney, Lester Worth, Abigail introduced herself and had Brady state his name and date of birth for the record.

"Brady Harvey," he replied. "My date of birth is Christmas Day, 1987."

She looked at his attorney and asked him to identify his law firm and his connection with Brady Harvey.

"Um, thank you, Miss, um, Kuhn. My firm, Worth and Worth, has been selected by the prisoner's mother, Mrs. Ruth Harvey, who lives on Conyers Farm Drive in Greenwich, to file a petition for release to home confinement so Brady can live in one of their family owned condominiums on Weaver Street in Greenwich Oaks."

Abigail recognized both addresses as desirable neighborhoods. She commented on that and asked the prisoner why he preferred to live in the smaller condominium rather than the more luxurious home on Conyers Drive if the court approved his petition for release.

He remained quiet and several seconds passed before his attorney spoke. "Brady has been very busy while in custody, completing college courses that met with the court's approval. He has also been engaged in becoming a novelist, which seems to be better pursued where he could work alone in the less-busy location in Greenwich Oaks."

"Please tell me more." Abigail looked past the attorney and into the eyes of the prisoner. "These efforts speak more directly to the interests the court has regarding the question of potential for recidivism."

Once again, only silence followed until the lawyer spoke. "Brady's interest while in custody focused on AI, you know, Artificial Intelligence. In fact, the novel that he's completing is titled *Algorithms and Blues*."

"I find that very interesting and most certainly an efficient use of the appellant's time," Abigail said. "Right now, though, I believe that this is the proper moment to discuss my role in the decision the court will make regarding your petition. If it's approved and you're released to home confinement, you will continue to be monitored by the Bureau of Prisons and required to follow the rules and limitations they determine necessary. Any violation must be reported to them by each of the persons they assign to assist in their efforts, such as myself."

"The prisoner understands that, Miss, um… and expresses no objection." Lester Worth seemed unsure whether to address the psychologist as Doctor.

Abigail added one more point that she hoped would be thoroughly understood by everyone. "I am a forensic psychologist, not a clinical psychologist, one who is generally an advocate for his or her client. The court is the client for the forensic psychologist, and my report is provided directly and exclusively to them. You will not be provided with the reasons I find appropriate for the court to use in making their decision. I hope that's understood from the very beginning."

A fifteen-minute break followed. The prisoner and his attorney conferred in private while Abigail reviewed her file listing the criminal offenses that resulted in Brady's various incarcerations since graduating from high school. His rap sheet rivaled those of older criminals.

The psychologist quickly read through the more recent activities ending with a summary of the incidents that resulted in Brady being sent to CVH for mental health care. It included charges of harassment, suspicion of pushing someone off a moving train, and causing an accidental vehicle death in Massachusetts, along with assorted other disturbance of the peace convictions. The statement from a Greenwich police detective that was made during the most recent court hearing for Brady's appeal for release to home confinement disturbed her the most. He testified that in his opinion anyone standing in Brady's way from getting whatever he wanted would be in mortal danger. *He is simply the most intelligent single minded person whom I have ever interrogated. He shows no ability to reason or understand or tolerate anyone else's' wishes.*

After they returned together, Abigail said she had reviewed the information provided by various police agencies along with reports of Brady's conduct while confined. For her recommendation to the superior court to approve his petition for release she would need answers about certain episodes that had caused Brady to require further limitations during home confinement.

"As you know, you have been diagnosed with bipolar disorder and you must receive certain medications on a prescribed schedule. While here at Connecticut Valley Hospital, you take these medications after they're given to you by a nurse, who records each dose. If the court approves your petition for home confinement, that routine will continue so that we're assured of your compliance."

Brady was surprised by that news as his attorney hadn't mentioned it when preparing the petition. "You said it will continue? Are you saying I have to come back here four times a day to take the medicine, like I do now?"

The psychologist looked at Brady's lawyer. "Didn't you go over these instructions with your client when you prepared your petition for the court?"

The attorney nodded but said that perhaps he needed to review those stipulations in more detail with his client.

Abigail Kuhn frowned. "Mr. Harvey has been diagnosed with bipolar disorder and is being treated with various types and doses of medications and mood stabilizers to control episodes of mania. These medications must be taken exactly as directed. Otherwise, there are withdrawal effects, and the symptoms may worsen or return. Mr. Harvey must continue to receive cognitive behavioral therapy to identify unhealthy negative beliefs and behaviors and replace them with positive ones. He must maintain a healthy lifestyle by getting enough sleep, eating a healthy diet, and being physically active." She stopped reading from her file and asked if Brady understood everything.

Lester Worth responded that Brady's mother had already arranged for a local therapist to meet with him regularly.

"A local therapist?"

Lester opened his file, apparently looking for the name of the therapist. "She is, um, Beverly Beckett Conforti, and her office is within walking distance of where Brady will be living while on home confinement."

3

Davis and Ellie

G RADUATION WAS SOMETHING I'LL remember for a lifetime," Davis told Ellie as they walked along Michigan Avenue and passed by the famous outdoor sculpture known officially as the Cloud Gate but commonly referred to as the Bean. "Learning that I've been accepted to law school makes it even better." They stopped and kissed. "What makes it most special is that it happened the day after the night when the love of my life said yes. Four tough but fun years of college are behind me now!"

"Whoa, there, Mr. Sunshine," Ellie looked up and replied. "Those were all the preliminary years. Next come the more difficult years of law school."

Davis smiled, accustomed to Ellie's wiser comments. "You know something, Sweet Pea?" He stole a quick look at her. "This is the last time we'll visit Millennium Park as free-spirited singles. Maybe we should take pictures of our reflections in the Bean now while we still have some time left before…"

Ellie put her index finger across his lips. "Hush now."

Something in her expression told Davis that her thoughts were somewhere else.

After crossing Randolph Street, he noticed that the traffic on Michigan Avenue was particularly busy and loud. Car horns blared as pedestrians dodged autos driven by anxious, impatient motorists. When they got to Monroe Street, the light changed, and they were almost trampled from behind after stopping abruptly at the curb. Across the wide street from the Cloud Gate sculpture, they could see much of what was reflected in the Bean, including the crowd around it, the surrounding green space, and much of the Chicago skyline.

"You'd think these people behind us are all going to the same place." Ellie laughed, holding tightly to his hand.

"I'm not sure that really matters," Davis said. "I think most are heading to the Bean, just like we are. Pretty clear, though, that they're determined not to be the last ones there."

A small boy pushed in front of Ellie causing her to slip off the curb as she reached for him. Just then a motorcycle sped between the cars and the curb trying to make a sharp right turn and beat the light. Davis lunged forwards trying to pull Ellie back to him. He reached for her hand as she twisted to find her balance. The motorcycle struck her, knocking her into oncoming traffic, where she and the motorcycle rider were then run over by a Toyota Corolla.

Davis rushed to where Ellie lay unmoving in a pool of blood. Turning back to the sidewalk where horrified onlookers stood locked in place, he screamed for someone to call an ambulance. "SHE'S BLEEDING!… HURRY!" He crouched next to her head but resisted touching her, not knowing how to stop the blood flowing out of her. He lowered close enough for her to hear him as he begged her to hold on while promising that help was coming. Her eyes remained closed, but she struggled to speak. Just as medical help arrived, Davis could barely hear Ellie's words.

"I... just found out..."

"TWO KILLED ON MICHIGAN BOULEVRD was the headline in the newspaper and on the breaking news on television and radio. News teams reported that a young woman had lost her life while trying to shield a small boy when a motorcyclist ran into a crowd of people waiting to cross the street. The motorcycle sent the young woman into the path of a passing Toyota. The injuries proved fatal for both the young woman and the motorcycle rider.

His best friend, Cooper Logan, came and stayed with Davis overnight. That evening and again the next morning, Davis' parents came to comfort their grieving son along with some friends and classmates. When Buffy, Ellie's younger sister, came by she was able to convince Davis to come away from the apartment where he had been living with Ellie and go for a walk outside.

"Why?" It was the same word that he'd repeated at the hospital when told that Ellie had died from her injuries. "Why?" he demanded over and over, unable to accept that there was any reason for the accident that took Ellie away. That was the only word he spoke while he and Buffy walked together. After reaching the corner a few blocks from his apartment, Davis began remembering more of the accident scene before the ambulance arrived.

"She was barely aware that I was right there next to her," he softly whispered.

Buffy wept and rested her head on Davis's chest and asked him what, if anything, her sister had said to him before the medics put Ellie into the ambulance. "When you called and told us about the accident, you mentioned that she said something, but you were still in shock and couldn't remember what it was."

Davis pulled back. "There was so much noise around us, and her voice was very weak. Her eyes were closed, so I'm not even sure she knew it was me."

Buffy sobbed as Davis revisited those last few moments of Ellie's life. "I think I might know what she wanted you to hear," she said.

"You think you know? You couldn't know. You weren't anywhere near us yesterday!"

Buffy stopped crying only to embrace Davis again. "I was with Ellie last week when she read the results on the pregnancy test strip."

Davis stopped and looked into Buffy's eyes, stunned. "Pregnancy… test strip?"

4

Career change

WHILE DAVIS WAS IN HIS THIRD year at Loyola, before he met Ellie, he landed a part-time job at WGN Radio, writing headlines and brief news reports. The job helped pay for his tuition, and since he worked only on weekends, from 6 a.m. to 3 p.m., he was free to spend Monday through Friday attending classes, studying, dating, and being involved in a social life. He found it satisfying when pieces he'd written were read on air.

He explained to friends that while the job would never be as lucrative as the legal career he was preparing for, it provided just enough income to meet his needs. "And it's better than stocking shelves at a grocery store," he always added.

After he fell in love with Ellie, their plans included getting him through law school and later practicing law, a career they expected to provide them with what they wanted while raising a family.

"Two boys and two girls," Ellie suggested, was the perfect number and combination. "We'll raise them in a nice home in a nearby suburb and send them off to college, when afterwards they might get married and do the same for their kids and our progeny."

The joy and hope he'd felt then had turned closer to despair as he remembered the last words she'd tried to tell him, words he understood only after her sister told him about the pregnancy test.

Following the accident, he struggled to find any sense in becoming a lawyer. No one would ever replace her or become the mother of his children quite like she would have done. No one else would help make any of those special dreams they shared come true. He worried about what he would do in life. Laws and lawyers would always be needed, but they weren't the solutions that he'd come to believe. *We already have laws.* He often considered that when alone in thought. The motorcyclist had broken the law by speeding and running through a red light. If the driver survived, he would surely have been held responsible. But even that outcome wasn't as certain as Davis's. He would never have Ellie in his life again.

"Perhaps we should look at the reason the man on the Harley decided to speed and gamble on his safety and that of others by running the stoplight," Davis told the dean of admissions at Loyola when explaining that he was delaying his entrance to law school. "It could provide some hope that such choices won't be made as often in the future."

"Could be" came the reply. "Perhaps you might find what you're looking for by studying for a degree in psychology."

The deferment request was subsequently approved after the dean considered the recent death of Davis's fiancée and its effect on him just as the starting date for law school approached.

When his boss at the radio station learned of Davis's decision not to attend law school, he offered him full-time work doing what Davis had previously been assigned for on weekends. Davis suspected that a new career choice was unwrapping and would likely reveal itself soon.

* * *

After working less than a few years in his job as a news writer for the evening radio broadcasts, Davis experienced a sense of self-betrayal. He believed he had more to offer than simply taking information from street reporters and turning it into news content to be read on air. His initial excitement about the work dimmed even more as time passed. He was at the same desk where he'd started after graduating from Loyola. The requirement to write only who, what, where, and when, made him suspect that those efforts resulted in only half truths. Worse, the work became so robotic that it made him believe that he was wasting his life, an awareness that frequently nagged at him.

The thoughts of his own self-betrayal reminded him of other times when he'd chosen to follow his gut in making life-altering decisions. While his father never voiced his disappointment that his son had put law school on hold following the accident, Davis saw it in his eyes. His education stalled after he had earned a bachelor's degree in liberal arts from Loyola University. There he had learned from his Jesuit professors that thinking was a synonym for living just as concluding was one for dying.

"Knowledge lives in a circle, constantly considering where it has been before moving forward, seeking its needs in pursuit of an unknown ultimate. The only straight lines are the ones that divide the circle into equal sections but with a lesser objective," Professor Sweeney emphasized in psychology classes. The accident effectively lowered Davis's enthusiasm to study for a degree that would employ a narrow, limited focus on a law's *definition* while falling short of accomplishing its *purpose*.

During his final two years at Loyola, Davis was happy to have a part-time job as an intern at WGN Radio. Not the pay though which was hardly an inducement to make the work a career, but he liked everything else about it—the constant excitement, accompanying street reporters on assignment, and learning from the news directors. Most of the people Davis worked with were veteran newsmen who taught him to dig beyond the headlines. The reasons people went to jail made for interesting copy just as much as their actual crimes.

"My mentor is Syd Esmaker," he told Cooper Logan one night while he and his friend were taking a break from their Wednesday chess game where they regularly competed against either themselves or other members at the Suburban Federation of Chess Club. "Sydney has been a city reporter for forty years now."

"Seems like he must have found something pretty life-ful-filling to be doing the same job since day one," Cooper said as they returned to the chess tables.

"Sydney loved everything about being involved with report-ing news," Davis replied. "He loved WGN first and foremost and everyone who worked there. He covered city hall and any news happening throughout the neighborhoods in each of the fifty wards. And it was ward politics that gave him his reputation for capturing real news from actual sources who otherwise trusted no one in the news business," Davis said. "Opinions are cheap," he once told me. 'They're a dime a dozen. People often think they're right about something because of their opinions. But opinions are the biggest enemy of the reporter if he happens to have any of them."

"Why?" Cooper asked urging Davis to finish placing his pieces on the chess board as he set the timer.

"Syd said that was because when you have enough knowledge to form an opinion, you decide that the search is finally over," Davis answered. "No need to hunt for truth if you already know what the truth is. And a reporter who stops hunting for truth is useless. His objectivity has been replaced with his bias. He's no longer writing news but just telling what he knows, at least what he thinks he knows. When he writes a sentence, he uses periods where commas are the more appropriate punctuation."

After losing Ellie Davis began the full-time job offer with WGN. That boosted his ambition to be a writer. He could try news writing for a while, and if he wasn't cut out for it, he could always apply to attend law school again.

"My mother, God bless her, was less able to hide her fading hopes that her only son would marry and give her grandchildren," Davis told his high school classmate Slim Patterson. After growing up with Davis and competing with him on intramural sports teams, Slim went on to college and now taught history at College of DuPage. "I've regretted not having children much more than I've missed out on becoming a lawyer," Davis told him while they got caught up enjoying a few beers at Otto's Pub.

During his first year of full-time radio work, Davis pulled various shifts, which required a flexible schedule. Serious dating was more difficult, and though he dated on occasion, he usually had no intention of pursuing a long-term relationship. Only once had he ever found himself in love with a girl that he wanted to share his life with. When that ended, in the way that it did, his life was abruptly altered. As time passed he wondered whether he could ever find that kind of love again.

There were moments when Davis' thoughts returned to when he began dating Ellie during his sophomore year at Loyola. She was finishing her senior year in high school. Surely it was fate that provided the coincidences that allowed them to meet and become a couple.

Ellie came to a party on Chicago's north side after a Loyola basketball game on a date with one of his fellow sophomores, Louie Turner. Davis was immediately attracted to her vitality and maturity. She showed no signs of the intimidation that might be expected from someone still in high school who was with an older, more sophisticated college crowd. She fit right in and seemed to enjoy the party as much as everyone there, which Louie saw as flirting. When she expressed a view different from

Louie's, he grew angry and embarrassed her. He insisted that she was simply too young to be with him and the other "adults" at the party. He told her he would be leaving and she could either follow him or find a ride home by herself. Ellie was taken aback by his outburst but responded with a mere shrug. That was the final straw for Louie, and he stormed out the door, feeling that he had just showed her, in his words, who was right and who was about to be left. Davis noticed no concern on Ellie's face after Louie departed.

And so it began. Davis came to her rescue and gave her a ride home. While the evening came to a strange end, it led to the beginning of a relationship that grew each time they were together, ultimately becoming a love that surprised them both. When it eventually got to that point, all they wanted was each other.

Syd Esmaker noticed Davis's fear that he hadn't yet written something more significant than what he provided to the radio station's breaking news teams—and probably never would.

"You're always upset that the crimes we report never seem to end without happening all over again," he said. "You wonder why that's the case, right?"

Davis nodded. "That's exactly the case. Sure, I think once a criminal is caught, he has to be put away. But all that does is solve one crime. Maybe taking it further and researching the reason a person robs or murders or kidnaps or rapes might lead to some solution that addresses the whole problem, bringing an end to such mayhem."

They were sharing their thoughts at McGillicuddy's, a favorite tavern for Chicago's news reporters. After Syd called the bartender over and suggested that his friend wanted to pay for one last sip of Irish whiskey—for each of them—he returned to their conversation. "Davis Q. Wiggley," he began. "No one in our newsroom shares your skill in capturing the right words that produce the reports that are later read on WGN Radio. But I can tell now how far ahead of those wonderful words your mind has begun to travel."

Davis always enjoyed spending time with Sydney and, after paying the bartender, turned to him. "Now, with business accomplished, just where were you going with that generous compliment?"

"Ha! You've been paying attention," he laughed. "Laddie, what you need to do—no, what you *must* do—is write a novel with your fine observations about how our justice system needs to fix itself."

"A novel? But novels are always fiction, aren't they?"

"Aye, that's true enough," Sydney assured him. "But it's in fiction that truth hides from its enemies. A good story has a purpose, something valuable to reveal. But it never tries to argue for anything or persuade someone to buy into it."

Davis listened earnestly to his mentor. "It's in fiction, you say, where the emotional truth will be the driver of the outcome being told throughout the story. Right?"

"If you add just one caveat, I'll be happy to say to all that you really have a chance."

"Just one caveat?"

"That's correct." Sydney waved the bartender over. "It stays hidden by never being observed... until the *whole* story is told."

That conversation with Sydney Esmaker prompted Davis to return to college part-time, taking fiction-writing courses in the evening at Roosevelt University and College of DuPage. He also wrote short stories in his spare time. Often, the stories were part of classroom assignments and were influenced by the same ones he'd written earlier at the news desk. But in the stories he wrote at college, he focused on the people involved. When characters were murdered, he wrote in terms of what had been lost forever. His fictional victims all had potential futures revealed earlier in the story, glimpses of what they might have become had they lived long enough. Their deaths left unfinished the responsibilities they'd had as parents, coaches, teachers, or sons or daughters. Someone left behind would pay for the life that was shortened.

While writing those stories, Davis discovered how lost he often got inside of them. Everything seemed to flow, prompting new questions and answers. His characters had depth and lived complex lives that weren't all good or evil. They had needs, some of which they ignored and others they should have. Some of their decisions fulfilled their lives, and others cost them or their loved ones dearly. Writing about the lives he created in his stories renewed Davis's faith in his own talent. His stories went beyond the incomplete news copy ones he wrote for the radio reports. Storytelling had to be done by a *writer*, he realized. Perhaps by a *novelist*, he hoped.

Ultimately, he decided to leave the radio station and commit at least a year to completing a novel. A small inheritance turned his decision into a reality, and the stories became a manuscript. Getting it published, he learned, would take much more time. Publishers were reluctant to invest in novelists who had no platform, reputation, or name recognition. His first step had to be making some connections. He needed an agent.

5

Sandra Pierce

WHILE HAVING BREAKFAST AT HIS neighborhood restaurant, Davis talked with his favorite waitress. "I'm twenty-five years old and changing careers. I'm going from being underpaid as a news writer for a top-five Chicago radio station to making a zero-income leap into what I can only hope is my future."

"Sounds like someone is having some serious second thoughts." Tina said while she refilled his cup. "I understand, you know, that being your waitress doesn't grant me the right to console or counsel you, or anyone else for that matter, but this change you're making is something you need to do. I've listened to you talk about something like this ever since I began working here at Buster's, and that was almost three years ago."

"Not having any second thoughts," he said, rising out of the booth. "Too late for that now. In fact, I'm on my way to DeKalb to attend a writers' seminar at Northern Illinois University where I hope to meet up with a lady who has the smarts to launch me on the new career path I was just mumbling about."

Tina feigned having hurt feelings. "What's this about a lady in DeKalb that you seem so eager to meet?"

Davis smiled. "Not jealous, are you?" He laughed. "She's someone who spoke at a writer's workshop in Iowa and impressed me with her knowledge of the ins and outs of the publishing business."

"I'm not *jealous*," Tina said. "I just know one thing, and that's when you mention a new woman at the same time you're talking about a new career, that means you're heading down two different roads, and one of them is sure to detour you from the other."

After Davis got past Aurora, the traffic was light along I-88. His thoughts returned to the first time he met Sandra Pierce following her presentation at a writers' seminar in Iowa. Her attractive but youthful appearance provided a less credible backdrop than she deserved for the brilliant business-oriented concepts she presented. At the luncheon following her talk, he approached her and thanked her for the helpful insights. He was pleasantly surprised when she invited him to send her a query about his manuscript.

Nearly two months passed and he all but gave up hope of hearing from her. Finally, she wrote, asking him for a synopsis and the first fifty pages of his novel. After carefully writing a synopsis, Davis attached the requested pages of *Dictated Choices* and emailed them to her. A week passed, then two. Finally, after six weeks of anticipation with each new email, Davis saw one from Sandra Pierce. At last, he said to himself but his mood quickly dampened as he read her message. She was merely informing him that she would be conducting a seminar at Northern Illinois University that month and hoped he would meet her there. Her brief response was disappointing, as he earlier sensed she might have a more personal interest in him—or at least in his story.

Davis had grown almost despondent about becoming an author. While he remained confident of his writing abilities, every day made it clear that he lacked the knowledge to convince an agent or publisher to give him a read. During all his efforts to find a publisher, Davis had learned one thing quite well, something he often mentioned when asked how his story was going. His response was always the same. "Many people fantasize about a future as an author, and almost as many people make a handsome living writing books or conducting seminars about how to make those dreams come true."

* * *

With cynical expectations as his companion, Davis arrived at the entryway to the NIU campus. Going into the auditorium for the seminar, he saw that the front-row seats were mostly filled. Davis found an open seat on the center aisle alongside a row of students who appeared anxious for the seminar to begin.

"Have you heard much about our speaker?" the young woman seated next to him asked.

Davis told her that he'd attended Sandra Pierce's Iowa seminar.

"That must have been nice, actually seeing her," the woman said. "I only know what I've read about her, and that impressed me enough to part with the reservation money, which I'd really intended for something else."

"I doubt you'll leave disappointed," he said. "You might be surprised by how young she looks, close to your age. Tell me, why are you interested in her? Are you a writer or planning on becoming one?"

The young woman opened a handbag and removed the seminar brochure. "It says here that she's considered to be on the fast track to success as a literary agent and that after graduating from Northwestern, she discovered Simon DuValle while on a post-graduation vacation in Montego Bay."

He noticed an inflection in the woman's voice when she spoke that author's name.

"Simon DuValle? I've heard that name somewhere," he said, hoping to add to the conversation.

"Of course you've heard that name before," she scolded. "Simon DuValle wrote *The Solitary Soul,* the book that was an overnight success and has been on the *New York Times* Bestseller list."

"Oh, that Simon DuValle." Davis faked awareness.

"Uh-huh, and I read a story in *Rolling Stone* that she followed that signing with a few other discoveries of unknown authors who have potential to make the list. They called her the agent with the Midas touch."

Davis thought about that comment during the seminar. Sandra Pierce's portion was scheduled for only an hour but ran over when the Q and A segment kept her on stage for an extra forty-five minutes. As soon as she finished, she walked directly to Davis.

"There you are! I spotted you just as that last question was asked," she said.

He liked being singled out by the celebrity speaker, and they shook hands. Not wanting her to get away before learning her impression of his novel's synopsis and first fifty pages, he asked if he could take her to lunch.

"I planned to meet with you today," she said. "But that extra time on the Q and A has created some difficulties with the time for my return flight."

She seemed to be considering another possibility, so he remained silent.

"You know," she said, "if you're available to take me to O'Hare, I could cancel my Uber, and we could spend that ninety minutes discussing your manuscript."

As they drove along I-88, through the peaceful farm country that separated the university from the Chicago suburbs, Sandra said she found promise in his "unique but awkward" style.

"I like very much that your story has a message yet is subtle enough to avoid being preachy. You focus as much on the why as you do on the how and the where of the crime that was committed. When I began reading your story, I suspected I was in for some bleeding-heart conclusions showing that the criminal had been deprived of his God-given right to be raised better by his parents, and so he grew up bitter and robbed banks to even the score."

They laughed freely at her observation.

"What made you conclude differently?"

"That happened deeper in your story when I couldn't help but feel that for some people the deck does, in fact, seemed stacked against their efforts or ambitions."

Sandra paused as if choosing her words carefully. "I want you to listen closely to what I'm going to tell you. You write beautiful words that manage to hold the reader's interest. You make observations that others subconsciously share. We nod with knowing agreement after we've read your words. Upon finishing a page or even a paragraph, I felt that I'd just read a revelation of my own thoughts that, until that moment, were still only rudimentary."

Her praise quickened his spirit. "I appreciate that. I really do," he said. "So how do I get anything published?"

She paused longer than Davis thought appropriate.

"That's just it," she finally responded. "Your observations lack credibility. To any publisher who considers getting your story into print, there's simply too much risk. They see you as an author whose résumé lists only his work as a news-desk writer at a Chicago radio station. You're just another someone with a liberal arts degree, writing stories that seem to persuade society that prisons and police, laws and lawyers, even judges and the entire justice system fail so often that they can't be relied upon anymore. Of course, the way you couch those criticisms within your novel is subtle enough not to interfere with the story line."

Sandra stopped talking and looked at Davis as if to gauge the effect of her comments. He remained silent and kept his eyes on the road. They had traveled beyond the quiet farmlands, and as they approached Chicago, the heavier traffic competed for Davis's attention.

As he slowed to pay a toll, Davis looked at Sandra. "What you said is true. I'm only a radio news writer. But I have been doing this work for five years, and that experience counts as part of my credentials, right?"

Sandra seemed relieved by his response. Seeing that he was neither bitter nor defensive, she was more hopeful now that she could work with him. They approached the passenger drop-off area for United Airlines where Davis pulled to a stop. Sandra gave him an affectionate squeeze.

"I'm sure I'll come up with something to address your lack of credentials," she offered.

Davis felt giddy, and the feeling stayed with him during his drive home. Sandra Pierce had impressed him both times they met. He was confident she knew the business end of publishing. And for the first time since he began writing his reality-based fiction, he sensed that he had a reasonable expectation of finding success. That hope explained his elevated spirit. Davis ignored and left uncontested a less-conscious awareness that somehow, someday, he might find a way to her bed.

6

Home Confinement

Brady Harvey removed the whistling kettle from the stove, poured the boiling water into a tall, narrow cup, and stirred in one teaspoon of Mount Hagen instant coffee. His mind was on the coming Sunday, when he would see her again. Catherine might be thinking about him at that very moment. Anything was possible. He was certain she knew he would be watching for her.

He recalled the saying about time healing all wounds working best when that time was used to forget. *But why should I spend time trying to forget her?* That was the most illogical suggestion his therapist had ever given to him.

"If you really, sincerely want to be happy, then you must clear your mind of everything about Catherine Dallas," Beverly Beckett Conforti coached him.

He liked his new therapist and was confident she was trying to help him dig out of depression. Forgetting Catherine might work, if that was even possible. But as long as she still needed him, he wasn't going to forget her.

He took another sip from his steaming cup and looked across the table at Angel, his Siamese cat and close confidante. "You wouldn't want me to forget you, either," he said, sounding self-righteous. "Of course you wouldn't. But then you would have found a way of staying close after they took me away from you."

Angel didn't understand Brady but seemed to sense where the conversation was headed and calmly left the breakfast table. She settled close by in his favorite chair, where he read books at night. As long as she stayed near, he would get over it eventually.

"You aren't fooling me, you know," he told her. "I know what's happening here. You expect me to think that you don't care, that you really don't need me." He took a bite of the blueberry bagel that he'd just warmed in the microwave. "But you do need me," he continued talking without looking in her direction. "Just like Catherine needs me in so many ways that she simply has no idea." He looked at Angel. "You two have so much in common, going on with your lives like I'm not even here. Maybe someday, she'll realize that the only reason I left her after high school was because I was taken away. I never did really leave her."

Brady adjusted the dial on his tabletop radio, turning to the classical music station that kept him company as he researched or read science news articles. He opened his laptop and clicked on his daily planner. The only entry was his weekly appointment with his therapist, scheduled for ten o'clock.

"And you?" Brady sneered after he closed his computer and pointed at the chair where Angel sat, showing her usual indifference. "You wouldn't even have food to eat or anything to drink if not for me."

The cell phone rang where he left it in his bedroom and Angel watched him walk away to answer it. She was glad that it took his attention away from whatever it was that set him off this morning. She turned and resumed looking out the window at the people below at street level waiting for the bus. They appeared so much smaller from her perch three floors above them.

"Good morning, son," Ruth Harvey said. "It looks like we can expect the same nice weather we had yesterday." Except for the current weather conditions, it was the same greeting he received from his mother almost daily. Brady appreciated her concern but knew that her morning telephone calls were designed for her to learn his plans for the day and see whether there were any changes.

After wishing her a wonderful day, he tried to rush through their conversation by telling her he was expecting a call from an agent.

"Agent?" She sounded surprised. "You've not mentioned that one before. Is this someone who can find you a publisher for your novel instead of you trying to self-publish it?"

Brady sighed. He could tell that her question was intended to lengthen their conversation. Ultimately, she would find a way to inquire about whether he was dating someone. He knew that this morning's call would be no exception.

"So, dear," she began. "With all the time that you've lost by writing your novel, and now with this new agent maybe helping, isn't there some time for you to find a lucky woman who's going to discover that you have all that talent to go along with your natural good looks? Maybe someone who's going to want you for her own?"

"Mother, while I would really like to talk a bit longer, I have to finish my breakfast and then get ready for my therapy appointment."

Before she could respond, Brady said goodbye and pushed the red button on his cell phone screen.

* * *

Beverly Beckett Conforti hurried into the Colgate Office Building's lobby, concerned that stopping at Starbucks had caused her to run late for her ten o'clock appointment. She was relieved to see that she'd managed to arrive before Brady Harvey. They were already in their third month of weekly sessions that began upon his release from the hospital and moving into his condominium after the court approved his petition for home confinement. With ten minutes to spare before their session, Beverly hurriedly reviewed her digital notes.

Brady is bipolar, his disorder first diagnosed when he entered high school. His father, James Harvey, was a victim of the 9/11 tragedy. His sudden loss resulted in Brady's deep depression, which worsened and led to various criminal activities. His neighbor, Catherine Dallas, was in the same year in high school, and they were involved in many activities and became close friends. Brady was convinced they needed each other and would one day marry.

By the time they were close to graduation, Catherine was dating other boys, leaving Brady to struggle with what he referred to as "pain worse than the loss of my father." Brady got into trouble soon after graduating. He caused a brawl at a party. Things happened, and his troubles escalated. That incident kicked off seven years of legal troubles that resulted at various times in him being confined in mental health care facilities like the one at Connecticut Valley Hospital.

At one of their therapy sessions, Brady mentioned how Catherine Dallas left Greenwich after winning a scholarship to Wellesley in Massachusetts. Later, while she was still a student she authored a bestseller, *Hounds of Hope*. He envied her for becoming a successful writer and was inspired to complete his own manuscript. Hopefully, if he became a published author that would convince her they were meant to reunite. Instead, her only contact with him—other than visits to their neighborhood during Christmas breaks—was limited to Twitter or Facebook messages. Even those ended after a few years.

Beverly planned to turn their discussion to perhaps more joyful and more current events in his life. She hoped she wouldn't detect any symptoms that could trigger additional episodes that might make him a danger to the community.

After Brady arrived and they exchanged greetings, Beverly asked about his novel.

"It's coming along pretty smooth since I'm more alone now and free to think when I write." He smiled while making a response.

"Yes, I'm sure that when you were constantly being checked up on at CVH and experienced other distractions, it must have been difficult to write," she said. "Tell me more about that book, or should I call it the manuscript?"

Brady looked puzzled. "What more can I add to what I've already told you?"

"How about the title? Have you given your novel a title yet?"

Brady shifted in the leather chair he always sat on during visits with Beverly. "Yes, my novel has a title, just not one that tells you enough to understand what it's about."

Beverly remained quiet, allowing her facial expression to indicate that the title would still be a good place to begin talking about the book.

Brady seemed to like that about her. She always waited to listen to what he wanted to talk about. "I've called it *Algorithms and Blues*," he finally responded.

"That's an interesting title," she said, unable to even guess about the contents. "Is it fiction? Or perhaps nonfiction?"

Brady said nothing, merely shrugged to indicate he'd clarified that when mentioning the title before.

The awkward silence continued until Beverly looked at her notes and asked whether he wanted to talk about his family or girlfriends or how he liked living away from Connecticut Valley Mental Hospital.

"I like my condo a helluva lot more than where I was being kept—uh, living at—until a few months ago. I have a cat, Angel, who provides me with more friendship than anyone else has in the last half decade."

"And I bet you're happy that you can have visits from maybe a new girlfriend or two?" She wanted to prompt more intimate conversation and hoped he wouldn't feel she was intruding.

"I write. I read. I listen to music that I select and want to hear. I call who I want to talk to. None of that was possible while I was being detained."

Beverly waited before pushing for more information noticing that Brady showed signs of becoming irritated. After more silence, she decided that the rest of the information that needed to be discussed could wait until their future appointments.

7

A published author

L ESS THAN A WEEK AFTER they'd said goodbye at the airport, Sandra telephoned with a suggestion that solved Davis's concern over his credentials.

"Your main character should have the academic background that you personally already have on the subject," she suggested. "For example, when that young defense lawyer argues her points to the jury, she should have previously earned academic credits in appropriate social science courses on her way to being admitted to law school. That's the kind of personal history that gives some weight to the wonderful words you wrote for her."

Davis listened to Sandra and instantly saw how his protagonist's educational achievements would provide the appropriate credibility for the arguments she made in his novel.

"Will doing this, rewriting the whole book with these changes, make my story work?" he asked. "Is anything else that is missing?"

"Whoa! Hold on there," Sandra cautioned. "You'll have to do a lot more than looking up what college courses you want her to have taken. What I want you to do entails many additional hours in interviews with real, accredited people in appropriate fields of social studies, law enforcement, and the judicial system. By incorporating their thoughts and vocabulary into the conclusions of your protagonist, you might address those concerns of a publisher."

"Do you think the people you recommend will be willing to answer my questions?"

"Some will and maybe some won't," she said. "But you've been gifted with an abundance of charisma that people welcome and should charm enough of them to offer their knowledge and time. You might also explain that each of the sources would be mentioned in the acknowledgments and that releases might be required."

His plan to get his novel published took a lot of legwork and hours of research and eleven long, lonely months of writing, rewriting, and incorporating changes. Sandra had suggested editors to help him with everything from content and plot to pacing and proofreading. Finally, Davis fulfilled his life's ambition and became a published author. Ballantine bought *Dictated Choices*, his story about a young, unemployed Puerto Rican father charged with bank robbery and whose defense used an argument with a fatalistic bent. Davis wound into the story facts and evidence he remembered from an actual trial that was reported on the radio news hour almost a half-decade earlier. An energetic young Latina lawyer was his protagonist and argued that the defendant's path from cradle to court was dictated by society's choices more than by any of his own free-will decisions.

The expertise needed to form that argument came from Davis's interviews with social workers, psychologists, economists, and law school professors. Characters in his novel held those same professions, and he had them present their ideas as testimony during the story's trial. The fictional defense attorney's summation to the jury featured her emotional appeal that society preaches equality for all but does little to level the playing field of opportunity for those handicapped by a different race, language, or lack of education.

Nearing tears, she raised her voice and asserted that people had no right to allow advertisements meant for "the haves"—showing products and lifestyles that only the wealthy could afford—to be flaunted before the "have-nots." The defendant, she argued, had neither the skill nor the means to provide his family with the products and lifestyle those advertisements persuaded him they needed and deserved. The action he took to address that lack was not only logical but also predictable.

Though the arguments failed to convince the jury in Davis's novel, he wrote of how the press coverage afterward increased public awareness and led to serious considerations for changes that were then argued in legislative discussions throughout the country later in the story. Also in the book, news coverage of the trial prompted new psychology and social science courses that progressive educators used to begin a more earnest study of reasons people act as they do.

The first printing was ten thousand books, and sales were slow for months. Reviews were good but few, appearing mostly in bookstores, Facebook, and advertisements that appeared in Amazon. His break came when nationally syndicated talk show host Augustine Samuel Skinner referred to the book on his radio program as just another example of a "blame the baby on a defective prophylactic" argument. He cursed the lack of responsibility on liberal journalism. Sandra Pierce acted fast and challenged Skinner to allow Davis to defend his book on air. While she waited for his response Sandra used the time to publicize her challenge by sending news releases to the media. Whether Skinner would yield to her challenge or not its publicity was feeding new interest in Davis' novel, Dictated Choices.

The radio interview was reluctantly scheduled. Initially nervous, Davis stood his ground with the outspoken Skinner. He fueled the controversy even more by challenging the largely conservative radio audience to come up with alternative reactions to the same advertisements that had influenced his fictional defendant. Skinner grew loud and intimidating and finally ordered Davis from the Hallowed Hall of Reason, as he referred to his studio.

Davis was surprised by the outburst and remained sitting across from Skinner until Sandra hurried to his side and urged him to leave. As they walked away, Skinner informed his listeners that the misguided liberal poof was being led out of the lions' den by a beautiful pussycat. With raised voice, he said Davis should spend more time with a pussy instead of acting like one. Hearing that, Davis lost it and went back into the studio. Two large security guards helped Sandra get him outside.

Davis was furious but apologized to Sandra for letting her down. When he was calm enough to look more closely at her, he was surprised that she was smiling.

"Quigley, my friend," she began, "you've just sold another thousand or more books tonight."

"I've just made all of Augustine Skinner's followers pissed at me. None of them will ever buy my book," he whispered back in a how-do-you-figure-that response.

"Trust me is all I'm going to say," she teased, taking his hands into hers.

He paused at the unexpected display of affection. Keeping her hands in his, he lowered them to his side and, yielding to impulse, leaned forward and softly kissed her on her forehead. He sensed her consent but stepped back almost immediately.

"I just wanted to thank you for what you've done for me tonight," he said. "You gave me the confidence I needed to go on the program and sit opposite that arrogant bastard."

8

Meet Catherine Lane

Sandra's prediction proved to be on the mark, and Davis's appearance on the Augustine Skinner radio program boosted sales of *Dictated Choices*. But the show's large national audience, comprised mostly of conservative followers of the outspoken and opinionated host, wasn't the most significant cause of the spike in book sales. Instead, the biggest buzz followed a fluke mention of the radio show incident—and that happened on TV.

Nationally syndicated columnist Will Jennings commented on the radio dispute during his appearance on the Sunday news program *Fox at the Front*. Davis happened to be watching and was startled when the title of his book came up.

"I cannot find any reason to condone the uncivil behavior displayed by Augustine the Great," Jennings laughingly said, a reference to the radio program's host. "However, I do find agreement with his keen conservative observation regarding the assertions made by the author of *Dictated Choices*."

Jennings, an admittedly proud conservative, had been engaged in a heated debate with other panel members who expressed sympathy for the plight of the twelve million undocumented aliens fighting harsh enforcement changes in immigration law. He refrained from referring to his opponents on the panel as left-wing sympathizers. Instead, he made his point using the criticism offered by Augustine Skinner that *Dictated Choices* revealed how weak the political left was when dealing with criminals.

"America has to stop coming up with reasons for those who break our laws," Jennings argued. "Reasons are never excuses and serve only to muddy the waters of the rivers of justice," he concluded just as the program broke for commercials.

Whether writing his column or participating on television talk shows, Jennings was well-known for choosing the right words at the right time to discourage dissenting views. The majority of his admirers were conservatives and Republicans. But the thoughtful, intelligent manner in which he articulated his views earned respect from even those who didn't share his conclusions.

When the program resumed, the screen showed a news clip of a recent demonstration in Washington, DC, with crowds holding signs demanding the relaxation of immigration laws. The signs and placards held by the marchers called for ending the harassment of Hispanics by the police and the courts. In English and Spanish, the signs declared that all people had the right to freedom in America.

Jennings bristled when the cameras focused on the words on the signs. "Freedom in America is the right of American citizens, not those who sneak into our country in the back of a truck or who wander in under the moonlight." He made no attempt to hide the indignation he apparently felt at what they were watching.

The moderator, looking for someone to make a rebuttal and provide some balance, turned to the only female on the panel, Catherine Lane.

"Has Mr. Jennings persuaded you yet, Mrs. Lane?" he asked, knowing quite well that the opposite was more likely the case.

The camera showed a close-up of her face. A soft smile surrounded her eyes and mouth, and the near perfect symmetry of her face prompted a "Wow!" from Davis, who was watching the show.

Catherine hesitated before answering the challenge from the moderator. Her expression indicated that she was in midthought when called upon.

"Instead of responding to Mr. Jennings's opinion of who has the most legitimate claim on freedom's privileges in America," she began, "I would first want to say how surprised I was by his earlier comments about reasons and excuses." Her tone was soft and feminine, yet it contained a hint of frustration and suggested her eagerness to challenge the analysis of her more tenured fellow panelist.

Catherine Dallas Lane had a following of her own that rivaled in passion, if not in numbers, that of the Will Jennings faithful. His national reputation had been gained over thirty-five years of writing syndicated columns containing his observations, opinions, and analysis of everyday life. While conservative and leaning heavily Republican, he was neither a follower nor an apologist when his opinion differed from the party line.

The public's awareness of Catherine was more recent. Her novel, *The Hounds of Hope*, written while she was still a graduate student at Wellesley, portrayed the triumphs and failures of people during their "coming of age" period of life. The book was an immediate success on university campuses. Its characters and their lives were as much a part of students' conversations as the wins and losses of their college football teams.

Catherine's novel focused on how new generations benefited from technology such as computers, cell phones, Alexa and Amazon, robots, and electric vehicles. But with the sudden appearance of the life-enhancing inventions came little to no guidance that previous generations had relied upon when accepting big changes into their lives.

Catherine created a hero who led everyone to consider new possibilities in life, ideas never even imagined before. Her heroine proclaimed the joys of individuality while celebrating the comfort of knowing one's purpose in the community.

Following her graduation, she wrote articles that appeared in the *Atlantic*, *Vanity Fair*, and the *New Yorker*. Her life had been chronicled in many of the country's major newspapers and magazines. She married at twenty-five and was widowed just short of a year later following the accidental death of her wealthy husband, Pemberton Lane.

"Mr. Jennings tells us to ignore reasons that influenced those he calls lawbreakers and that reasons only muddy the waters." Catherine faced the television camera. "Yet it was reasons that gave birth to those very same laws he now relies on."

Jennings was smiling when the camera caught his response. Catherine had employed one of his special tactics by twisting his own words to score the counterpoint. She was also talking past him to the large audience of television viewers. That, too, was one of his skills. She proved to be a worthy opponent in the joust, and he knew just how to parry her attack.

"For sure it was reasons, as you mentioned, that prompted the lawmakers," he said. "Laws always have reasons. Violators have only excuses."

Jennings extended his arm with the palm of his hand up, implying that he had served the ball back to Catherine's side of the court. His expression indicated that while he anticipated her attempt at a return volley, he doubted it would score inside the lines.

"You mentioned the novel *Dictated Choices*," Catherine said in a subdued voice. She seemed to be leaving his last observation unchallenged. "But the defendant in that story was vindicated when reasons such as his were later determined by many to have been ignored at the time those laws he was charged with violating were made."

When the set director signaled that it was time for the moderator to wrap up, Catherine spoke over Jennings as he attempted to rebut.

"The rivers of justice are indeed muddy," she said again, using Jennings's earlier comment. "And that is why we include judges and juries as well as universities and studies in our effort to navigate toward the truth."

Jennings was unaccustomed to being checkmated, which was how he was portrayed in Monday's newspapers. The *Post*'s entertainment section carried a brief report on his television debate with Catherine Lane. Both the *Times* and the *Tribune* mentioned it in the editorial portion of their newspapers. All agreed that Will Jennings had finally met his match, and all of them mentioned *Dictated Choices*.

*   *   *

Over the next few weeks, Sandra Pierce was besieged with media requests for interviews with Davis.

"There are as many conservative-leaning choices as there are liberal ones," Sandra joyfully explained after calling and waking Davis with the news that he had become the buzz on radio and cable TV talk shows. "That shouldn't surprise you. The liberal shows like those on MSNBC want you to expand on how your stories unveil the unfairness in our current justice system. The conservative programs like those on Fox want to portray you and your novel as presenting a more revolutionary challenge to the very principles that our country was founded upon."

Davis struggled to wake up. He understood that he was learning something positive about his book's success, but he didn't know what it all meant. "Are you saying that I should respond to those requests for interviews? And which ones? And how should I prepare?"

"All good questions, Davis, and all in good time I'll have your answers." She laughed. "But yes, we will respond to them. Maybe not all of them. And after a day or two, we'll put together a plan of who and when and where to begin full speed on your very first book tour."

Davis liked her calm, confident tone. He struggled to mask his excitement. "So, I guess that I'll leave this part up to you, right?"

"That's exactly right, and even now, I see that another interview request has arrived, this one from GMA. I fully expect that means *The Today Show*'s request will arrive within minutes."

Davis was thrilled with all the requests for TV and radio interviews. He was also interested in the prospect of working with Sandra more closely.

"Should I expect to hear more from you later today or…?"

"Actually, you and I won't be doing any of the prep work together," Sandra interupted. "But I'll always be watching over your progress as I continue the preliminary meetings with various talk show producers."

Davis was confused by the turn in their business relationship. "Watching over my progress?"

"Yes. As you may know, here at the Pradle Literary Agency, we use various media connections that are very good at preparing our authors for interviews on these book tours."

"But I thought with everything I heard from you at the seminars in Iowa and NIU that, well, that you and I would be a team for this type of stuff."

Sandra was familiar with the disappointment her new authors felt when told that other people would take over at times. It had happened with Simon DuValle and each of the other "finds" that she'd brought into the Pradle Agency.

"We are a team, Davis." She spoke in a soft, motherly tone. "But a team has many members who contribute to the success that we all want to happen. The Ballantine Publishing Group has arranged for you to work with someone from McHale Media, who will likely contact you within a day or two. And remember, I'll always be available for any questions or concerns that may arise. You understand now, don't you?"

Davis's disappointment came not from being pushed on to a different agency for the prep work but instead from the sad awareness that Sandra's priorities meant there was little potential for their relationship to grow beyond his novel.

9

Pradle Literary Agency

CHARLOTTE OLSON'S DESK DID LITTLE to indicate the workload that Sandra Pierce had delegated to her. Clear of everything except a single client file that she was currently updating, her desktop gave the appearance that she was either highly organized or had little to do. Only she and her boss knew that "highly organized" was the correct answer.

Charlotte's office was actually larger than Sandra's, a necessity since two other Pradle Literary Agency employees shared that space with her. Amy Wang, whose desk was closest to Charlotte, answered telephones, responded to emails, managed the websites, arranged travel and hotels, and served as default office gopher. Sitting across from her was Randy Turley, the firm's wizard of all things digital. He maintained the computer software that tracked client appearances on radio and TV as well as book signings and speaking engagements. His systems tracked book sales, publishers' deadlines, clients' advances, royalties, book returns, and any special needs of the firm's authors.

Charlotte's desk was in the center of the room, a sufficient distance away from Sandra's office to ensure privacy. A leather sofa and matching chairs along the other side of the office accommodated visitors. Charlotte thought of herself as similar to an orchestra leader. She coordinated everything on her side of the wall separating her office from Sandra's. As busy as Amy and Randy were, everything they were involved in went through Charlotte. She gave to them assignments and deadlines that allowed her to address any problems. It was all programmed into her DNA. Everything had to run smoothly, and nothing was left to chance. Ultimately, her job was to accomplish everything Sandra asked for and anticipate anything Sandra might have forgotten. Sandra had to be free to do whatever it was she did so well. She should never be bogged down by details. Sandra wrote the musical score, but left Charlotte alone to lead the orchestra.

Charlotte had run things for many years, even when it was just Arthur Pradle and her. In 1984, in her mid-twenties, she gave up a promising career and followed Arthur after he left the William Morris Agency. He'd been recruiting writers for studio-produced dramas during what was known as the Second Golden Age of Television. Charlotte was his personal secretary and right hand. The new agency was a success almost overnight. Pradle took with him many of the clients he'd personally handled for the William Morris Agency. He was a major player until everything ground to a halt in 1988, the year of the Writers Guild of America strike.

During the twenty-two weeks of the strike, the studios shut down production of all shows that depended on writers for new scripts. Pradle's clients, comprised mostly of Guild members, were out of work, and the revenue that came from representing them dried up fast. Hoping to avoid bankruptcy, Pradle took on and represented new writers who weren't members of the Guild. The qualifications for membership in the WGA required having at least one script accepted by a studio. Once the strike began, the only writers working were all novices and, by definition, nonmembers of the Guild. Those "scabs" were blacklisted for life. During the strike, Pradle supplied the studios with writers who hadn't yet qualified for Guild membership. The revenue was much needed by his new agency and saved it from bankruptcy. However, once the strike was settled, the Pradle Agency and all the writers they'd hired were fired and blacklisted by the Writers Guild. Any writer who remained loyal to the Guild during the strike couldn't dare be represented by or associated with the Pradle Agency.

The fired writers still needed an agent if they were to find work. They were talented writers, and Arthur found good uses for their skills, not by the studios but by publishing houses. During the decade following the WGA strike, seventeen best-selling books were written about the strike, and Pradle was the agent for twelve of the authors. The money that the authors earned for his agency paled in comparison to the income he lost from the studios after the strike was settled. But it was enough to pay the bills and keep himself and one employee working.

Charlotte Olson never forgot Arthur's loyalty not only to his clients but also to her during those bleak years. Even when months passed without any incoming revenue, she never missed a paycheck. She accepted his explanation that it came from "reserves." But she suspected it was more likely that to keep the business going, he had taken an additional mortgage on his house in Brentwood. The two of them were a team in Charlotte's mind and somehow managed to make it through the tough times.

* * *

In the spring of 2013, Sandra Pierce earned a Master of Fine Arts degree in Creative Writing at Northwestern University but had virtually no experience in publishing or marketing. Arthur

Pradle agreed to interview her—and for a job he doubted his agency could afford—only as a favor to his sister Elaine, who taught playwriting to graduate students at Northwestern.

"I will tell you this, Arthur, she is the brightest student I've ever had during my teaching career."

Elaine didn't doubt that Sandra could succeed in the writing business. And just before she knew Arthur was about to say that he was in no position to hire anyone, Elaine mentioned that her bright, industrious student had recently brought to her a manuscript for a novel that would take the publishing world by storm. Pradle relented and told Elaine to mail him the manuscript.

The manuscript was on his desk by the time he returned from lunch. That surprised Arthur, as he knew his sister was at home in Park Ridge, Illinois, when she called. Since the manuscript was in an unwrapped box with no address or postage on it, he called Charlotte into his office for an explanation.

"A young woman brought this in just as I was about to leave this afternoon," Charlotte said. "She told me that you knew all about it, and when I said you had already left for the day, she wanted your home address."

"My home address?"

"That's correct. I told her that would be out of the question and that she could leave the package with me and I would see to it that you received it when you returned."

Arthur listened as he looked at the title sheet. "You mentioned a young woman, but the author of this manuscript is someone named Simon DuValle. That doesn't sound like a woman's name."

Charlotte seemed taken aback. Her posture stiffened, and she sounded annoyed at being questioned about a mere delivery person. She spoke slowly and deliberately. "I am certain that the delivery of this manuscript was made by a woman, a young woman perhaps but most definitely a woman. And I did not even concern myself with asking if she was someone named Simon DuValle."

Arthur laughed softly. "Now, don't get all upset." He moved away from Charlotte and toward his desk. "I wasn't suggesting that you were supposed to know the name of the person who delivered this. It's just that, you see, my sister told me that her student, a young woman, wrote this manuscript."

"This package must have had something urgent in it," Charlotte said, getting the final word as she left Arthur's office.

Before deciding whether to keep his promise to his sister, he called her and asked how she managed to get the manuscript delivered on the same day they talked on the phone.

"You mean you have it already?" Elaine asked. "When I called Sandra and told her that you agreed to read the manuscript, I used her cell phone number. I didn't know she was already in Los Angeles."

Half of his concerns answered, Arthur asked about the author's identity.

"You asked me to read a manuscript that one of your prized students wrote, a Sandra Somebody, and now I'm having a hard time understanding why this material on my desk says the author is a Simon DuValle. Is this a nom de plume?"

"Simon DuValle?" Elaine repeated. "Oh, that's the author."

"Then what's the relationship between your Sandra Somebody and this author?" Arthur was slowly becoming more frustrated.

"It's not Sandra Somebody," Elaine said. "Her name is Sandra Pierce, and she's not the author of *The Solitary Soul*."

"Then who is this Simon DuValle, and why do I now have a homework assignment from you to read his manuscript?"

Their discussion had progressed from friendly inquiry to big sister—little brother spat. That wasn't an out-of-the-ordinary outcome whenever one of them wanted something from the other.

"Sandra met Mr. DuValle while vacationing in Montego Bay." Elaine sighed, clearly frustrated that her brother simply didn't get it yet. "It seems that he impressed her enough to read some of his unpublished works, and after reading *The Solitary Soul*, she told me she had just discovered a genius. She brought me the manuscript, and if you pass on it, I'm sure you'll regret it for a long time."

Arthur decided that the only way to restore peace with his older sibling was to either read the manuscript or interview Sandra Pierce. His time was too precious to spend reading unpublished authors from the Caribbean Islands, but he reluctantly decided to skim the manuscript prior to interviewing and then rejecting that "ambitious student."

Reading that manuscript was one of the best decisions of Arthur Pradle's business career. It was everything his sister said it was, and that was something he observed before he finished reading the first chapter. The story centered on the innate need to find expression of the self within the community role one must have for completeness in their lifetime. The allegorical story featured characters who communicated with both animals and plants. The protagonist was a small girl who had the same abilities as everyone else but also communicated with nature.

Reading the typewritten pages, Arthur felt drawn to the author's characters and their stories, and he lost any sense of time or place outside of the book. Through his subtle use of dialogue and the experiences of his characters, DuValle shared concepts that the reader understood only in retrospect. Sufficient conflict gave the story the necessary tension to hook the reader without distracting from the enlightening revelations from the characters.

At times, Arthur felt he wasn't merely reading the story but had become an observer within it. It was the nearest experience to existing inside of a dream that he'd ever realized with any book or movie or play. When he finished reading the book, Arthur knew two things—he wanted to have Simon DuValle as a client, and he needed Sandra Pierce to help get him do that.

Within two years, the fortunes of Arthur Pradle and his agency rose. Instead of just scraping by to meet rent on his office in Los Angeles, he needed a second office in New York to accommodate the increased business on the East Coast. Sandra Pierce turned out to be everything his sister had promised. She signed DuValle within a week of being hired. Then she persuaded Arthur to auction the right to publish the manuscript.

In his thirty years in business, Arthur had never offered a script to top publishers simultaneously. He'd heard of such auctions, but they all featured books written by famous authors. As exceptional as he knew *Solitary Soul* was, Simon DuValle was an unknown. And as a rule, publishers didn't vie against each other for the right to publish such manuscripts.

Arthur found that trying to convince his new employee of the unlikely success of an auction proved more difficult than giving in to her. Besides, Sandra held all the cards. Simon DuValle wanted things done her way. He wouldn't meet with or even take telephone calls from anyone except Sandra. So Arthur gave in and turned the auction over to her. She would fail, but that wouldn't be a disaster. Sandra would then turn the project over to him, and he would find a publisher willing to take a chance on the novel.

To the surprise of everyone except Sandra, the auction was a huge success. Four major publishing houses participated, and the story of their bidding war was featured in *Publishers Weekly*. Little Brown topped a final bid from Putnam Books and won the rights to publish *The Solitary Soul*.

The hype that began with the bidding war seemed mild once the reviews came out. With a first print run of twenty thousand, the book was soon in its fifth printing. Almost overnight, the unknown author from Montego Bay could afford to buy a good portion of that island paradise. Back in Los Angeles, the little-known Arthur Pradle agency could hardly keep up with all the interview requests for their new in-demand client.

Arthur sent Sandra and Simon on a nationwide promotional tour that was planned to last off-and-on for six months. During the first three months, *The Solitary Soul* remained number one on the *New York Times* Best Seller List, and it still sold well enough to rank number ten at the completion of the book tour. Rumors that Sandra and Simon had more than an author agent relationship concerned Arthur, but such rumors seemed newsworthy only when book sales showed signs of lagging, and they coincidentally always helped renew interest in the novel.

By the time Sandra settled back home in Los Angeles, she had signed a dozen other talented but unknown writers. When a few of their novels received favorable reviews and appeared lower on bestseller lists, Arthur split the agency in two. Sandra was in charge of talent and remained in Los Angeles and he moved to New York to manage the remaining aspects of the business.

Meanwhile, Sandra had become a celebrity herself. The rumors about her and Simon DuValle dwindled to a whisper after he returned to Montego Bay. But every time she appeared on the LA nightclub scene, a new rumor started. No matter who she was seen with—another new writer, an upcoming movie actor, or Arthur Pradle himself when he came for a short stay—the paparazzi followed. And it wasn't just the cameras that provided the flashing. The beautiful, sexy literary agent was always good for at least a page-two photo with story.

When Arthur split their duties and moved to New York, he made another important business decision. Seeing how in-demand Sandra had suddenly become, he feared she would be lured away or tempted to start her own agency. By then, her clients were responsible for more than three-quarters of his agency's annual revenue.

So Arthur made Sandra a partner. It was only a junior partnership since he retained seventy-five percent ownership, but giving Sandra a stake in the company did the job and kept her from moving elsewhere. To keep a close eye on his junior partner, Arthur "gave" Charlotte Olson to her as one last token of gratitude. Charlotte's home was in Los Angeles, and he knew she would be hesitant to move away.

10

Marketing

MᴄHᴀʟᴇ Mᴇᴅɪᴀ ɪɴ Lᴏs Aɴɢᴇʟᴇs was located on Wilshire Boulevard, only blocks from Pradle Literary Agency. It was the convenient choice, as was the nearby Ramada Hotel where Davis would stay during the three days of training for his book tour.

Jeanne McHale met Davis with a warm greeting. "I read your novel immediately after getting the call from PLA and am excited about helping you market it," she said. "Your story just might wake us all up to something badly needed in how we look at justice in our country."

After touring McHale Media and going over the schedule for training, Davis was impressed. "I appreciate everything that's on the agenda, but I do have a few questions," he said as they entered the audio and video studio.

"Of course. Anytime questions arise, feel free to fire away," she said.

"You told me that you read *Dictated Choices* after getting called by the PLA?"

Mild confusion showed in her eyes before she grasped his question. "Yes, the PLA is how we at McHale Media refer to the Pradle Literary Agency." She smiled. "Certainly not the Palestine Liberation Army," she reassured him.

"That was one of the possibilities that crossed my mind," he laughed. "But you also said this training is to help in marketing my novel. I thought that was something my agent or publisher would do."

Jeanne smiled as she reached back to her credenza and retrieved a brochure. "Marketing a novel is just another way of saying that you're building a platform for becoming better known and getting out news you hope will promote sales." She offered him the brochure while she explained certain points in it.

"In today's world, we depend on maximum exposure in social media. I'm talking about apps like Facebook, Instagram, Twitter, Snapchat, Tik Tok, and the like. You'll need a website where you create podcasts and share information with your readers."

The news troubled Davis. "I don't know beans about setting up those things."

Again, the media guru smiled. "Stay calm," she said. "PLA has all of these tools available. A fellow by the name of Randy Turley works that end of things there. Our goal here is to familiarize you with them so that you can use them."

He nodded while continuing to read the brochure. "I see that getting interviewed is also listed here. That's what I thought Sandra had in mind for me, as she's already lined up various radio and TV interviews for me to be on."

"That's right, and now you can see how all of this comes together with your agent, you, and your publisher. They line up the inter-views for you, and when you're finished here, you'll be prepared when you show up for them. I suspect Sandra or your publisher will also line up some public speaking presentations at bookstores and universities or YouTube. We'll make suggestions that I'm sure will prove quite helpful perhaps even having a Ted Talk."

He looked up from the brochure. "I've already been interviewed on the radio, and that went rather ugly."

Jeanne McHale smiled. "I listened to a recording of that interview, and quite frankly, I thought you were marvelous. I still have a few ideas about that for future dates."

Davis's media training passed quickly. Near the end, he returned to his room at the Ramada as his cell phone pinged with a text from Sandra, asking him to call her as soon as possible.

"I texted instead of phoning so that I wouldn't interrupt anything," she said.

Davis paused, wondering what she'd worried she might be interrupting. "No problem. I'm back at the Ramada right now, almost finished at McHale."

"Actually, you *are* finished there," Sandra said. "I have you booked on the Bull Ripley show tomorrow, and Amy Wang is on her way to pick you up for the drive to the airport."

"Amy Wang?"

"Yes. Amy has your plane ticket for the flight to New York on the red-eye."

Davis was overwhelmed. "You got me on the Bull Ripley program? The number-one cable talk show? Tomorrow?"

Sandra sounded almost as excited. "That's right. I've been trying to nab that interview all week, and they just called and said they had a cancellation, so our one chance was to be there and be the replacement. Amy will fill you in on the way to the airport, and I know you'll be completely fine. Just keep your head, let Ripley have his way, and remember, it's his show and our book that'll both be winners when it's over."

As expected, the proud host of the most-watched cable TV talk show in America blasted Davis's credentials as an author and said that Augustine Skinner had correctly pegged him as a bleeding-heart liberal. Davis spoke only twice without being interrupted or shouted over by the nation's top conservative commentator. But Ripley did allow a camera shot of Dictated Choices book cover and suggested that viewers might find it an interesting tearjerker.

Four nights later, Sandra used her influence to get Davis another prime-time cable TV interview, this time on the *Kent Knott News Hour*. The program aired opposite the Bull Ripley show and had a more liberal bent, so Davis felt welcome and was pleased that the interview focused on the research in he did writing his novel. Knott was open about his distaste for everything Bull Ripley stood for and congratulated Davis on surviving the slaughter.

Sandra accompanied Davis to the interviews. Afterward, she reviewed the parts that had gone well and those that could use improvement.

"Always keep the big picture in mind, regardless of how you feel about the questions," she counseled. "You don't want to appear angry or defensive. Those who've purchased *Dictated Choices*, or who might, want to like and admire you."

"I can understand that," he argued, "but I don't appreciate being made to look like a pussy, like that bastard Augustine Skinner was attempting to do."

"What's the matter with letting them say whatever they want to say?" Sandra asked. "Each of these TV and cable talk shows have millions of viewers, and whatever they say about you or *Dictated Choices* translates into book sales."

If the whirlwind of TV interviews wasn't enough to make his head spin, the first-class treatment that his publisher arranged for his brief stay in New York City certainly made him feel like a celebrity. Sandra herself wasn't budgeted for a stay at the legendary Four Seasons Hotel for their three day media blitz.

"How was this hotel selected?" he asked. "Don't get me wrong. It's super, but it's also so expensive."

Sandra smiled at his naiveté. "There are two answers to that question."

"Okay, I'll bite," Davis said.

"Let's go back to when you signed with Ballantine. They gave you an advance, which was completely their gamble. If the book didn't earn out, it made no difference to your wallet, as you're never required to pay back any of it. But you also earn royalties, and those depend on how many books are actually sold."

Davis's expression told Sandra that he still hadn't heard an answer regarding the expensive hotel.

"The costs of marketing your novel will be deducted from any royalties that may come later. They figured you would draw media attention during your stay in New York, and putting you in this wonderful famous hotel adds to the magic they're creating around you."

Davis nodded. "But I have to ask, what about you? You're not booked at this hotel. Why not?"

She laughed. "The publisher isn't worried about enhancing my mystique. Otherwise, we'd be together almost every waking hour."

Before the Augustine Skinner radio interview, Davis had difficulty restraining his feelings for Sandra. Beyond her physical attractiveness, he was drawn to her because of her cleverness and high energy, evident in almost everything she said or did. Sandra had more ambition and self-confidence than many women he knew. Being with her boosted those same qualities in him. Still, Davis was unsure of her feelings for him and wanted to avoid anything that might damage their author-and-agent relationship. Sandra would have to make the first move.

11

Writers Words

WRITERS WORDS APPEARED IN ALMOST every publication Brady Harvey subscribed to. Along with informative articles, it often included a column by Cora Charles that he enjoyed. Brady liked her and the way she described the effort to get a novel published as teamwork between an author and an agent. She wrote about how that could be accomplished without him leaving home, and when she described her condominium in Santa Monica, her appeal to potential clients became even more convincing.

Although Brady's novel was unfinished it was nearing its conclusion and he was pleased with his progress. Cora's address was in Santa Monica, and she explained on her website that her location made her available to meet new authors and work with them. Sometimes, she offered opportunities for new writers to participate for a fee on one of her podcast conference calls that she organized from her home studio. That was just what Brady needed, as his home confinement rules kept him from going anywhere to meet people. After Brady paid the fee and participated in the conference call, she suggested that those listening from home could send to her the first ten pages of their manuscript along with a query letter.

When he emailed the required information, Brady added a postscript saying he would like to talk with her some more about his novel and asked that she would call him the following Monday before noon. When noon arrived and she hadn't called, he decided she was probably attending a meeting that had lasted longer than anticipated. Rather than waiting, he googled the website for Writers Words and found her telephone number and mailing address. She answered his call on the first ring.

"Yes, this is Cora." She sounded curious but impatient.

"Cora Charles, right?" Brady had heard her voice only on that conference call and wanted to be sure it was her.

"That's who I am," she snapped. "So now it's your turn, and that's where you can say who you are and why you've just interrupted my busy schedule."

Brady was disappointed by what he considered to be a less-than-professional attitude but simply replied that he was Brady Harvey from Greenwich, Connecticut, and was calling because she hadn't yet called him.

Nearly half a minute of silence followed before Cora spoke. "Mr. Harvey, have we met somewhere? Have I forgotten something about our relationship?"

Brady grew frustrated. "Yes! You and I talked during a conference call only seven days ago, and you asked me to email you a query letter along with the first ten pages of my novel. You're now acting like you didn't even read my email."

Again, Cora paused. "Oh, yes," she said with faux enthusiasm. "I remember you and how you stood out during the conference call where there were, what… twenty-seven others asking me all kinds of beginner-writer questions."

Brady was relieved that she seemed to remember him. "Well? What did you think about my first ten pages? I'm a lot further than that and can send at least a hundred more. Right now, if you'd like."

Suddenly, the call became disconnected.

12

A Fine Romance

AFTER ARRIVING AT WORK, Charlotte looked around and not see-ing Kirsch she was wondering whether the Rayburn Towers doorman was taking another sick day. Ever since Arthur Pradle had opened the office there on the fourth floor nearly twenty-two years ago, the doorman and Charlotte had repeated the same greeting almost every day. Upon offering a welcoming smile, he walked just a bit faster than her to hold open the elevator.

"He treats me like I'm an old lady," she told Arthur once as he rode up with her. "I mean, I know his intentions are good, but really, we're probably the same age, and yet he always greets me that same way. 'Good morning, Miss Olson. My, doesn't this look like it's going to be a fine day?'"

Their friendship never progressed into anything much more than that. They were just two people who saw each other every weekday morning, exchanging pleasantries at lunchtime, then again as they left for the day. Though each seemed to love their job, it was still the same one they'd had when first they met. Kirsch was always in the same doorman's uniform, always with the same morning greeting. As the years passed, it reminded Charlotte of her own lack of personal advancement.

Soon after Sandra was named a junior partner at the Pradle Agency, she asked Charlotte about Kirsch. "I find him rather handsome," Sandra teased. "You surely must be aware of how he fawns over you."

Charlotte was uncomfortable with any conversation with her much younger boss that wasn't strictly concerned with agency business. She'd had many opportunities to ask questions about the gossip columns covering Sandra's social exploits, but she'd never wanted Sandra to feel ill at ease discussing her personal life. Charlotte wished Sandra would show the same regard for her privacy.

"With all due respect, Miss Pierce"—her tone expressed how she felt about Sandra's intrusion into her personal life—"I also think our doorman is handsome, and yes, I have some suspicions about how Kirsch feels toward me. But I haven't yet decided if I have the same intensity in my feelings for him. When or if I reach any definite conclusion in that respect, I promise to make you the second person that I so inform."

The message was delivered, and Sandra never broached the subject with her again.

After Charlotte arrived at her desk she noticed that Sandra was already in her office and on the telephone. That was no surprise, as Sandra always seemed to be the early bird. Considering how frequently Sandra was seen clubbing or attending some gala or Hollywood party, Charlotte often wondered if the woman ever slept for more than a few hours. "Ah, sweet youth," she murmured.

Apparently hearing someone was in the outer office, Sandra called for Charlotte while remaining on her phone conversation. "Charlotte, if that's you out there, hurry and locate our Davis Quigley for me. I have some exciting news." Then she returned to her telephone call.

While waiting for Davis to answer, Charlotte noted there was more than excitement in Sandra's voice. Charlotte sensed something troubling in the way Sandra had pronounced "exciting news." Her suspicions were confirmed when Sandra abruptly ended her call after Charlotte signaled that the author was on line 4.

"Davis? I sent you an email an hour ago. You what? Okay, I hoped that I might have heard more excitement. Wait a minute! Did I just wake you up?"

"Sandra, I got in very late, and yes, your call did wake me," Davis admitted. "I'm reading that email right now. Wow!"

"That's more like it." Sandra laughed. "It looks like the week we spent in New York doing those interviews has paid off—big!"

"How do you find out these things so fast?" He was shocked to learn that Ballantine had scheduled another printing of his book, twice the size of the last one.

"When there's any large spike in book sales, there's always a way to explain it," she said. "It always follows news, any kind of news, good or bad."

"And as you mentioned on that last night we spent together, things are beginning to happen," Davis said. He was both disappointed and grateful.

Sandra picked up on the nuance right away. "Hey, sleepyhead." She laughed again. "Sounds to me like you're either falling back asleep or perhaps you have something other than business bothering you."

He was surprised at how fast she'd caught on to his slip-up. When Sandra said things were beginning to happen, Davis had hoped Sandra meant something much more personal than business. If he'd misunderstood, it was only because they were in bed together the last time she'd spoken those words.

"No, no. You were right the first time. Guess I am still a bit of a sleepyhead." Davis hoped to cover his mistake.

The part about "something besides business" jolted Davis back to reality. His feelings for Sandra were escalating beyond what he had any reason to expect her to have with him. Sandra Pierce was a celebrity and socialized with people far more famous than himself. Davis had heard the gossip about her and her busy social life. But he wasn't interested in being famous. His attraction to Sandra grew from being with her, seeing and talking with her, and teaming up with her to make his novel successful. Her confidence, energy, and brilliance were more evident each time they were together. Their periods of time apart left him longing for her in ways he'd forgotten since he lost Ellie, still the only love he'd ever known. Davis hoped Sandra shared some of those same longings. But if he was mistaken about her affections for him, he had no doubt regarding the significant role she played in his writing career.

"Okay, then. All is okay?" she asked.

Before Davis could respond completely, she interrupted.

"You did watch that *Fox at the Front* show last Sunday, right? Well, here's something that might cheer you up. Catherine Lane—you remember her, the lady who put old Will Jennings on the has-been list for talk show invitees—called here yesterday."

Davis reluctantly returned to agent-writer business and knew it wasn't a good time to discuss his feelings. "Yes, sure." He tried to sound more focused. "I laughed out loud watching her handle that only-my-opinion-counts Jennings. Doesn't she already have an agent?"

"I'm sure she does, but that wasn't the purpose of her calling here. She wants to meet with you. Something about discussing the research that you did for *Dictated Choices*."

"She wants to... meet with me?"

Before she could respond to Davis' question she saw people gathering around Charlotte's desk. "Sorry, Davis. I have to go. Something weird is going on outside my office. I'll have Charlotte call you, or you can call Charlotte and get the information you'll need to contact Mrs. Lane."

Without so much as a goodbye, Sandra ended the call.

After returning to the office from buying a snack, Randy Turley had news regarding "Charlotte's doorman," a name he and Amy Wang quietly referred to for Kirsch. "Old Kirsch had a heart attack…" was as far as he got before Charlotte slumped into a near faint. Amy rushed to Charlotte's aid while Randy stood dumbstruck at the effect of his news.

"Bring some water," Amy told him as she steadied Charlotte into a chair. Seeing Amy taking charge calmed Randy enough to think clearly, and he hustled to the cooler along the opposite wall. When he returned, he found Charlotte back on her feet.

"Tell me everything you heard." Her voice was uneven, displaying her anxiety.

Randy sneaked a peek at Amy, looking for her guidance on whether it was all right to tell everything to Charlotte, who still looked like she might collapse any minute.

"I was coming back from the lobby, and old Carl Hobbs, who works in the Franklin law firm mailroom—"

"WILL YOU PLEASE LEAVE OUT THE DETAILS OF HOW YOU HEARD AND JUST TELL ME WHAT YOUR HEARD?" Charlotte screamed in desperation to know what Randy meant when he said Kirsch was in Cardiac Care. By now she had grabbed Randy's shirt and was shaking it so hard he thought it might rip right off of him.

"All I know is he is in Cardiac Care at St. Johns in Santa Monica." Randy's voice moved from 33 RPM to 78 RPM and sounded so much like a chipmunk that it would have been comical under other circumstances.

By the time Sandra arrived alongside of them, she heard only the last part of Randy's news. Using Charlotte's telephone, she contacted Sam Fortman in the building manager's office. Learning all she needed to know, she told Randy to get her car and have it ready for her to drive Charlotte to the hospital.

Turning to Charlotte, who was losing all color, Sandra eased her back on to the desk chair. "Kirsch suffered a heart attack earlier and was taken to St. John's Heart Institute. Sam told me that Kirsch was conscious and that tests are being run to see what needs to be done. Hopefully, he'll be allowed visitors, so we're going there now, you and me. Grab whatever you need, and let's get on our way."

If there was any part of life that Charlotte was least equipped to handle, it was the unexpected or the traumatic ones. She prided herself on always being prepared for anything. Things could and did go wrong, but if alternatives were previously considered—*if this, then that*—appropriate action followed almost automatically. But if something happened out of the blue, something she'd never imagined, panic took over.

Absent any time to think things through, she couldn't decide how to act or how to react. Thoughts rushed through her synapses—Kirsch lying on the marble lobby floor, ambulance personnel loading him onto a rolling stretcher, emergency lights flashing. She was left feeling drained and helpless. Seeing Sandra take charge gave Charlotte the strength to slow her mind down. She was happy to turn the orchestra over to Sandra.

The hospital visit went by faster than Sandra would have expected. After she returned from St. John's Heart Institute, she called Arthur in New York with the news about Kirsch. Arthur was surprised about him but not about Charlotte's reaction to his hospitalization.

"I've suspected this all along, right since we moved into our offices at Rayburn Towers," he said. "They were made for each other, both too private to acknowledge even their own feelings for the other. Too bad they never did, as that's the stuff that makes romance work." He laughed.

"Why, Mr. Pradle," Sandra said, sounding like a Southern belle. "I do believe that you care about our poor little Charlotte Olson."

Arthur admitted that was true and wondered if he should plan a trip back to Los Angeles. Sandra reminded him that the two of them would be together soon in New York when one of their authors, Franz Graber, was scheduled to be interviewed on *The Today Show*. In the meantime, she would keep him up to date on Kirsch.

Before ending the call, Sandra told Arthur about Catherine Lane's efforts to reach Davis Quigley. She wondered if that was anything they should be concerned about.

"You aren't referring to that blip in *Writers Monthly*, are you?"

"I wasn't concerned, to use your word, when I read it," she said. "I mean, just because they quoted an anonymous source at Hurd Patterson saying that whenever they blew out candles on birthday cakes, they wished to get Davis Quigley into their camp."

"If that didn't push any of your buttons, what has you wondering whether we should worry about why Mrs. Lane wants to contact Davis?"

"Arthur, my wise and respected mentor slash partner." Sandra sounded like she was about to say something nice before dropping a bomb. "Mrs. Lane is under contract with none other than that jealous literary agency known as Hurd Patterson."

A loud throat-clearing cough was all the response that Sandra heard for the next few seconds. When Arthur recovered enough to continue their conversation, his voice sounded bruised.

"Sandra, Davis loves being represented by Pradle Literary Agency, particularly by Sandra Pierce," he said cautiously. "You discovered him, and that along with the other rationale that men use when making decisions leaves me feeling comfortable about the prospects of our continued future with Davis Quigley and each of your male writers."

That little extra dialogue about "the other rationale that men use" was unnecessary and convinced Sandra to draw the conversation to a close. Without showing any sign of the insult she felt hidden inside Arthur's remarks, Sandra ended the call and said she had every confidence that her entire cadre of writers, male and female, would remain faithful to Pradle Literary Agency.

After she hung up, she felt sad that every now and then, Arthur threw a dig at her. His extraneous remarks, always demeaning, usually concerned something about her nightlife that had appeared in a gossip column. It was designed to show her he was boss. Or perhaps he'd suffered guilt over his own extracurricular activities with her.

Sandra clicked open her password-protected Microsoft journal and typed.

Well, Arthur is at it again. He waited until just before we finished our call to remind me that he thinks of me as the slut he has for a junior partner. Oh, he didn't use that word. Never does. But that's what he was referring to by implying that I'm sleeping with writers to get and keep them as clients. But really, did Arthur think that I was going to only go to him for my body's needs? He's a married man, and I have no interest in changing his status there. I slept with him, twice. Both times because I wanted to, not because I wanted him to hire me (our first) and not because I wanted to own a part of the business here at PLA (the second and FINAL time). Speaking about such misunderstandings: Simon DuValle, that beautiful man from Montego Bay... I know that he thinks I used him too. Yes, I made love with him (many more times than Arthur Pradle would even care to guess). But never for any reason other than that I was so damn attracted to him. He is a Black warrior, and I am his white slave, whom he captured one night in the moonlight and never let me free. But then Arthur found out about us and threatened to fire me if I didn't break it off with Simon. Of course, I didn't want to do that, but at the time, I had no future as an agent without Arthur's backing. So, from then on, Simon and I had separate hotel rooms when we went out on tour and took pains to never be seen together outside of business situations. I taught Simon the meaning of the word discreet. *We didn't stop what we were doing. We stopped doing it where we could be caught.*

13

Sunday with the Press

D URING THE MONTH FOLLOWING his appearance on *Fox at the Front,* Will Jennings walked a tightrope. The reviews were brutal and, to his way of thinking, unfair and insulting. But responding to them made him appear defensive and often led to lashing out at friend and foe alike. It didn't bother him that his comments found little agreement outside of his regular readers. Strangely, he felt belittled by the condescending efforts used by those fans who came to his defense. Those who called or wrote letters to the editors of the papers that carried his column, *Just Jennings,* didn't support what he said so much as express sympathy for the "mean things" being said about him in the press.

"People don't understand," he told Patricia Flood, a *Sunday with the Press* producer who had just invited him to appear on the program. "My reputation hasn't suffered, at least not by anything that I've said or, for that matter, anything that Catherine Lane said on that damn Fox show. It's all those well-wishers who are causing this role reversal, this poor-picked-on Will Jennings stuff. They have it all wrong."

That was a side of Will Jennings that surprised the producer. Defending his reputation while casting his apologists as his newest enemies seemed to unmask either a narcissistic or paranoid personality. It wasn't only the words he spoke. His voice lacked his trademark self-assurance and sounded almost whiny.

Patricia wondered if he would allow her to quote him. *Did Will Jennings just expose an Achilles heel?* It would certainly be a scoop for *Sunday with the Press* viewers to learn that the nationally syndicated columnist and champion of conservatives, a man known and admired for his strong opinions on what it meant to be American, secretly suffered from insecurity.

She needed to be delicate with her invite. If she upset him, he wouldn't agree to be on the show and take questions from her boss, Ted Richmond. She decided to put the invitation in a different form.

"You haven't yet told me whether you'll be with us on a coming edition of *Sunday with the Press*." She tried to sound as meek as possible. "But if, as you suspect, people are suddenly looking at you as a victim…"

When he heard that word *victim*, Will Jennings's eyes widened, his jaw stiffened, and anger seemed to pulse throughout his body. For years, he'd seen that word as a sign of weakness, of surrender. People called themselves a *victim* when they wanted charity. They were people who couldn't succeed on their own and quit trying. They survived by being lifted on the backs of the sympathetic and misguided fools who bought into their stories.

He wasn't a victim. He was Will Jennings, someone who understood, like Charles Darwin, that only the fittest survived. Crying counted for nothing. Guilt counted for even less. Conquer or be conquered.

He rose from his chair and walked over to his visitor. "You can tell Mr. Richmond that Will Jennings will be happy to accept that invitation." He sounded like someone who had just accepted a challenge to a duel.

Patricia was excited by his acceptance but wondered if it would be the best time to mention that Catherine Lane had already agreed to appear and would be seated alongside him. Her decision was made easier when Jennings, explaining that he faced a column deadline, rushed her out of his office. She was in her car and returning to NBC when her caller ID indicated the big man himself was on the line. Pushing the talk button, she barely had time to say hello before hearing a familiar voice asking how things had gone with Jennings.

"Well?"

She loved the brevity that her boss employed when he wanted a report. Patricia paused to heighten the suspense. "You can call in the promotion squad and tell them to begin hyping. The rematch is on. Jennings wants a second chance."

"Cheers for you, Patricia." Richmond said adding that he was surprised that she beat the other Sunday morning shows who wanted the same guests. "We'll talk later about how you got him to agree. But for now, shake a leg and get back here and work on the research that I'll need to moderate this rematch."

When Davis called Sandra's office to get the Catherine Lane information from Charlotte, he also learned about the incident regarding Kirsch. Amy Wang didn't know anything about how to contact Catherine. Sandra had earlier promised to leave a note on Charlotte's desk, asking her to get in touch with Davis when she returned to work.

Davis decided to call Sandra's cell phone number but had to settle for leaving a message. He explained that he'd never received Catherine's contact information. A minute later, his cell phone buzzed.

"Sandra," he said without checking the screen, "how am I supposed to contact anyone when no one tells me anything about anything? There's no telephone number or maybe her agent's number or...?"

The voice that spoke next wasn't Sandra's.

"Mr. Quigley?" she asked. "My name is Catherine Lane, and Sandra Pierce gave me your telephone number and—"

"Oh my. I'm sorry." Davis felt compelled to explain that he knew the reason for her call. "Sandra did, in fact, tell me to contact you, but then before I got your number, all hell broke loose in Los Angeles. I was expecting a call back from Sandra on this very matter." Davis was babbling, aware that it all sounded like an excuse to blow her off.

"Please don't apologize," she said. "I talked with Sandra and know all about the excitement that happened there. As it turns out, I'm in Chicago right now, between flights at O'Hare, and I wondered if we might meet."

Relieved that it no longer looked like he was avoiding her, Davis quickly agreed. He said he could be at the airport within a half hour and wondered how much time she had.

"Actually, I have less than an hour before boarding. But if you're really not too inconvenienced, I can schedule a later flight. Perhaps we can have lunch?"

Davis said that if she had a longer time between flights, he could pick her up at Arrivals and have their lunch meeting away from the airport. She sounded pleased by his suggestion and agreed to let him pick her up where he suggested would work best for their meeting.

14

Death of a Friend, the novel

Sandra Pierce's flight to New York encountered strong head-winds and arrived twenty-five minutes late. After checking in at the Lombardy Hotel, where Charlotte had booked her a room, Sandra texted Franz Graber to ask whether he wanted to meet for a late breakfast. She knew Franz was also staying at the Lombardy but decided a text was preferable to a phone call. Her author-client might be entertaining someone overnight. She was surprised when he responded by calling her cell phone.

"Sandra?" He sounded enthusiastic. "Yes, let's meet. Right now, if you're available."

Sandra smiled. They were both in New York for his appearance on *The Today Show*, and the alertness in his voice assured her that he wasn't nervous. She suggested they meet at Ninth Street Espresso. "They're right next door, and besides, they have the absolute best coffee selection, everything from espresso to iced lattes."

"Since you like it, I know I will too." Franz laughed.

Earlier in the week, Arthur Pradle had booked Franz on *The Today Show* to discuss his book on Bruno Richard Hauptmann, the man convicted in the Lindbergh-baby kidnapping case. The television interview date marked the eighty-sixth anniversary of the crime. Pradle also called Sandra with the good news and told her to come to New York a day early to prepare their author.

"It hardly seems possible, but it was almost four years ago that we first met," Sandra recalled after they ordered breakfast. "I was accompanying Simon DuValle on his book tour for *The Solitary Soul* and suddenly noticed you standing very close to me while Simon was busy autographing books."

"I do remember," Franz acknowledged. "Earlier, I read somewhere how you discovered Simon while you were on vacation in Montego Bay and that you turned a chance reading of his typed pages into what became *The Solitary Soul*. I guess I was hoping you might read my manuscript."

Sandra gave him a wide smile. "Yes, that's how it all began." She remembered how attractive and soft spoken he was and recalled that was the reason she decided to accept the manuscript outline he just happened to have with him.

"I was surprised to discover later how impressed I was with your outline. I mean, there had already been many books published about the case, but the ones I was familiar with focused on either the guilt or innocence of Hauptmann. What I found so interesting was the information you revealed about who Hauptmann claimed was the real kidnapper."

"Isidor Fisch," Franz said. "It was actually my grandmother who suggested that would be an interesting subject for the thesis for my PhD in history."

"I was happy to hear that but wondered why your grandmother would be so interested in that case," Sandra said.

Franz took a bite of his breakfast. The look in his eyes told Sandra he was reliving that time period in his life.

"I was born fifty years after the kidnapping took place," he said. "The most important evidence used to convict Hauptmann was the fourteen thousand dollars in ransom money that was discovered in his home when the police arrested him. He claimed that Fisch gave him a sealed box before he returned to Germany for treatment of a lung disease. Investigators later tracked Fisch to Germany, only to discover he had already died from a pulmonary illness."

"And your grandmother?"

"She grew up in Leipzig, Germany," Franz said, "and she was acquainted with Fisch. She was certain Fisch was the man who met with Lindbergh's intermediary in the cemetery when the ransom money was handed over."

"But how did she reach that conclusion? Did she ever explain that to you?"

Franz looked puzzled. "You already know how my grandmother's involvement came about. You suggested much of it yourself."

Sandra sighed. "Franz, I'm helping you prepare for the questions they may throw at you when you appear on *The Today Show.* Everything we just rehashed is perfect for your responses to any of the questions," Sandra said. "But the part about your grandmother and how she decided Isidor Fisch was the man who accepted the ransom money is not something that I want you to discuss on that morning show—or ever!"

Again, Franz looked confused and taken aback.

Sandra noticed his troubled expression. "I was impressed with your style and thorough research but knew that turning nonfiction about such a famous kidnapping case into a mystery needed something more than the known facts. Your story needed to show that it was offering something new, something not yet looked at by all those who'd studied the crime of the century."

The confusion showing in Franz's eyes gave Sandra pause.

"Surely, you remember that I even told you then that your manuscript wasn't one I could present with any confidence to publishing houses," she reminded him. "I told you how it needed something that no one else had ever discovered. The secret that you then added was just what I knew your book needed. I never asked you more about that, and I hope it can stay that way."

"But you did decide to help me. That cheered me enough to take you to the pub where my fellow grad students were gathered."

"Ah, yes." Sandra laughed. "Hemingway's Hideaway. What a first impression that made on me. A small tavern with no more than six barstools right off the entrance, where two middle-aged men were engaged in debate. Nearby was a large table filled with friends of yours from the university."

"Right. My friends who then became your friends too," he added.

"I remember how within minutes, I felt completely accepted. Nothing seemed off-limits, and when they learned I rejected your manuscript, they even booed me." She laughed.

Franz left his seat in the booth across the table from Sandra and slid alongside her. Putting an arm around her, he whispered, *"Last... call!"*

Sandra knew immediately what that meant, and together, they quietly sang the Whiffenpoof Song like they did that night along with his chums at Hemingway's.

Later that morning, while unpacking in her room, Sandra remembered more about that wonderful night they'd been talking about. It had been raining all night, and she and Franz got soaked running the two blocks to the hotel where he'd earlier found a parking spot. Their dripping clothes made them discard their wet garments once they were inside her hotel suite. Four hours later, they awoke in each other's arms. Sandra was already late for a planned breakfast with Simon. Franz was also running late for his job. Their hurried departure left both with a sense of absence. After a final goodbye when their elevator reached the hotel lobby, they kissed and pledged to find a way to be together again… soon.

Sandra remembered watching as Franz hurried out the large revolving glass door and ran down the sidewalk to where he'd left his car. It was raining again, which had made her smile as she thought about poor Franz showing up at his job dripping wet. A strange warmth filled her as she recalled their night together with his friends at Hemingway's. She loved the singing, the drinking, and the storytelling. She even loved the cozy atmosphere at Hemingway's. And Franz? She'd wondered whether she was in an early stage of falling in love with him.

While she relived old memories, a voice from behind asked if she had forgotten their breakfast date. She turned around and saw Simon. He looked down at her as she approached, then without another word being spoken, he pressed a button that closed the elevator door.

"Simon?" she'd called after him. "How long…?" It was useless to continue speaking. The elevator doors had closed, and he was gone. Simon had witnessed her and Franz's goodbyes, and he could guess at all the rest. That didn't bode well for her relationship with Simon and definitely not for her relationship with Arthur Pradle.

Sandra later wrote in her journal:

That morning in Seattle when Simon caught Franz and me leaving the elevator and kissing goodbye nearly ended my career again. Why? Did Simon think I was his exclusive bed partner? Yes, I know that he loved me and that in his island religion, when a woman sleeps with a man, she becomes his and his alone. He, of course, is not so bound by that custom. So, seeing me with Franz makes me a slut and entitles him to seek revenge. Arthur had to resolve it all by flying into Seattle and convincing Simon to stay with the Pradle Agency by sending me back to Los Angeles and completing the book tour with Simon. Actually, Arthur did fire me but then rescinded that when I told him that my tryst with Franz was about to produce our next best-selling author. (I left out the part about how I had told Franz the previous night that his manuscript was unlikely to find a publisher.)

I spent the next week with Franz, going over various changes in his manuscript that might make it special. Finally, it dawned on me to convince him to write that after all his investigations were complete, he'd discovered that the secret that his grandmother had hidden throughout her entire life was that Isidor Fisch was her lover and the real father of Franz's dad. Franz was reluctant at first, but it was this little white lie that gave him the unique historical account. I sold his book, Death of a Friend, *to Doubleday. I knew what Franz wrote would cause attention, since he alleged that the state executed an innocent man in the Lindbergh-baby kidnapping case. Doubleday did a fantastic promotion for the book, and within a month, it was number five on the* New York Times *Best Seller List. And now, two years later,* The Today Show *will be interviewing Franz Graber to mark the eighty-sixth anniversary of what was called the crime of the century.*

And, dear diary, no one outside of these pages knows that Franz Graber only agreed to my suggested changes for his book the morning after we enjoyed the most passionate lovemaking in our lives.

Slut? Seems a bit unfair when one looks at results... don't you think?

15

Preparing for the rematch

I ACCEPTED THE INVITATION TO appear on *Sunday with the Press* because it seemed to give me an opportunity to respond to the perception that my reputation and my conservative views took a beating on the *Fox at the Front* program, Will Jennings explained during his meeting with Richard Drake. "The moderator, Ted Richmond, is considered by most observers to be an Independent in his political preference. Whatever his questions might be, at least they will be fair and show respect. Don't you agree?"

"I do agree," Drake responded. "You'll also be afforded time to fully respond, unlike the opinion programs on cable, like Ripley's on Fox or those on MSNBC."

"Exactly!" Jennings said. "That's why learning now that they will also have Catherine Lane on the same segment of the show with me is such a slap in the face."

"It's all for the ratings," Drake added. "They're promoting it big with ads on TV and in newspapers too."

"I'm not afraid to be presenting the conservative views, even with Mrs. Lane doing her subtle best to make everything I say and stand for look intolerable or plain ignorant." Jennings allowed some disgust to sneak into his response. "I just do not accept all the hoopla that this is a rematch. Put me in a debate with Obama or Bill Clinton, and then you might have a discussion that could deserve to be billed as a match." Left unsaid was the complete disregard he had for Catherine Lane as a competitor.

Richard Drake and Will Jennings greatly respected each other's skills and achievements in their occupations. While Jennings's style had brought success and fame on a much larger scale, Drake's reputation was based on being the most sought-after consultant on what was happening within the clandestine world of politics. His insights and advice left others marveling about his sources.

Whenever Jennings needed information that wasn't available in the public sphere, he called on Richard Drake. After discovering that he was to be joined by Catherine Lane on the Sunday program, he sensed that his preparations might benefit from having as much knowledge of her background as he could get his hands on. With less than two weeks remaining before the program, he called on his old friend.

Patricia Flood came up with only enough information to fill maybe half the airtime on *Sunday with the Press.* That included the quotes that Ted Richmond always put on the screen and read aloud to his guests just before dropping a bombshell. His producers were responsible for gathering the information and having it at the ready. The questions or comments regarding that information came only from the inquisitive mind of the show's moderator, Ted Richmond.

During an update with producers, it became evident that something more might be required to sustain audience interest. As much as everyone hoped for it, they couldn't count on Catherine Lane to sparkle as brightly as she had earlier when contesting the formidable Will Jennings on *Fox at the Front.*

"I'm just afraid that now that Jennings has had time to measure her as an opponent, he'll murder her," Richmond concluded after sitting through the staff's presentations around the conference table. "Mrs. Lane was obviously better prepared for Will Jennings than he was for her then." The moderator stood up and looked each of the four people in the eyes before settling on his producer.

Patricia Flood sorted through some notes she'd written earlier on a yellow legal pad. "Perhaps we might invite a third guest, someone related to this rematch concept that we're using to promote the program."

"Do you have someone in mind?" Richmond seemed to be growing impatient when little more than a week remained to prepare.

"I can think of two people who could certainly fill empty airtime," Patricia said. "Perhaps we could bring on the author of that novel that was referred to on the Fox program, a Mr. Davis?"

"No, his name is Davis Quigley," an assistant seated next to her clarified.

"I read his book and also watched him on Bull Ripley's program," Ted Richmond told the group. "Ripley murdered him, and it won't be any easier for Quigley to do combat with the brilliant Mr. Jennings." He paused. "You said you had two ideas for a guest?"

"The other is a reach," Patricia said. "But one sure way to add fire would be to include Augustine Skinner."

The three others around the long oval conference table looked back and forth from Patricia to Richmond. Patricia was also curious how her suggestion was being received but almost laughed at the bobble head performance of her coworkers.

"I like that one," Richmond finally responded. But then his expression changed.

"No, it won't work after all." He sighed. "In a best-case scenario, it would become Jennings and Skinner piling on poor Catherine

Lane. In a more likely worst-case scenario, the pompous, loud-mouthed, belligerent Augustine Skinner would monopolize the whole program."

Richmond left the conference room after deciding to do the program with only Jennings and Catherine Lane and told his producers and staff they each had much work remaining before their program date. The bobble heads all turned back to Patricia.

16

At last, they meet!

DAVIS WAS RELIEVED TO FIND Catherine Lane waiting exactly where he'd expected her to be at Arrivals but was surprised she had her luggage with her. She explained that upon learning the earliest available flight was going to be on the red-eye departing shortly before midnight, she opted instead for a mid-morning departure the following day and had already booked a reservation at the Palmer House.

"I always allow for an extra day or two when traveling for speaking engagements or book signings and promotions," Catherine explained. "I'm more comfortable avoiding anything that's rush-rush and prefer arriving a day early. It gives me time to recover."

The afternoon traffic on the Kennedy Expressway was unusually light and trouble-free, allowing Davis to focus on Catherine. Her comment about wanting time to recover seemed more suitable to someone older and revealed how little she was aware of the impression she left on others. He recalled seeing her on the *Fox at the Front* program, where her face had captured his attention. In person, he was drawn to her other attributes.

Catherine was about his age, thirty-two. Yet she could have easily passed for someone much younger. She appeared to be a few inches shorter than Sandra and had a less slimmer figure, all of which complemented her persona. She spoke with a soft sincerity that revealed an underlying vulnerability. Davis had the urge to stop driving, pull over, and hold her close. Only the briefness of their recent acquaintance interrupted that impulse and returned his attention to the purpose of their meeting.

They enjoyed lunch at the Palmer House Café, and Davis discussed much of the background he'd used for *Dictated Choices.* Her questions were few, and she seemed drawn to stories of his days at the radio station. She was most interested in the female lawyer in his novel. A progressive young public defender who argued eloquently on behalf of the accused, pitting wealth and ability to fill wants versus poverty and a subsequent smaller ability to provide for needs.

"The words you wrote for her summation to the jury stung not only my consciousness but also my heart," Catherine told him. "When you described the emotion in that courtroom when the guilty verdict was delivered by the hushed and ashamed-sounding jury foreman, you were speaking not only about them. Your words made me feel ashamed too, and I suspect many of your readers felt that way as well."

She got it! Davis had written *Dictated Choices* for a reason, and until that moment, he believed he'd failed. True, he wanted to write a novel, get it published, and hopefully become a bit richer and perhaps even famous. But the story he wrote came from the frustrations that he'd experienced writing about crime in Chicago.

Early in his job, he'd observed that justice was only a reaction to something that had already been done. "Ignoring the reason something was done left no hope for addressing the crime, only the criminal," he told Catherine. "And that course of action leaves only one obvious result, more crimes."

Davis looked into Catherine's eyes and explained that he'd written his novel to bring some attention to the problem. If society could be persuaded that studying the motivations of people who broke laws wasn't the same as making excuses for them, the root causes of crime would be better addressed.

"When I wrote about street crimes in the city for the radio news, I sometimes found they were often followed by a story about a new wonder drug," he recalled. "I was struck by the difference in how we seek solutions to diseases compared with our efforts to reduce crime."

Catherine's smile indicated that she shared his beliefs. "You seem to be saying that if we still relied only on surgery and not on finding the cause, disease would never be eliminated."

"Exactly!" Davis smiled. "Many learned people at the universities have proposed that motivations have to be understood when addressing criminal behavior, but their suggestions are passed off as nothing more than liberal tears."

"So, you decided to cloak their efforts in a fictional story, hoping to sneak their conclusions into public awareness," Catherine said.

"Exactly! Talking with you now, I feel much like someone who has just seen his invention working outside of the laboratory. I'm sorry, but I feel like shouting."

Catherine laughed then sheepishly looked around at the neighboring tables, where heads quickly turned away, betraying their eavesdropping. She looked at Davis, who'd noticed the same activity. He apologized for being so caught up in their conversation that he forgot they were in a crowded café. Catherine smiled and said she too had fallen unaware of the other diners.

While Davis took care of the check, Catherine visited the powder room. She was pleased with the information she'd learned.

Everything they discussed during lunch would help her prepare for her *Sunday with the Press* appearance. She'd gained great insight into the reality of living in poverty. Still, that helpful information alone didn't account for the buoyancy of her current emotional state. Something else seemed to be happening.

17

Suspicions and a therapist

IMMEDIATELY AFTER HER UNSCHEDULED surprise visit to Brady Harvey's condominium, Miranda Esquivel phoned his therapist, Beverly Beckett Conforti, and left a message asking Beverly to call her back as soon as possible. Miranda had just enough time to get back to her office before the call was returned.

"I'm afraid that he's slipping," Miranda began. "I noticed something different in him during my regular phone check-up recently and decided it was time for another on-site visit."

"Tell me," the therapist asked, "just what you noticed that was so different. Was he angry? Was his speech slurred?"

Beverly retrieved Brady's file and looked at her notes.

Miranda continued, "I mean that something just seemed different, you know. It was his reluctance to let me inside his condo when I first got there that told me he was hiding something," she said. "He knows the rules. He knows he can't keep me from checking up in person to be sure he's complying with the restrictions the court placed on him before releasing him from the hospital and—"

"Okay, Mrs. Esquivel," Beverly interrupted. "I understand that he must have close scrutiny, and I'm certain he understands that also. What is it that you saw once he let you inside? He did let you in, didn't he?"

"Oh yes, he let me in but not without trying to keep me outside waiting until he could hide what he didn't want me to find."

"And once you went inside, what did you discover that has you convinced he is, as you said, slipping?"

Miranda thought that she detected indifference or something worse. Perhaps the therapist was hurrying her along because she had a client waiting. Perhaps she was annoyed at spending her valuable time listening to the analysis of her client's behavior from someone she considered unqualified in that role, merely interfering in her territory. Whatever the reason, Miranda felt disrespected. Her job required her to do just what she was trying to do. If Brady was returning to a stage where he might become dangerous, she had to get the therapist to agree before taking the next steps to have him returned to custody.

"Yes, Mrs. Conforti, I know you must be busy, so let me tell you everything. The first thing I saw was that the newspaper on his table had something cut from it. I looked around and saw something that looked like a small piece of a newspaper under a dish towel, and when I removed the towel, I saw it was a picture."

"And you feel that cutting pictures out of newspapers is a sign of what?"

Miranda ignored the question. "It was her in that newspaper picture. It was the same woman in the framed photographs in his living room, bedroom, and on the kitchen table. In the picture he cut out of the newspaper, she was with a man. They sat across from each other at a table in a café, and she had his hands in hers. And a big *X* was scribbled across the man's face."

Beverly didn't immediately respond. During the previous six months, she thought she had seen progress in Brady's openness to her suggestions about how to deal with his painful childhood memories. He was fixated on his neighbor and schoolmate Catherine Dallas and believed their high school romance had ruled and ruined his life, even though their relationship had ended more than a decade ago.

Beverly could see that her client was perhaps moving past those memories only by zeroing in on another woman, so there was definitely cause for concern. The problems that had landed him at Connecticut Valley Hospital wouldn't be resolved by fixating on a different woman—if in fact the woman in the pictures was not Catherine Dallas. Having pictures of the same woman all over his apartment sounded like another fixation, especially when he cut out newspaper pictures of her and kept them.

"Mrs. Conforti?" Miranda asked as the silence lingered. "Are you still there?"

"If what you're telling me is accurate," the therapist finally responded, "I find all of that to be very disappointing news. When you said that it was the same woman—"

"Yes, I'm certain that it's her in the picture. But you can see for yourself if you buy yesterday's *Daily News* and go to the front page of the entertainment section. Look for the gossip column, Seen at the Scene."

"Yes, I'll be sure to do that," Beverly told her. "I'm writing that information down now. But you're confident it's the same woman?"

"I wasn't sure at first," Miranda said. "But when I found a scrapbook lying on the couch and opened it, all the pictures inside were of only one woman, the same woman whose picture is in that newspaper cutout."

"Were those photos that Brady took? Or were they also newspaper clippings?"

"Some in the scrapbook were newspaper or magazine cutouts," Miranda said. "Other photos looked like they might have come from back covers on books. You know, where they show the author's bio? I think one of the newspaper photos was at a cemetery, and at least one or two pages in the scrapbook showed that woman at her wedding. There were a lot more, and I wanted to ask him about them but figured it might upset him to know that I—"

"Did he become upset when he found you going through the scrapbook?"

Miranda knew that her job description required her to avoid doing anything that might unnecessarily upset a client. Her responsibilities were unambiguous—monitor behavior and file reports that her immediate supervisor then forwarded to the appropriate manager for evaluation. Miranda wondered if the therapist was setting her up.

"No, not at all." Miranda hoped to nip that suspicion in the bud. "In fact, he was talking to Angel in his bedroom when I opened the scrapbook. I don't think he even saw me look inside it."

"He was talking to Angel?"

"Yes, that's right. He tells her everything. This time, I overheard him saying that Vladimir will be avenged, and the new Onegin will have to be eliminated."

"Miranda, that sounds very much like something that should have prompted you to leave and then call me."

"Oh no, Mrs. Conforti. I didn't take that to mean that Brady was planning on eliminating someone. He often listens to operas when I'm there, and his favorite one is *Eugene Onegin*. Vladimir Lensky was eliminated in that opera by Onegin, and Brady always says it only proves how no one should trust anyone."

"Are you saying that he was just talking about that opera and wasn't angry that you were snooping around?"

"No, and he didn't seem upset about anything. He likes me, you know?"

"Yes, I know he likes you," Beverly responded. "I believe that you've mentioned that a few times recently. But for now, all I need to know is how he was when you left."

"He stayed in his living room, doing his weight lifts and other exercises. When I said I was leaving, he just said goodbye." Miranda knew she probably sounded defensive. "Just 'Goodbye, Miranda.' That's what he usually says when I leave. Just goodbye. Nothing else. Just—"

"Then let me use that same parting right now," the therapist said with only a twinge of guilt for being unable to resist that opening. "Arrivederci, Miranda."

Beverly Conforti then swiftly pushed the off button on her phone.

If in fact Brady was obsessed with a new woman instead of Catherine Dallas that was news to Beverly. Her client had never mentioned being interested in someone else. Also, that part about another man being in the picture—literally and figuratively—concerned her as well.

Completing her review of the Harvey case file, Beverly believed she was still missing something, and that unrest stirred mysteriously inside her mind. She sensed that someone in Brady's current life was going to experience something bad, something awful. Her intuition screamed that trouble lay ahead. She had nothing more than feelings to go on, but she had to do something to stop that awful thing from occurring.

Beverly checked her calendar and saw that Brady was scheduled for a session the following Wednesday. *Should I wait until then to do anything?* She closed her calendar and left for the Kiwanis Club luncheon where she was the scheduled guest speaker.

18

Will Jennings

WILL JENNINGS LOOKED OUT THE window of his office on the eighth floor of the Watergate complex. It wasn't yet seven o'clock, and the sun was just beginning to shine enough early light to move the sensors that controlled the streetlamps along Virginia Avenue to their off positions. Most employees hadn't yet arrived for work, allowing him a brief solace that would all too soon become a busy madness for the remainder of the day. Living in one of the three apartment buildings within the Watergate complex meant he was less than ten minutes' walking distance to his office.

He enjoyed being Will Jennings, both the private one who relished his solitary life away from public scrutiny and the other one who was loved or hated by many yet respected by most. While he enjoyed the last of the coffee he'd bought before boarding the elevator next to the delicatessen in the lower level, Jennings reflected on his life in the limelight.

Ninety percent of his waking hours involved his syndicated column that appeared twice weekly in seventy-four newspapers in print and online. Although his reputation had taken a mild hit following his appearance on *Fox at the Front*, he was still considered the most eloquent proponent of political conservatism in America. His readers quoted from his column just as earnestly as evangelicals quoted from the Bible. Before they had Jennings, they suffered merciless taunts from coworkers, friends, and neighbors influenced by those they considered to be upper-crust Ivy League pseudo-intellectuals who ridiculed their opinions as nothing more than redneck ignorance.

His followers had grown used to being the butt of jokes on late-night comedy shows, especially on *The Daily Show*, where Jon Stewart regularly savaged their views, and even worse, on *Real Time with Bill Maher*. But when those shows displayed sufficient courage to have Will Jennings appear as a guest, the playing field suddenly leveled. Jennings wasn't some rube from the rubble who spit seeds in his spare time. Jennings was an honest-to-goodness nationally respected scholar whose knowledge on the subjects he wrote or spoke about surpassed all challenges. Just as important, he was confident when combatting any left-wing liberal who dared to step up against him.

He understood that was the reason thousands of letters to the editor in newspapers across the country were written in his defense after critics wrote that Catherine Lane had topped him on the Fox program. As much as it galled him to be perceived as one needing to be defended, it proved that his large following was as passionate about his reputation as they were about his ideas. It was that overwhelming reaction from his readers that gave *Sunday with the Press* the idea to have a rematch, and before he understood the real purpose behind their invitation, he had agreed. Others had maneuvered him into feeling he needed to prove something. Still, it was a simple task that lay ahead and not an especially difficult one for someone as well schooled as

Jennings. The expression "on with the show" had just come to mind when the first call of the day rang on his desk phone.

"Mr. Jennings?" the caller asked. "It's me, Mike, downstairs in the lobby. A messenger just dropped off a thick envelope for you. Can you send someone down here to fetch it, or would you prefer to wait for when the eight o'clock crew from the mailroom makes their rounds?"

After being told that the sender was a Richard Drake, Jennings told the lobby manager that he was alone but would come down immediately.

It had been less than one week since he'd asked for Drake's assistance in gathering background on Catherine Lane. After he opened the envelope and saw that it contained not only her biography but also some old news clippings and two large photographs, he quickly dismissed any concern that Drake wasn't taking his request seriously.

Both photographs showed Catherine Lane with a man inside a restaurant, and Jennings wondered why the photos were included. He examined the news clips, and they were taken from newspapers nine and twelve years old. Jennings also wondered about their relevance, as he had specifically requested current information that he could use immediately. Reading the cover letter from Drake, he searched for answers.

Will,

Enclosed is the information that I was able to get on our subject. The section marked biography at first appears to contain nothing more than early background information. But it was while gathering that data that I made contact with a retired reporter from her hometown newspaper. The information that I received from him and where that led me is not included in this report. Instead, I'll call you later this morning and make arrangements for us to share that portion of my investigation. It will save time if you first get a chance to review the enclosed files.

Sincerely,
Richard Drake Associates

<u>*Catherine Lane:*</u>

DOB: August 15, 1987, to Wallace and Kay Dallas (Dallas Shipping LTD)
Height: 5'4"   Weight: 130

Education: Greenwich Academy 2000-2005, Wellesley College 2005-2010

Marriage: March 4, 2010, to Pemberton Lane, the wealthy father of her roommate at Wellesley. He was eighteen years older than Catherine. He died within six months of their marriage after a passing car cut him off while driving along US 95. He missed the turn and drove-or was forced into Long Island Sound and drowned. Lane's five grown children successfully contested his will that granted Catherine half of his fortune. The settlement they finally reached three years later left her with five million dollars.

Other: During her last year at Wellesley, Catherine authored a novel, The Hounds of Hope *that after being published climbed to number one on the* Times *Best Seller List. She subsequently wrote two other novels that were both very successful in sales.*

Address: 20525 Conyers Farm Drive, Greenwich, Connecticut 06807

The photos didn't identify the man that Catherine was with in the restaurant and didn't indicate when or why they were there. Jennings wondered why the photos were included and made a mental note to discuss their importance when he next met with Richard Drake.

19

Visiting Time

CHARLOTTE VISITED KIRSCH EVERY evening while he remained a patient at the hospital. They talked about the temporary replacement who had taken Kirsch's job at Rayburn Towers and how he looked confused and knew nothing about the people who worked in the building. Charlotte even read up on the Dodgers, Kirsch's favorite team, telling him that she'd always liked their retired announcer Vin Scully and missed his hopeful, friendly commentary. She told him about the weather, and he kept her apprised of any new celebrity patients who'd arrived on his floor. Neither of them talked about themselves.

Soon, the nurses and technicians in Kirsch's wing got to know Charlotte quite well. She avoided discussing Kirsch's medical condition with him during her visits. But after leaving his room, she badgered the staff with questions so frequently that before long, she knew more about his medical status than any nurse or doctor who wasn't reading his chart at the time.

One evening, Amy Wang accompanied Charlotte to the

hospital, and later, on their ride home, she asked why Kirsch's legs looked swollen.

"They looked swollen because they *are* swollen," Charlotte said, stating the obvious.

"Were his legs swollen like that before his heart attack?"

Charlotte didn't respond immediately. She drove on and paid attention to the traffic along busy Twenty-Second Street, leaving Amy to wonder if she'd even heard the question. But when she stopped at the next red light, Charlotte turned and looked at her.

"To answer your question, yes," she said pausing long enough to decide whether to tell Amy everything she had learned about Kirsch. When the light changed and she resumed driving, Charlotte decided to share more. "Kirsch's legs were swollen before because, as it turns out, he was suffering from heart failure."

Amy seemed surprised. "Are you saying he had heart failure first and then had a heart attack?"

"No. What I'm telling you is that he only thought he was having a heart attack. He started getting very dizzy then couldn't seem to catch his breath. His heartbeats grew rapid, and he guessed it was a full-blown heart attack."

"Well, it was, wasn't it?" Amy sounded confused. "When my grandfather had those symptoms, they called it a heart attack."

Charlotte sighed, second-guessing her decision to delve into the facts surrounding Kirsch's illness. "After he was taken to St. John's and they stabilized him, they ran a lot of tests and discovered he was suffering from congenital heart disease."

"Congen… what?"

"He has a hole in an upper chamber of his heart." Charlotte hoped that explanation might bring the discussion to an end.

They drove another few miles without talking. When they pulled up in front of Amy's apartment building, Charlotte thanked her for showing interest in Kirsch and for going along to visit him.

"It sounds like something horrible," Charlotte said calmly. "They're going to do an ASD closure on him tomorrow right there at St. John's, and we're very confident that will be all he needs."

Amy looked more confused than before. "What's an ASD closure?"

Charlotte realized it had been a mistake to give Amy so much information. After all, she herself had required a second explanation when Dr. Fremi first informed her of the treatment plan. Because she appreciated Amy's concern for poor Kirsch, Charlotte would make one final attempt to explain things.

"ASD stands for atrial septal defect, which is the same thing as calling it a hole in the upper chamber in his heart. They've decided to have surgery and to insert an umbrella-like device via a catheter into his heart. Once it's there, the device expands to block the passageway between the atria and closes the hole."

The look in Amy's eyes told Charlotte how miserably she'd failed to clear up any confusion. With a wave of her hand, she indicated for Amy to go ahead and leave her vehicle. First, though, Charlotte smiled and, with a nod, assured Amy all was going to be okay.

20

Richard Drake

ON THE WEDNESDAY BEFORE HIS *Sunday with the Press* appearance, Will Jennings received a telephone call from Richard Drake, who wanted to meet to discuss the information that he hadn't included in his report on Catherine Lane. Jennings was scheduled to speak at a breakfast conference of the Log Cabin Republicans at nine o'clock that morning and told Richard to pick a restaurant nearby where they could meet later for lunch.

"Have you ever been to Green Top?" Drake asked.

"What is that? Some environmentalist restaurant where they serve only food that doesn't cause ozone problems?" Jennings was clearly aware that Richard was active in a few environmental organizations.

"Hold on there, old wise one who's not yet a wizard." Richard laughed. "No, Green Top is anything but an environmentalist's hangout. They serve the best hamburgers on that side of town. You know, across the street from the Pavilion Café on Ninth Street, just around the corner from your meeting with the gay guys and gals in the Republican Party."

"So, you picked that place because they serve hamburgers?" Jennings sounded doubtful.

"No, I picked that place because they have a huge green awning over the entrance, and I was sure that even someone as nearly blind as you would find it," Richard mocked. "I picked it for that reason and because it's your turn to buy lunch, and they're the most expensive restaurant in that area."

Drake was already seated at a corner table when Will arrived. The young woman at the reservations podium escorted him to Richard's table, which sat beside a wall with a mural of springtime on Capitol Hill.

"What kind of Irish restaurant features hamburgers?" Jennings laughed after sitting across from Richard.

Drake was finishing one of the stuffed celery sticks he'd selected from the list of appetizers and merely pointed at the history of Green Top printed inside the menu.

Jennings quickly scanned the information, which read, "Green is a symbol of Ireland, often referred to as the Emerald Isle. Green is the color used in many Islamic flags, as green is considered sacred in Islam. Green is used to symbolize nature in folklore and literature. Green signifies immortality in ancient Egypt. Green is used to signify witchcraft in English folklore. Green is used in politics to establish a connection with environmentalism."

"See, it's just as I suspected when I asked why Green Top was your choice of restaurant." Jennings looked up from the list.

"Huh?" Richard's mouth was busy with another tasty stuffed celery stick.

Jennings laughed and read aloud about the color green and environmentalism.

It was true that Richard focused on the alarms sounded by Al Gore and other environmentalists more than Jennings did. Perhaps it was only because of the popularity of Obama and other Democrats that the conservative Jennings turned such a deaf ear to the problem. In any case, Richard wasn't going to be successful in matching wits with Jennings on that or any other topic. He decided to change the subject.

"So, do you have any questions?"

"I most definitely do," Jennings responded. "First, let me say that the entire biography section of your report contained nothing one wouldn't discover in an internet search. The newspaper clips with the obits on her husband had nothing for me either."

"Maybe so, maybe no." The burly investigator rolled his hands. "But you do understand there's more than I included in the written portion."

"Oh, I understand that," Jennings assured him. "But if all we're going to discuss now is a photograph of Catherine Lane with some unidentified man while they were eating somewhere—

"I'll get to that in a minute," Drake said. "What about the high school kids at the cast party that I mentioned? Didn't that capture your interest?"

"That's nothing that I imagine will be helpful for me to know when I'm on *Sunday with the Press*. But why don't I just allow you to explain all these things and their relevance for my purposes? How much you can add will determine which one of us picks up the tab today."

Drake observed the smile on Jennings's face, the expression he often wore when moving toward a checkmate.

"Okay, it's a deal. Let's explain that photo first. It was taken while they had lunch at the Chaz cafe in the Palmer House. They were observed in close conversation that included occasional hand-holding and that lasted for almost two hours."

"So, she has a man friend." Jennings sounded unimpressed. "Anyway, after I received your report with that photograph in it, I saw the same photo on an Associated Press blog. They reported that it appeared in the *Daily News* in an entertainment column known as Seen at the Scene. So, tell me, what's there?"

"It's what *isn't* there," Drake said. "The newspaper referred to Catherine Lane and an unidentified man. I wouldn't call him an unidentified man. I would call him by his name, Davis Quigley."

Jennings looked like he was about to interrupt, but on hearing that the photograph was of Davis Quigley, he waited for Drake to continue.

"One of my sources in Chicago discovered the two of them in the restaurant, snapped the picture using his cell phone, and sold it to the Seen at the Scene columnist. With the attention that *Sunday with the Press* is giving to that rematch between you and Catherine Lane, she's become more of a celebrity than she had been. So, my source figures a photo of her is something he can sell and then takes off without getting the identity of the guy with her. The *Daily News* gets in hurry-up mode to be sure they don't get scooped and ran it in their gossip column."

"Okay, maybe knowing that she's in bed, so to speak, with the author of a book that Auggie Skinner refers to as "all that's left to be read," with emphasis on the words *left* and read, maybe that might be of some interest. But I'm paying for pure background on her, not for anything I would never use in my column or on any TV program I happen to appear on."

"I know that. You're certainly above using garbage on anyone," the investigator acknowledged. "But that part about her being in bed…"

"That was a figure of speech," Jennings explained.

"Okay, a figure of speech, then. And you should understand that we don't have any further information beyond those two holding hands and having lunch in a hotel restaurant. Yet it does seem likely that they're involved in some adult behavior when alone and not in some public place."

At that point Jennings got up to leave. The waitress let him pass and then hurried to Drake's table. "I apologize for the wait," she offered. "We have two girls out with the flu that's going around."

Richard smiled. "Not to worry, my pet. I think my dinner companion was suddenly feeling a bit ill himself."

21

On with the show

GOOD MORNING FROM OUR nation's capital. It's Sunday, and once more, you're invited to spend your *Sunday with the Press*. I'm Ted Richmond, and today, we have something very special to share with you. We'll spend the entire show this morning with only two guests. On your left is the author of four novels, two of which have found their way into the top twenty-five on the *Times* Best Seller List, Catherine Dallas Lane. And on the right is the nationally well-known syndicated columnist, the man most frequently referred to as the voice of intelligent conservatism, Will Jennings. Good morning to you both."

Earlier, Catherine had been surprised by the unexpected nervousness that gripped her just before airtime. She was anxious when producer Patricia Flood led her from the greenroom to the set but felt at ease while being introduced to the moderator, Ted Richmond. His relaxed manner and the fact that she was a frequent viewer of the program allowed her to quickly lose any looming stage fright. She was comfortable, confident, and composed. There was no discomfort brewing even after she was seated and in came

Will Jennings, who gave her a friendly enough smile then and turned away and said something very quietly to Ted Richmond.

When the director signaled the countdown for going live on air, with each descending number Catherine's blood pressure rose. Her palms grew moist, and something at the back of her throat threatened to restrict her voice. She reached for the cup in front of her and sipped the water, hoping to avoid the panic surging in the back channels of her nervous system.

Just as suddenly as it overtook her, the nervousness was gone. Almost at the very instant that Ted Richmond greeted the viewers and introduced her and Jennings, Catherine felt her calmness return. Control of her emotions had resumed, and her ability to focus was restored.

The moderator began by looking first at Catherine then at Jennings. "Three weeks ago, both of you appeared on *Fox at the Front* and became involved in a rather heated debate that began on the subject of illegal immigrants and in very short order segued into the absence of real justice being even possible for our nation's poor. I'll begin with you, Will Jennings. Have things cooled down between the two of you since then?"

"Ted, there has been way too much said by way too many about which way too little was deserved," Jennings answered. Both he and Richmond smiled. "I'm not saying that what we talked about was insignificant, only that what others said later about our conversation was nothing short of exaggerated hype."

"Exaggerated hype? Is that how you would describe your discussion with Will Jennings?" Richmond turned to Catherine.

"I'm not sure I would have used those same words." She smiled. "But I do agree with the substance of how Mr. Jennings described the subsequent analysis that was given to our discussion on that program."

Richmond wouldn't yield to their efforts to downplay the public comments following their earlier squabble. "You both seem like it's all peaches and cream now," he said with a hint of sarcasm. "But take a look up at the screen, where we've pasted some of the descriptions used by various media to describe your performances on that program. The *Washington Post* ran this headline over their review of your appearance on *Fox at the Front.* **Jennings Checkmated!** Or how about the way the *LA Times* saw it? **Jennings picked the wrong Lane and is passed on the final turn in Fox at the Front's match-up on immigration.**"

Will Jennings appeared prepared for just such an opening salvo. "Ted, it's like I just told you. Media people need to find ways to describe something that was viewed by millions in a way that makes it appear they discovered something that was missed. It's what gives them a purpose, a different slant, if you will, to offer as their raison d'etre. What they reported as a debate or a fight or a match or whatever they chose to call it was in reality a rather civil examination of a problem that has our country at present divided."

The moderator stole a peek at his producer, who, off camera, looked concerned. Patricia sold the show as a rematch where sparks would fly between two well-informed combatants. So far, all she saw was Will Jennings manning a fire hose and Catherine Lane wearing asbestos attire.

"A civil examination?" Richmond asked Catherine. "I'm not implying that either of you were anything less than civil in your discussions. But wouldn't you agree with the pundits who found your responses to Will Jennings's assertions regarding the immigration problem as being more powerful? More on point?"

Catherine recognized the purpose of the question. She, too, had noticed that their appearance was being advertised as a rematch and that, so far, the program had failed to elicit any signs of acrimony. Still, that was their problem. She simply saw herself as someone who might provide information that seemed to be ignored by proponents of harsh laws for immigrants.

"Yes, I also think that what we provided is best described as Mr. Jennings just did, a civil examination." Catherine immediately regretted her short response but was uncertain whether it was the time for her to speak about poverty and how it overwhelmed the majority of immigrants. She remained mute and waited for a signal to continue.

Richmond seemed disappointed by the tone of peaceful coexistence that thwarted his every effort to get his guests back into the ring. With a signal to Patricia Flood, he moved away from the rematch theme and on to the subject of illegal immigration. Up in the booth, Patricia hurried through the briefing material on the prompter screen, settling on background information her boss might want to use.

"Let's return to something you said on *Fox at the Front* a few weeks back." Richmond looked at Will Jennings, obviously making one final stab at encouraging attacks and counterattacks from his guests. "I'll ask our producer to put this up on the screen, where you and our viewers at home can see what you said then."

"What's he want up there?" the director asked Patricia.

The moderator shuffled through the papers in front of him to allow them time to figure out where he was headed. "You said something about not accepting reasons from lawbreakers, and we're going to show the exact words now, on the screen."

"I've got it!" Patricia screamed into the headphones. "Roll 7-22."

"Ah, there it is now." Richmond sounded relieved as he read aloud.

"America has to stop coming up with reasons for those who break our laws.' Then you added this. "Reasons are never excuses and only serve to muddy the waters of the rivers of justice."' Richmond stopped reading and stared at Jennings. "You had immigrants in mind when you spoke those words. Am I correct?"

"I was making reference to a video that was shown immediately prior to the moment I said that," Jennings responded. "The video was a news clip showing a near riot during a demonstration that was organized to lay guilt upon those of us who prefer that all our immigration laws are enforced. My reference there was directed not at all immigrants but specifically those who are illegal ones."

Richmond stayed with him, not trusting Catherine to enter the fight. "Yes, illegal immigrants. That's when you said this about rights illegal immigrants want or should have."

As the moderator phrased his question, Patricia scanned the comments they had previously extracted from video of the Fox program. "He wants the Freedom in America blast," she said into her headphone mic. The movement of Richmond's right hand as he adjusted his glasses signaled his concurrence. Almost immediately, those words appeared on the screen.

"You said, 'Freedom in America is the right of American citizens, not those who sneak into our country in the back of a truck or who wander in under the moonlight.' You seemed to be making a direct reference to those who enter from Mexico."

"We have borders on our northern boundaries too," Jennings pointed out. "I didn't specify any nationality, only the legal status of these people. When they cross our borders without a visa, they become illegal immigrants."

Richmond looked in Catherine's direction.

"I must object to the use of that term illegal immigrants," she said. "It's time that we stop demonizing these people."

"Ah, but they have broken our laws, Mrs. Lane." Jennings jumped back in. "What word could be suggested as a sufficient replacement for *illegal* and still demonstrate the difference between these people and those who enter legally?"

"Here we go," the producer said with renewed enthusiasm.

A smile appeared on Ted Richmond's face too. That was what they'd hoped would happen—the shrewd conservative attacking a weakness.

"I would prefer the term 'undocumented,'" Catherine responded.

"So your objection is merely based on semantics?" the moderator suggested.

"Being undocumented has quite a larger difference than being grouped with rapists and robbers, murderers and molesters," Catherine explained.

Jennings turned and looked directly at Catherine. His outrage was evident even before he spoke.

"I don't think it is necessary to continue finding ways to coddle these illegals, many of whom are in fact guilty of doing all those nasty things you just described as matching the description given to criminals," he said. "When one violates the law, he is performing an illegal action, which fits any definition of the word 'criminal.'"

Catherine didn't look away from the moderator when Jennings faced her. Instead, she appeared undisturbed by both his words and the rudeness of his turning to stare at her, which in many ways violated her space.

"I'm sure that you didn't intend to paint with such a broad brush, implying that all or most undocumented aliens are also guilty of the crimes that you mentioned." She took special care to avoid sounding condescending. "Of course, all the known data establishes that quite the opposite is true. These people don't come to America to steal, rape, or murder our citizens. They come because they're poor and jobless and their families are starving. They come because of the wonderful things they've heard about America."

"Whoa, now. Let's not go making any heart-tugging speeches," Jennings interrupted. "Why not try staying on point? I asked you a specific question, and you seem hesitant to give a response."

Catherine looked to Ted Richmond to see if a response was even necessary.

"Yes, he did ask you why someone who is guilty of breaking our laws should be exempt from owning the description of being a criminal," the moderator concluded.

Catherine paused long enough to make it appear that she had not been lying in wait for just such a question.

"We don't choose to call someone who gets a speeding ticket a criminal," she began. "Nor do we identify as criminals those who spit on our sidewalks or who hunt and fish without getting the appropriate license first. I could go on, but my point is—"

"Your point is not persuasive, Mrs. Lane," Jennings broke in. "People who commit those minor violations are fined, and all is well beyond that. But for your people who cross our borders illegally, there are much larger problems." Jennings was primed and wouldn't yield his position, even when the moderator tried to allow Catherine to respond.

Jennings turned his attention away from the two people sharing the set with him and looked directly into the TV camera. "Right now, there are over twenty-one million illegal immigrants in our country. More than four million of their children attend our public schools at taxpayer expense. An estimated ten million of these illegal immigrants hold skilled jobs, taking those opportunities away from American citizens. Our jails house more than three hundred and fifty thousand illegal immigrants who have been convicted of crimes beyond their illegal status, crowding our prisons and burdening the taxpayers with further costs."

Ted Richmond was caught off guard by the information that Will Jennings was sharing and tried to wrestle back control long enough to at least address the veracity of it. But Jennings wouldn't yield.

"As we speak today, there are well over a half-million illegal immigrants who have been charged with a crime and are in hiding," Jennings said before observing that the program director was giving a cut-to-commercial signal. He decided to wrap up his argument. Speaking in almost a whisper, the conservative orator circled back to the original discussion.

"The fugitives from justice have been charged with the very crimes that Mrs. Lane objected to being named when we referred to them as what they were even before they raped, robbed, or murdered American citizens—illegal immigrants."

During the ninety-second commercial break, Ted Richmond asked Jennings about the source of his statistics. Jennings said they were well reported by ICE and also by DHS. Richmond stepped away from the set and spoke hurriedly with his producer.

"Jennings said those statistics were reported by Immigrations and Customs Enforcement and the Department of Homeland Security. See what you can verify and signal me so that I can confirm or rebut them while we're on air."

When the program resumed, the moderator explained the FCC regulations and told the viewers that his producer was trying to verify the information.

"Oh, they're accurate," Jennings said. "I stand by their accuracy."

"Fine with me, Will," Richmond said, retaking control. "Let's allow Catherine an opportunity to respond."

The shift to her was unexpected. Catherine was caught unprepared to deal with the statistics that described the scope of the immigration problems. Her interest was always on the suffering endured by those who were locked in the throes of poverty and who sought a better life for their families by coming to America.

"Mr. Jennings knows all about the numbers, and I don't have information at hand to suggest whether he is correct or not," she began. Her voice was soft but not weak, and she sounded as determined in the righteousness of her position as Will Jennings had been. "But the immigration problem is not all numbers, just as undocumented immigrants are not all to be considered as risks."

Catherine paused briefly, collecting her thoughts. "One of the very first to die in Iraq was a United States Marine corporal, Victor Torres, one of those street children living in Guatemala after being orphaned before reaching his fourth birthday. He first entered the United States in 1975 without the necessary papers, someone Mr. Jennings would call an illegal immigrant. He came with others wanting to escape the hopeless poverty in their lives. His young dream was to study and become a doctor. That ended years later in Iraq, where he gave his life fighting a war not for Guatemala, where he was born, but for America, the country he wanted to call his home."

Will Jennings had suspected that Catherine would somehow use an emotional story during their discussions and planned to use it to his advantage by calling it just another bleeding-heart liberal's fallback. But while she was telling that story, he wondered if she was setting a trap. How could he blast away at her when her sob story wasn't about a poor wayward illegal who'd stolen food for his dying mother? She was using a Marine corporal, a hero.

When she finished and Richmond turned to him, anticipating a counterattack, Jennings remained silent. It was the only strategy he could decide upon. He was the early winner, spouting numbers on the evil effects of illegal immigration. Catherine had closed with a rally that carried just as strong a punch as any he'd landed. So far, the rematch was a draw, and mocking her story about the hero from Guatemala would be seen as a low blow. He would become the loser by disqualification.

Once again, the program went to commercial. When they returned to air, Richmond began the wrap-up. "We have only a few minutes remaining, and I want to thank each of you for being here today."

Will Jennings's mind raced to find anything he could say that might address the position where Catherine had cornered him.

"Ted, if I can, I would just like to say a few last things now." He appeared to be about to offer an apology. "Those of us who want our immigration laws enforced are not acting out of selfishness. We are not anti-Mexican or anti-anyone. Most countries have immigration laws and enforce them. Without them, security is threatened, as is the very identity of their own citizens. That's all. Just secure borders and enforcement of our immigration laws. And one last thing. If we stop employers from breaking our laws by giving jobs to illegals and also limit or eliminate the free social services for them, then we are more properly addressing this problem."

Noticing that the moderator was getting the signal to conclude, Jennings spoke faster. "If we remove the things that present such a draw to citizens from foreign countries, we take away the motivation that drives them to be here."

The program director waved harder, and Richmond signaled that they were out of time.

"That's it from Washington," he said, smiling victoriously. "Thank you for spending some of your morning with us at *Sunday with the Press.*"

22

Where there's smoke

CHARLOTTE FELT RELIEVED THAT Kirsch gave in when she offered to do his shopping and other chores until he recovered from his surgery. She knew he cherished his independence. Finding that he was unable to care for himself was going to seem not only strange but also a challenge to his self-esteem.

"Too bad you never married," she told him when they quarreled over letting her fill in after his heart surgery. "If you had a wife, then we wouldn't be having this discussion."

"And if you had a husband, you wouldn't be here at my home, looking after me now," Kirsch said with a get-even tone.

They both laughed. It was sad, but it was how life had turned out for them. Still, the fact that they shared this flawed outcome made it much more tolerable. True, it had taken a major event like Kirsch's debilitating illness to bring their mutual affections out into the open. That no longer seemed to matter much. Kirsch found that someone had feelings for him, and he felt the same way about her. It was a first-in-a-lifetime event and left no room for feeling ashamed about how long it had taken to happen.

"You may want to thank Sandra Pierce for accommodating us by letting me work half days while I run errands for you. It makes it much easier that I can do these things during the mornings," Charlotte said.

"I agree," Kirsch added. "I also have been surprised by how supportive she's been."

"I formed an early opinion about her after Arthur made her a junior partner and placed her in charge here when he opened the New York office," Charlotte said. "Sandra struck me as self-centered and someone who wasn't to be trusted."

"You probably were put off by her after-work partying and those frequent mentions in the entertainment columns," Kirsch observed.

"Well, I guess you're right there too," she agreed. "But my loyalty will always remain with Arthur if those two have any difficulties between themselves. Whatever side Arthur Pradle is on is where I want to be."

The weekly visit with Kirsch's cardiologist went longer than usual and left him feeling fatigued. Charlotte decided to catch up at the office while Kirsch rested and perhaps slept for a few hours.

"I'm not expected until noon," Charlotte said. "But I've fallen behind on some work that Arthur sent from New York. After your nap, you can make yourself some lunch from the leftover tuna salad from yesterday."

Kirsch was asleep five minutes after she watched him go back to bed. Charlotte made sure that the prescription on his bedside table was within reach then quickly left for the office.

Masons Restaurant was two doors down from Rayburn Towers, so Charlotte stopped in and ordered a ham and cheese on rye to take with her to the office so that she wouldn't need to leave again for lunch. While she waited for the counter girl to arrive with her order, her mind was on the assignment she'd left for

Amy Wang. It wasn't something urgent, but it was aggravating that it wasn't being completed in a timely manner. She decided that Amy might require a good talking-to if it was still unfinished.

"Good morning, boss." Randy Turley greeted her as she walked past him and placed the bag with her sandwich inside her lower desk drawer.

"Good morning," she finally responded. "Where is everybody?"

"Uh, Amy is in Miss Pierce's office." He nodded toward the front office.

Sandra's office door was closed, which was never the case unless she was in conference with a client. Charlotte turned again toward Randy, who was clearly trying to appear as busy as possible.

"Do you know why they needed to close the office door?" she asked.

At first, Randy pretended not to hear the question, but when he saw Charlotte approaching his desk, he tried avoiding her question by merely shrugging and raising his eyebrows in an "I don't know" gesture.

"Well, it's out of the ordinary," Charlotte muttered, returning to her desk. "Unless something very urgent happened recently that required Amy to take dictation from Sandra, then this is against our usual office procedure."

Amy remained in Sandra's office for almost a half hour, raising more suspicions from the office manager. When Amy finally emerged, Charlotte was going through some of the paperwork Amy had left on her desk when Sandra called her in.

"Do you mind telling me what was so important that it couldn't wait for me?" Charlotte asked.

The look on Amy's face told Charlotte that she wasn't about to get an honest answer. "I was just in there because…" Amy appeared to struggle to come up with something believable.

"Yes, because why?" Charlotte persisted.

Amy was definitely trying to hide something, and her hesitation to answer did nothing to assuage Charlotte's growing concern. Then Sandra came out of her office.

"Why, Charlotte!" she said. "We didn't expect you until after the lunch hour. I hope everything's okay with Kirsch."

"Yes, he's doing fine. I drove him over to Santa Monica this morning for his checkup with the cardiologist, and he seemed a bit tuckered out afterward. As long as he's going to be resting, I figured I might as well be here," Charlotte explained. "Looks like you needed something done quick, and it couldn't wait for me," she added, hoping to prompt an explanation.

"Oh, you must be referring to why Amy was in my office," Sandra said. "But no, nothing special. Don't bother yourself about it. By the way, Arthur asked about the file on Wilson Farthing's expenses on that book tour he's on and said that you promised to complete it and send it to him."

Charlotte knew that Sandra was either exaggerating the importance of the file or that Arthur had never even mentioned it. But it did change the subject. Charlotte concluded it was best to play along and give up on finding out why Amy had been in Sandra's office.

As Sandra returned to her office, Amy hurried to her desk and placed the notebook she'd had with her in the lower left drawer. It was the drawer where she kept her purse and other personal items. Charlotte's suspicions only grew as she watched Amy lock the drawer.

When Sandra was in town, she was usually already at Pradle Literary Agency by the time Charlotte got to work. Usually the next to arrive was Amy Wang, often five minutes ahead of her scheduled starting time, followed by Randy Turley, who was always five minutes later than his. Lunch times were staggered so that one of the three was always present in the office. All of them left at five o'clock, and Randy was always first out the door. Amy tidied up and left a few minutes later. Charlotte, who always checked everything twice, was usually last to leave.

That all changed abruptly for two days following Amy's closed-door session with Sandra. Amy suddenly needed to stay after everyone else went home for the day. The explanation she gave Charlotte was that she was completing a research paper for a night course on the history of television that she was taking at Los Angeles Community College. She said Sandra had given her permission to use her office computer, which had better software, as long as the schoolwork occurred after work hours.

That was the first time Amy or anyone else had mentioned that she was taking a night course. Charlotte was even more suspicious when she remembered that Amy had asked Randy to go with her last month to purchase a new laptop. What type of research on television history, Charlotte wondered, required more than Amy would find by googling the subject on her new laptop?

Charlotte decided that asking any more questions would only make Sandra and Amy guard their secret even more closely.

The next day, Arthur Pradle was surprised to receive an early-morning call from Charlotte Olson. He feared Kirsch might have suffered a setback, and his first question was about Kirsch.

"No, everything's on schedule for Kirsch to make a full recovery," she told him. "I'm at his apartment right now. I wanted to talk with you about some things going on at the office and needed to have some privacy."

Charlotte told Arthur about showing up unexpectedly and finding Amy in seclusion with Sandra. "At first, I was concerned only about being usurped by Amy. But when the two of them made it a point to be secretive, coming up with that far-fetched excuse about a night school research paper, I just thought it was time to let you know what's happening in your West Coast office."

"What do you suspect Amy's keeping in that locked drawer?" Arthur asked.

"That's what I'm asking you," Charlotte said. "Can you think of a reason Sandra doesn't trust me with whatever that project is all about?"

Arthur hesitated to consider her question. "I can only think that Sandra's aware of how close you and I are and doesn't want me to know whatever this involves."

Charlotte waited through more silence, knowing that Arthur was giving the matter some serious thought.

"There's another key that can be used to unlock that drawer," he began. "The same key that locks the cabinet door where you keep the revenue statements."

"But I thought that I had the only key that opened that cabinet." Charlotte was surprised.

"No. You have a key, I have another, and Sandra has one also."

"But you just explained that Amy's key also opens that cabinet," Charlotte pointed out.

"That's true," Arthur said, "but the difference is that Amy doesn't know that her desk drawer's lock is keyed to match the lock in the cabinet. The important thing for you to understand is that you do have access to the drawer where Amy hides their little secret."

It was clear what Arthur wanted her to do. She told him that they would have their answer the next time both Amy and Randy were out of the office on their lunch break.

23

An invitation

THE JOURNALISTS WHO REPORTED AND commented on the *Sunday with the Press* debate between Catherine Lane and Will Jennings were the same ones who'd written about the earlier appearance on *Fox at the Front*. Where most were much kinder to Catherine then, noting how well she stood up to Jennings, they all saw Jennings as winner of the rematch. While some wrote favorably about Catherine's inclusion of the Marine hero in her response, others observed that even then, she failed to address the statistics and other arguments made by the wiser and quicker-on-his-feet Jennings.

Neither Catherine nor Will gave an interview afterward. Both seemed to realize that anything they said would fan the flames of the misperception that they were having a quarrel. Each preferred to let their position on immigration take precedence over their personality differences.

Their brief truce abruptly ended when it became the subject of the Just Jennings column the following week. He repeated the statistics he'd spoken of on *Sunday with the Press* that had proven the extent of the immigration problems. Once again, he mentioned the twenty-one million illegal immigrants in the United States and said that four million of their children were enrolled in public schools. He referred to Catherine's objection to the use of the term "illegal" since it was used to identify rapists, robbers, and molesters. But he justified that description, arguing that there were now more than three hundred fifty thousand of them incarcerated in jails for just such crimes. He finished his lengthy column by thanking those who wrote so cogently with their evaluations, declaring him the winner.

Davis was at home having a light breakfast when he read the Just Jennings column in the *Internet Tribune*. He almost choked as he read the single-sided version of the facts that Jennings used to slant his reporting. Davis knew that Catherine didn't feel she had done as well as she did on the Fox program. But the tone of Jennings's column was unfair when it lacked her rebuttals. Davis suspected Catherine would feel she had let down the undocumented immigrants she cared so deeply about. He decided to call her and offer support.

"Catherine, I'm so glad I caught you at your hotel. I was afraid that once you'd checked out, I wouldn't be able to reach you until you got back to Greenwich."

"Why, Davis, how sweet you are." Catherine responded warmly, perhaps trying to hide her disappointment. "But your concern about not being able to reach me while I'm traveling reminds me that I never left my cell phone number with you. Here. Write this down, then we can get back to why you called. The area code is 203 and—"

"Wait," Davis said. "You did give me your cell phone number. It's on the notepad that you used when you wrote down the name of the hotel you're staying at in Washington. I'm sorry. I didn't notice that earlier."

"Good," she answered. "Now keep that somewhere that only you can find it. I don't want to start receiving calls from crazies."

"You mean like the way Will Jennings used his biased column to argue on *Sunday with the Press* that you did nothing to inspire the notion that liberal views on immigration have any standing in logic?"

"Oh, you've been reading his column." She sighed. "Poor Davis. I hope you don't think I would let anything that man said or wrote ever hurt my gentle feelings. Do you?"

Davis was relieved to hear her say that. "I was concerned that the way he summarized the program, showing only the few salient points that he did make, could be something you might find disturbing," he said. "Especially since you were so brilliant by comparison."

"Now, Davis Quigley," Catherine said in a Deep Southern accent. "Hush your mouth. You're causing a blush to appear upon my very cheeks."

"Anytime you feel the need to blush, I'm happy to be the reason." Davis laughed.

Catherine changed the subject, telling him that her publisher, Hurd Patterson, was hosting a dinner party during the Mystery Writers Conference in Los Angeles the next week.

"They're honoring me for having two books that have been on the *Times* Best Seller List. Won't you come too? Before you even try finding some bogus excuse, I'm writing your name down right now on the list that Lloyd Patterson asked me to give them listing my personal guests. What do you say? It will make me so much happier if you—"

"Hold it!" Davis spoke over her. "Surely you know that I would love to be at that party, celebrating your success. Yes, have Lloyd save me a place at your table. But isn't mystery a different genre than your novels?"

Catherine laughed. "Surely you realize that Hurd Patterson represents many mystery authors. Lloyd knows that honoring me for having two of my novels on the *Times* Best Seller List is just the thing to attract more coverage for my books. Anyway, a lot of authors are going to be there, and the conference always has plenty of news-making events and surprises each year."

24

Erotomania, you say?

Beverly Beckett Conforti looked again at the desk clock that was turned so that only she could see the time when she was with a client. Brady Harvey's appointment was the same time as usual, ten o'clock every Wednesday except during her vacations or on a holiday. Neither of those exceptions was the case, yet it was 10:20 a.m., and Brady hadn't shown up or called in.

There were times over the past few months that he'd arrived ten minutes late or so. On each occasion, she'd insisted that frequent tardiness could result in her reporting it to the CVH Committee. He always promised to improve and sometimes arrived fifteen minutes early. He would then wait quietly until she opened the door from her office to the waiting area and beckoned him inside. After a few months, the cycle would start all over again.

By ten thirty, she still had not received any word from Brady. Even if he did arrive, she would have to send him away, as she couldn't conduct a productive therapy session in only twenty minutes. Her next client's appointment was scheduled too soon later, allowing her little wiggle room. This time, she decided, she would report his tardiness—or absence, if he failed to show.

While she waited in case Brady might still arrive, she listened to recordings of their earlier sessions from a digital voice recorder that she'd kept on her credenza. One recent session was a breakthrough for Brady, as until then he had been reluctant to discuss his mother and father. On that occasion, he opened up about his relationship with his parents after she asked if he still loved either of them.

"My father was my hero until I reached my teenage years," he slowly began.

"And? What happened that affected that feeling?" she urged more of an explanation.

Beverly remembered how Brady's expression revealed mixed emotions. He was obviously living through incidents that caused hurt, perhaps betrayal, and definitely anger.

"My father left our family soon after I started high school," he replied.

Hearing his voice on the recording, she recalled how he'd avoided eye contact with her and looked out the window. "Oh? He died when you were only fourteen?" Her question caused him to turn and look directly at her.

"I was only thirteen years old when I started out in high school," Brady corrected. "I didn't say he died," Brady sneered. "He was killed. He was taken from us on September 11, 2001 when terrorists flew the plane he was on, United Airlines Flight 175, into the South Tower of the World Trade Center. Mother explained to me later that sometimes, changes such as a death occur in a person's life and are difficult to understand, let alone accept. She told me that her religious faith provided the comfort we need during such times and to understand that it happened according to God's will."

Almost two minutes passed on the recording without any further dialogue.

"I was crushed," he finally said. "Mother later assured me that we would still have our lives as they always were. We wouldn't need to move or anything and still had the home that I grew up in... and really, everything else!"

Once again, the recording went silent for another minute before a noise indicated that Brady had gotten up from his chair and raised his voice.

"My mother kept repeating that these things happen to the best of families and life goes on, but she just didn't get it. She never seemed to get it that there was a real bond between my father and me. Just because I still had the house that he raised me in didn't solve anything. I wouldn't have him, his guidance, his everything that we shared together!"

The next sound Beverly heard on the recording was from Brady, apparently using his handkerchief. "Mother later explained that her good friend Corwin would soon be more available and that our needs would always be taken care of."

"Corwin? Are you saying she planned on being remarried?"

Brady's laughter on the tape did little to hide the bitterness that he was obviously feeling.

"No way would they ever get married," Brady scoffed. "Corwin Wellington is her pastor at the evangelical church. They had been best friends as long as I can remember. What I meant was that Mother felt that Reverend Wellington could provide the adult friendship that I had with my dad. All of a sudden, he was always there in our house when I was back from school or whatever."

Almost a full minute of silence followed as Brady seemed lost in the memory. When he resumed talking, he discussed how his mother had taken command and seemed more eager to offer helpful suggestions than she ever had while his father was alive.

"Mother took me out for long drives in the country and told me that she always found the best way to handle sadness, like when my father was killed, was to just change with the times that were changing anyway. I remember her mantra; *Sometimes things happen that are sad because they're beyond anything you can do about them. Just say it doesn't matter. Say it often. Soon, the sad thing seems less and less tragic.*"

"Do you find that saying things don't matter helps, just by repeating that?"

"Oh yes," he said with bold confidence in his voice. Then he quietly sang and hummed the melody from "Bohemian Rhapsody," finishing with the words about how nothing really mattered anyhow, anymore.

Beverly recalled feeling surprised and a bit threatened when he began singing. But those concerns melted as she watched him move and act like he was holding a microphone as if performing before an audience. Brady was capable of doing anything when it seemed, at least to him, that it was the thing to do and the time to be doing it. From each of their previous weekly sessions, the therapist had become well aware that his impulses influenced his thoughts, words, and actions. His impulses were what had led him into all the difficulties he experienced following high school.

Beverly recalled that when she later informed him that she had diagnosed his psychosis as something called *erotomania*, it seemed to stop Brady cold. Confusion was displayed on his face and in his body language and he slumped down, just looking at her.

After several minutes of silence, he asked, "What the fuck is eroto… what?"

Beverly arrived with that diagnosis after she earlier researched Brady's difficult life, especially since his father died, and how he'd bonded with his neighbor, Catherine Dallas. He told her about the violence and misconduct that followed while he was still in high school and afterward, especially when he was required to remain in Greenwich, Connecticut after high school while Catherine went to college at Wellesley in Massachusetts. That separation revealed more definitively his obsession with Catherine and his inability to control his impulses. Beverly hesitated to share her observations with Brady until she researched the disease further. However, as additional sessions provided more information that confirmed her diagnosis, she thought it was important to inform him of it.

"No, the word is erotomania," she corrected him. "Erotomania is a rare mental health condition that happens when someone is fixated on the idea that another person has intense love for them. This fixation on being loved by the other person is considered delusional because it's not based in reality."

Brady became more agitated. "Are you trying to tell me that the woman I've loved as sincerely as anyone might ever love another person, that our love isn't based on reality?"

His question was expected, but what she hadn't anticipated was his threatening tone. Knowing that Brady had, in the past, slipped into violence when he was in that state, she decided to wait until a future session to continue with her analysis of his illness. But Brady would have no part of waiting to learn more about the emotional illness he'd just heard about.

He rose, left her office, and slammed the door. She remembered now being frightened by his actions but not for long, as he quickly returned. With both hands raised in a hush hush manner, he indicated for Beverly to just stop talking and say not another word. His body language and facial expression indicated that his outburst wasn't meant to harm her. He returned to the seat across from her.

"First, I apologize for the tantrum," he began. "But as smart as I know that you definitely are, how could your diagnosis of what's been causing my depression to have anything that connects with that word you just used, erotomania?"

His demeanor was calm and pretty much as he usually was during their therapy sessions. But suspecting that anything she said might ignite another outburst, she chose to be calm and explained to him how erotomania had controlled his emotional life.

"Brady," she began, "you have indeed shown me that you loved two people during your life."

"Two?"

"Yes, I'm referring to your father and, of course, Catherine."

"Please do *not* say that my love for Catherine mimicked my feelings for my father." He angrily said as he clenched his teeth. "I loved my father until he was taken away from me, which told me that the love I could always depend on might someday be taken—stolen!—and never be replaced. I say this because I never thought about anything then that would separate us. I think from all we've discussed, that you can understand what I'm saying now, right?"

Beverly remembered looking at him, unsure whether his question was meant to invite a response.

"Brady, there are many more than two types of love, something I'm certain you already know. Love for parents or siblings is one special type but miles apart from our love meant for another who is desired to become a life partner. Surely your love of Catherine began and developed following your father's tragic death. In her, you discovered that your role changed. You became the person being depended upon. You were able to address what she wanted or needed. It's not as evident that you understood how she was meanwhile doing much the same for you."

While listening to the recording Beverly recalled realizing that her words kept him from interrupting. He sat quiet thinking about what she'd said.

She continued, "You needed the guidance you received early in your life that was available from your father. This, along with the many other connections between you two, was the basis for the feelings of love you had for him and felt that he had for you."

"Okay, I can see where you're going," Brady said. "But you didn't mention how much those things proved so wrong. I was merely guessing about his feelings. That's never been the case with Catherine. She *knows* that I love her, and knowing that doesn't interfere with the feelings she has for me. Those feelings merely get suspended from her awareness when she seeks others for comparisons. And of that, I'm certain!"

"Yes, you're certain, but have you asked yourself if she's just as certain?"

Brady leaned toward Beverly. "Can't you see? Can't you understand that once we fell in love with each other, that it was real then, and it's just as real now?"

"Yes, it's just as real now for you," she responded. "But imposing your certainty into her feelings is perhaps fooling yourself. That's the very definition of erotomania. You feeling that you know that she loves you as much as you love her, all the while making excuses for when she does things that clearly demonstrate the error of your conclusion. Think about this. She told you to stay away from her. She even got married to someone."

Brady then rolled his eyes, indicating that his therapist just didn't get it.

*　*　*

The cell phone on her desk rang and startled her. The caller ID read Harvey. Beverly hesitated, but after a few extra rings, she picked up her phone.

"Dr. Conforti?" Brady always ignored her suggestion that he refer to her as Mrs. Conforti. Beverly also saw that she had less than twenty minutes before her next appointment.

"Brady, you're too late for your time with me today. What is it?"

"Doctor, I lost track of time this morning, but I really do need to see you today."

"You say you lost track of time, yet there's some urgent need to see me?" Her tone left no confusion about her dissatisfaction with his excuse.

"Yes. I spent this week since our last therapy session going over those things you talked about. I have so many questions now about your diagnosis of the erotomania."

Beverly was happy that he pronounced the word properly. *Maybe he's been doing some research.*

"That's all good," she said, "but by the time you arrive, there'll probably be very little time available for me to spend with you this morning."

"Wait!" he said. "I'm already here. I'm standing on the sidewalk outside."

Minutes later, Brady was inside Beverly's office, seated where he usually was during his therapy.

"From the information I've found on Google regarding the diagnosis of erotomania, there's really nothing that even remotely reflects the love I've always had for Catherine. Mostly, it says that emotional impairment fits people like young schoolgirls, the ones who fall in love with a rock star or movie star and then believe that they're equally loved by the person."

"No, that's not an accurate explanation of an erotomanic delusion," Beverly argued. "That is perhaps one of the ways that fit, but there are many others."

"Well, I chose this one because it seems to establish that the person just imagining another's love may not have ever known that person. The schoolgirl has maybe her first real crush, and she reasons that it alone must prove that her idol feels the same way. In mine and Catherine's relationship, we actually know each other and have lived and played and gone to school together for many years. When we grew old enough to develop feelings of love and not just a teenage crush, each of us was beginning a new phase in life, and we really needed each other to go through it. When love did come to us, it hit hard and went deep. We knew how special it had become between us. It was a feeling neither of us had ever experienced or could ever experience again in our lives. The only way that this *true love* could end is when life itself ends!"

Beverly silently listened to Brady explain his understanding of erotomania and its applications. Her objections were many, but she realized that anything she might say would be seen by Brady as argumentative. As sincere as he seemed, he wasn't addressing the many times that his Catherine gave clues that she wanted someone else's love. He found reasons or excuses for her behavior that he considered as only temporary obstacles for them to overcome together. Beverly knew she would have to find a way to encourage Brady to reexamine his longed-for relationship with Catherine.

Remembering the recording of their earlier session reminded Beverly of how alarmed she became when Brady said that true love ended only when life ends. She'd been focused on his explanation of how the death of his father had ended the love he always felt existed with him. She felt a sudden chill that could be a warning that she needed now to be concerned about someone in the present.

Peeking at the time on her cell phone and seeing that it was already five minutes past ten o'clock, she ended the session and thanked Brady for his explanations and research. She concluded by emphasizing the necessity of maintaining full compliance with his appointment dates and times.

25

Perhaps a plot

I T TOOK ONLY ONE DAY AFTER her call to Arthur Pradle for Charlotte to find the opportunity to use the cabinet key. It was Amy's birthday, and Charlotte earlier gave Randy permission to take ninety minutes for lunch. He explained that he wanted to take Amy to Zax's in Brentwood. Charlotte was happy to oblige since she knew that the restaurant was all the way over on San Vicente Boulevard. Sandra had already left the office for the remainder of the day. Charlotte would have more than ample time to accomplish her task.

She waited almost fifteen minutes after Randy and Amy left just to be sure there were no sudden changes in plans. While she waited, she wondered what she would find. She also wondered if she would find anything at all since it was possible that Amy had already completed the assignment Sandra had given her. There might be nothing out of the ordinary inside that drawer.

Finally, her curiosity reaching the boiling point, Charlotte took the key and walked over to Amy's desk. When she looked down, the drawer that she was certain to have contained all of those secrets was open.

"Open?" Charlotte almost shouted for all the world to hear. *How can that drawer be open unless Amy was onto my little plan and managed to take the secret stash with her when she left for lunch?*

Charlotte thought about how disappointed Arthur would be when she told him that Amy had left the drawer open while away celebrating her birthday with Randy. Arthur's disappointment would involve more than just the news about the drawer being open. His faith in Charlotte would probably be shaken. That gnawed inside her as she bent down to shut the drawer. Then she glimpsed inside the partially open drawer and saw something under the box of Kleenex. Charlotte pulled the drawer wide open and removed the box of tissues. Underneath was a binder with a label that read Contracts.

Charlotte removed the three-inch-thick binder, took it to her desk, and sat down. Inside the binder was a letter addressed to Arthur Pradle at the New York office. Her eyes dropped to the space at the bottom of the letter. The space provided room for a signature but wasn't yet signed. Under the space was typed "Davis Quigley."

Charlotte read the body of the letter, and saw that it was a thirty-day notice, beginning on a date left blank, to terminate the contract between Davis Quigley and the Pradle Literary Agency. Underneath was an identical letter for Franz Graber and another for Simon DuValle.

All the remaining letters were identical to Quigley's, Graber's, and DuValle's and each was the name of an author that Sandra had brought aboard to Pradle. Charlotte was flabbergasted. There had been no indications that any of the authors were displeased with anything or anyone at Pradle Literary Agency, at least none that she was aware of. And why did Sandra assign the preparation of the termination letters to Charlotte's subordinate, Amy?

Charlotte decided it was urgent that she get Arthur on the phone. Something bad was going down, and she was certain it was being done behind his back. She first attempted to reach Arthur at his office, where his secretary spent the first few minutes inquiring about Kirsch.

"Oh, Kirsch is feeling much better, thanks for asking." Charlotte hoped to avoid sounding rude. "But I really must speak with Arthur."

"You know, Mr. Pradle talks a lot about how you and Kirsch met and—"

"I'm sorry, Florence, but it's urgent that I speak with Arthur. Please connect me with him **now!**"

Florence was clearly taken aback by Charlotte's demand. Even though office managers held equal rank in the agency, Charlotte did have the advantage of being Mr. Pradle's first secretary.

Sounding completely businesslike, Florence responded, "I will be happy to tell Mr. Pradle that you called and want him to return your call when he returns to the office later this afternoon." Then she hung up.

Charlotte was furious with the way Florence handled her call, but the important thing was to focus on the reason she'd made the call in the first place. Wherever Arthur was right then, he had his cell phone on him. Quickly, she called that number.

Arthur was meeting with Taylor Forest from the mayor's committee for the arts when he took the call from Charlotte. He excused himself and went outside into the hallway so he could speak without distracting the other committee members who were giving their reports.

Charlotte got right to the point. After reading the first letter to him in its entirety, she told Arthur that all of the others read the same way, using the same words and dates about the thirty-day notice but each having a different author's name typed under the signature line.

"So, none of these letters are signed?" Arthur asked.

"None of them," Charlotte answered. "Not yet, anyway."

"Yes. Okay," Arthur said. "It appears that my junior partner has plans for something else. She may be moving on to another agency, or perhaps she plans on starting one herself."

"But why?" Charlotte asked. "Why would Sandra leave her position as a junior partner?"

Arthur paused, considering whether to share what he already knew. "A few weeks ago, I had lunch with Lloyd Patterson," he finally resumed. "He wanted to discuss a range of possibilities that could result in combining our two literary agencies, and when I said that wasn't something I wanted to pursue, that ended our conversation on this subject."

"But why? How could either agency profit from a merger? Or was Mr. Patterson indicating that he wanted to buy you out?"

Arthur merely sighed. "You know that the Authors Guild of America has been using their writers to stir discontent with all of us agencies."

"Yes," Charlotte answered. "I've read somewhere that they want to share in the packaging profits that we make when we hook up a writer with a screenwriter, a director, and an actor for a TV series or movie. But how would a merger between us and Hurd Patterson get involved in that problem?"

Once again, Arthur paused. "Lloyd Patterson mentioned that he thought the new Code of Conduct that the Authors Guild had come up with would require that on any packaging endeavors, agents would receive only the same percentage that they initially had with the writer. He's worried that if we don't band together, they may eventually persuade enough writers to demand that we share profits on the packaging even though we do all that work by ourselves without them."

"Does Sandra know about that?" Charlotte asked.

"No. That's only speculation that has Lloyd concerned," he said. "But not much later, Sandra called to tell me she thought Catherine Lane was trying to lure Davis away from us, and if she succeeded, Sandra worried that might begin a steady exit of the writers we have under contract. When I told her that would be most unlikely since I knew that Davis was very attracted to Sandra as his agent, she responded that she thinks Catherine Lane would like to share her future with Davis."

"So, was that all there was to that whole thing?" Charlotte asked.

Arthur laughed. "You know Sandra. She leaves nothing to chance, and only a few days afterward, she managed to get published in the Writers on the loose blog that blip about Catherine Lane hoping to share her future with Davis Quigley."

"Really?" Charlotte blurted out. "I didn't hear anything about that."

"No, and you wouldn't. Actually, Lloyd saw it first and called me, wanting to make sure I didn't think it was him planting seeds of misinformation. Together, we contacted the blogger, and she arranged to delete it a few days later from the Twitter account that she uses to promote her blog."

Charlotte had never trusted Sandra Pierce, and the betrayal business prompted Charlotte to warn her boss never to completely trust her either.

"So do you wonder why Sandra is now having Amy Wang type those letters for her writers to end their contracts with us? If she knows that we have no intention of selling or of merging with Hurd Patterson, what purpose would those letters have unless she's thinking about starting her own agency?"

"It's beginning to look that way," he answered. "For now, all I want you to do is put those letters back exactly where you found them. It might be to our advantage to let them think we're still in the dark. And don't forget that the drawer was ajar when you approached it. Be sure it's left that same way. Amy was careless, but she'll probably discover that she goofed. If she returns and sees the drawer closed, it'll be a dead giveaway that you found the letters."

26

Making the decision

HE WAS GOING OFF AGAIN, and about what didn't matter. Sometimes, nothing at all would seem to send him into a rage, an uncontrollable fury. Then just as suddenly, he would look for her to come near and offer comfort. His outbursts occasionally startled her, not so much causing her to feel threatened as much as surprised or maybe even shocked. He might be watching television when *bang!* He would jump up from the sofa, cursing a blue streak. Other times, it happened when he read the newspaper. She couldn't always predict when he would go off on a tangent, but Angel knew it was nothing that wouldn't pass. All she needed to do during those angry periods was sneak away, just leaving him alone. Sometimes she went to her window seat where she could feign disinterest by looking at the traffic below.

"She's at it again," Brady growled. "Look here, Angel. See my Catherine with the man in this picture and just look at how they're clutching hands. Sure looks like they just did something in secret, don't you think?"

Brady rose from the kitchen chair, holding out his newspaper, and walked over to Angel, who was sitting by the bookcase.

"This isn't just an innocent situation where someone is interviewing her about her books," he said derisively. "Take a good look. They're holding hands, and see this? They're looking right into each other's eyes. Those are sinful looks they're giving each other."

He threw the paper toward Angel.

Running away wasn't an option. Not yet, anyway. Often that made him all the more agitated.

"How much more does she think I can take?" Again, his question was rhetorical. "I've tried. Lord knows that's the truth. I've tried to do just what the good therapist lady wanted me to do, but gaud almighty!"

He stopped moving and looked off into the distance. Then it began all over again.

"Hell's fire," he moaned. "I've gone and missed my appointment with the nice therapy doctor lady. Jeez, Angel. This time, she's going to have my balls served on a saucer. She warned me the last time when I was late that she wasn't about to ignore it anymore. If being tardy got her that pissed off, then blowing the whole damn appointment has to leave me with no chance at all. Damn!"

Brady stormed into his kitchen and then just as fast turned around and walked even faster toward Angel. Her head rose straight up as her eyes widened, wondering if that might be her exit cue. *No sense staying where I might get hurt.* He had been that angry before but not by a whole lot. She'd seen him throw things, sometimes dangerous things like scissors or one of those sharp knives he used to cut up his pork chops.

Angel saw her chance when Brady turned back on the return path to the kitchen. She hustled away quietly, carefully watching him in her peripheral vision, and managed to escape to the bedroom closet. There, she found safety behind the long overcoat hanging in the corner. He could find her there if he really meant to, but he wasn't thinking about her right then, Angel guessed. He was thinking about doing something besides looking for her.

27

An absence for an appointment

BEVERLY BECKETT CONFORTI, PHD, prided herself on having the ability to understand and handle any situation that developed with her clients. That business of Brady being tardy and then absent from his scheduled session prompted her to consider what needed to be done about him. While she preferred not to be contentious with her clients, there were times when a "supportive confrontation" might be the critical choice if therapy was to be effective. Knowing that he'd become her client not on his own but through a decision of the Connecticut Valley Outpatient Evaluation Committee, which had oversight responsibilities, she decided it was time to inform them of his attendance failures. But first things first, she reviewed her summary notes inside his case jacket.

The case was assigned to her after Brady's mother, Ruth Harvey, petitioned Fairfield County Mental Health Department to release her son from his involuntary confinement at Connecticut Valley Hospital for the Criminally Insane. When they declined to approve Brady's release, she brought suit in superior court.

The Fairfield County Sheriff's Office and the Greenwich Police Department joined the government agencies in fighting his release.

They argued that Brady required prescribed medicines at precise times along with the regular cognitive behavioral therapy that he was receiving at CVH. They pointed to the petitioner's responses to their pretrial discovery requests. Nothing guaranteed that Brady would continue the required therapy once he was outside of their control. Further, they argued that he had been found guilty in Criminal Case FC 20MK2007 on charges that included intent to do bodily harm, arson, stalking, and attempted kidnapping.

To reinforce their belief that he should still be considered dangerous, they listed all of his escapes and attempted escapes while an inmate at Connecticut Valley Hospital. Following one escape, he was captured in Wellesley Massachusetts after he was discovered at the scene where a car had lost control along US Route 1 and crashed into the ocean. The driver was killed. Brady could provide no explanation for being at that location and said he only stopped there to watch the car sink. There were no witnesses, and although police investigating the accident suspected he was involved, they returned him to Connecticut Valley Hospital.

Judge Wolfgang Charmer ruled on behalf of the petitioner, Mrs. Harvey. In his decision, the judged cited the fact that Harvey had already been under the medical care of the Riverview Hospital and later the Connecticut Valley Hospital for a term that by then exceeded seven years. During some of those years, he had voluntarily signed himself into Riverview, seeking treatment for depression and anxiety. Other years, he was in Connecticut Valley Hospital for the Criminally Insane after being found guilty of violent assaults, arson, and other crimes.

The judge's order released Brady to live at the condominium the Harvey family owned in Greenwich Oaks near downtown

Greenwich. Judge Charmer's verdict indicated that CVH would administer the medical requirements in his decision and oversee Brady's progress while he remained in home confinement. He ordered the Fairfield County sheriff to monitor Brady's conduct and his compliance with all instructions from CVH.

The judge authorized CVH to contract with an outside psychologist to provide Brady with regular and appropriate therapy until that service was determined by CVH to cease being of value.

Beverly set the case file on her desk and smiled. Who could ask for anything better than that? She recalled the joke that one of her colleagues had told at a recent seminar.

"The best clients are policemen. They have the best-paying mental health plans in the country, and no matter how long they remain in therapy, they never get well."

She lifted the phone to call the office of the CVH Evaluations Committee then paused and hung up. On second thought, it was probably better to send her report in writing.

28

Some surprises

AMY WANG'S BIRTHDAY WOULD definitely be one to remember. She was surprised when Randy asked Charlotte if he could treat her to lunch to celebrate. Surprise number two came when Charlotte allowed them the extended lunch break. Amy was impressed more when she learned that Randy had reservations at Zax's, where many celebrities ate, and she hoped to see a few of them there.

Her biggest surprise came when she and Randy returned from lunch. Sitting down at her desk, she noticed it. The drawer where she kept the letters Sandra had asked her to prepare was unlocked. *Unlocked? But how? Did Sandra return to the office while Randy and she were at lunch and open the drawer?* No, Sandra had left the office earlier for the rest of the day. Amy was certain that she hadn't left the drawer unlocked. Maybe Charlotte had opened it. She was acting very nosy after catching her coming out of Sandra's office. But Charlotte didn't have a key to that drawer. Nobody else in the office had a key to the drawer where she kept her purse and other personal belongings. She was sure of that.

Amy looked to see if Charlotte was watching her, and saw that her boss was talking to Randy about their lunch date. Trying to be as nonchalant as possible, Amy used her foot to pull open the drawer enough that she might see whether the file with the letters was still there. Seeing it relieved her jangled nerves. She could wait until the coast was clear before examining it to be sure all the letters were inside the file. But for the moment, she could relax. She thought back to just before she'd left for lunch. *Did I close and lock the drawer?* She did that automatically any time she got up and left the office. But with Randy surprising her with the lunch date then watching him ask Charlotte for the extra time before totally surprising her with lunch at Zax's, she might have forgotten the drawer. She could have left everything and hurried out the door with Randy.

Angry at her own carelessness, Amy was nonetheless relieved that the puzzle was solved and the little secret she shared with Sandra Pierce hadn't been breached. She wouldn't even bother telling Sandra about it. Nothing had happened.

Then she saw the Kleenex box on her desk, and the soup she'd had at Zax's came dangerously close to making a return appearance. The box would need to be taken out only so that the file with the letters could be retrieved. Someone else had seen the letters.

29

Urgent call from Charlotte

THE ANNUAL PACIFIC COAST MYSTERY Writers Conference always attracted the best-known and biggest-selling authors for their conference speakers. That was only part of the reason for the huge success marking the conference's fiftieth anniversary. Attendance was expected to exceed last year's record of one thousand participants. The registration fee included up to four sessions in the mystery and crime fiction genres. Sessions for writing suspense and romantic suspense were the most sought-after tickets of the year. Other sessions provided insights into engaging readers with a strong hook and planting red herrings, those clues that made it difficult for readers to discover the perp until the mystery was solved.

The conference location was the InterContinental Hotel on Wilshire Boulevard. Many of the writers who registered for the conference booked rooms at hotels close by that had more affordable rates. Davis was pleased to learn that Hurd Patterson had a block of rooms reserved at the luxurious Carlyle Hotel, almost twenty minutes away.

"Surprised?" Catherine laughed.

"Yes, I guess I am," he replied. "Surprised but not at all disappointed. I'm guessing that the reception honoring your successes will be in this same hotel where we're staying?"

Catherine smiled, noting that Lloyd Patterson always did everything first class, and said she was sure the reception would have as much news interest as anything happening at the Mystery Writers Conference.

"Will any authors represented by Hurd Patterson be speaking at any of the sessions at the Mystery Writers?" Davis asked. "I learned just before we left that Pradle Literary Agency will have one of our authors, Franz Graber, speaking in the session on police procedurals. And Arthur Pradle himself will speak at the closing banquet, where he'll receive the Amos Nettleton Award for the literary agency that represented the most authors of novels that made best-seller lists during the past year."

Catherine seemed unaware of that news. "Lloyd Patterson is scheduled to address the conference in a session dealing with the ethical responsibilities that agents have with authors." Learning that Arthur Pradle would not only attend but also be given the prestigious Nettleton Award made her concerned that Sandra Pierce might attend.

"I asked Charlotte about that when she mentioned that Franz and Arthur would be speaking. She surprised me by saying something about Sandra being in Arthur's doghouse at this time and that Sandra wasn't even told about the Pradle participation in the Mystery Writers Conference. I called Sandra but got no answer and had to leave a message."

Catherine grew more concerned and wondered whether she should tell Davis that she'd heard something that might have caused the fallout between Sandra and the Pradle agency.

"I do know that Sandra and Lloyd Patterson met a few weeks back, but..." She stopped. She seemed concerned that she might be revealing more than Davis should know.

"They met? A few weeks ago?"

Catherine nodded. Then, looking around the hotel lobby and seeing Lloyd Patterson coming in, she took Davis's hand and walked toward her agent.

"Here's Lloyd now," she said as they drew closer. "Why don't you tell him what you mentioned about being so surprised by our accommodations?"

Lloyd seemed eager to greet Davis and said how much he'd enjoyed reading *Dictated Choices*.

"That means a lot to me," Davis responded. "But a lot of my recent success must go to Catherine after she referred to it often while sparring with Will Jennings on television."

Patterson smiled, acknowledging that an author he represented had contributed to another's book sales. "Perhaps we can spend a little time together this week," Lloyd suggested. "You know, talking about things like book tours here and in Europe."

Davis agreed and said he would appreciate discussing the subjects when an opportunity arose. Still, he wondered why Catherine's agent would want to discuss things that he must know Sandra Pierce would consider to be tampering with the agent-author relationship.

Before their conversation could continue, Davis's cell phone buzzed showing the caller to be Pradle Agency in Los Angeles. Thinking it was probably Sandra answering his earlier call, he excused himself and walked into the corridor, where he could talk in privacy.

"Sandra? Thanks for calling me back—"

"Wait, Davis. This is Charlotte calling." Her voice was almost a whisper, and she sounded cautious and concerned. "We have a visitor who says he must get in touch with you as soon as possible. Says it's an emergency regarding a Catherine somebody who was hiding something."

Charlotte was obviously trying to talk as silently as possible, indicating that the visitor must be standing close by. "He wants to know where you are right now and who you're with, and I said that I really can't divulge that kind of information. When I said I would call you and see if you wanted to talk with him, he just said something like, 'It doesn't matter!'"

Seconds passed before Davis responded. Whoever had shown up at Pradle's office needed or wanted to get in touch with him and sounded desperate. The comment about having something to do with someone named Catherine—and hiding something—left Davis struggling to make a connection.

"Davis? Davis, can you hear me?"

Hearing Charlotte calling his name in a louder, almost panicked way snapped his focus away from his own questions and back to the strange visitor. "Did he give you his name?"

"No. And I did ask for it, but all he said was, 'Doesn't matter!'"

"Well, put him on. Let me ask some questions. I have no idea what this can be about."

Davis heard Charlotte tell the man that he could talk to Mr. Quigley then suddenly heard her screaming. Then came a moan. Next, the phone went silent as if it were gently being hung up.

Emergency!

Before Davis could address the confusion about the man who'd wanted to talk with him and the obvious attack on Charlotte, his cell phone buzzed again.

"Hi, Davis." She sounded distracted. "You called earlier?"

"Sandra." He seemed to be in panic mode. "Forget about why I called. Something bad is happening at the agency. Charlotte might have been attacked. I'm on my way there right now."

Sandra was shocked by what Davis just told her. She'd called merely to respond to Davis's earlier message saying he needed to talk to her. She figured then that Catherine might have told him about Sandra's secret plan to leave the Pradle Literary Agency and maybe hook up with Hurd Patterson. All of that was still being worked out as of that morning. But something was happening at her office, and her office manager, Charlotte, might have just been attacked. *By whom? Why? And was Davis on his way there?*

"Davis," she said when he stopped talking. "I'm at McHale Media right now, near the office. Just ten minutes away. Where are you?"

Davis had just finished clicking off his Uber app. "I'm at The Carlyle Hotel, probably fifteen minutes away from your office."

"Did you call the police?" Sandra asked.

"No. Right after Charlotte's phone went dead, you called. I'm catching an Uber ride and can be at the office and meet you there. Wait! Yes, I mean no. I haven't called the police. What can I tell them?"

Sandra thought quickly and said she was going to contact their doorman, who could get there in seconds.

"Kirsch was supposed to drive Charlotte in today and may be with her. I can check this out right away. This being Sunday, almost no one else in the building is working there today. Charlotte was only going to work briefly this morning and then—"

Davis interrupted to tell her that his Uber driver had just texted and said a car would arrive in three minutes.

"Okay, then. I'm on my way. I'm with Jeanne at McHale Media, and she's going to drive me there."

In Davis's and Sandra's haste to get to Charlotte, the police were never called.

* * *

As the doorman at Rayburn Towers Office Building on busy Wilshire Boulevard, Kirsch was normally in uniform, greeting tenants, office employees, and neighbors working in other buildings on the street. He'd had the job since getting out of the army in 1989. His military service was, as they said, between wars. The Vietnam War was well past when he enlisted in 1984, and the Gulf War didn't fire up until the year after he was honorably discharged and began working as an elevator starter at Rayburn Towers.

"Hey, Doorman," Officer Tuttle yelled before entering Masons Restaurant next door. "This is Sunday. God said you can rest and be off work today!"

Kirsch laughed and waved hello. "Can't you see that I'm not working? I mean, look at me. No uniform. That should tell you something."

"So, I suppose you're really asleep, and this must be when you wake up, out of uniform and still holding doors open for important people."

Again, Kirsch laughed. "No. Charlotte Olson had to stop by the office for some important business thing for her boss this morning, and since we spent the night together, the least I could do was get up when she did and drive her downtown."

While Officer Tuttle placed his order for a mini breakfast—two eclairs and a cup of coffee—Kirsch's cell phone buzzed.

"Your lady friend missing you?" Tuttle teased.

"No, it's from Charlotte's boss, Sandra Pierce. I better take this outside."

Sandra spoke as fast as she could and still expect to be understood.

"Kirsch," she began. "Charlotte might be in some kind of trouble upstairs in the office. Where are you right now?"

As soon as he heard the words about Charlotte needing help, Kirsch took off to enter the Rayburn building and headed straight for the elevators. While riding up to the fourth floor, he kept the cell phone to his ear and listened as Sandra told him what she'd heard from Davis. Kirsch began panting with worry.

"Davis is on his way, and I'm just a few moments from there," Sandra said.

"When you get here at Rayburn, go next door to Masons first and find Officer Tuttle. Tell him what you know about what's happening and that I need his help," Kirsch said. "I'm in the lobby just outside their office already, and I'm going to knock down that fucking door if it's locked."

31

The scene

UPON REACHING THE FOURTH FLOOR, Sandra Pierce and Officer Tuttle raced from the elevator into the darkness inside the Pradle Literary Agency office.

Officer Tuttle, his handgun already removed from its holster, cautiously sneaked through the open doorway. Aware that Sandra was close behind him he waved for her to stay back. Knowing only what Kirsch told him earlier, he quietly called for Charlotte. All of the office lights were off. A window inside Sandra's personal office provided light from the outside and showed someone at the desk, slouched over as if carefully examining a document. Sandra quietly called out Charlotte's name without getting a response.

"Is that her?" the policeman asked as they snuck forward.

From her crouched position behind the policeman, Sandra saw only a shadow of the person and hesitated before responding.

"She's not moving," she finally whispered. "Why is she just sitting there?"

The policeman edged farther in front of Sandra and signaled again for her to stay put. Grabbing an office chair as a shield, he charged ahead, yelling that he was a policeman and for anyone inside to put their hands up. He stopped abruptly once he got to the door to Sandra's office. A body lay on the rug between him and the seated woman. Using the radio mic clipped to his uniform shirt, he called the precinct and requested backup.

"Officer?" Sandra's voice was choked with fear as she snuck closer and looked into the room.

"Stay back, ma'am," he instructed. "There may be someone in here we haven't seen yet."

Once more, the policeman ordered anyone inside the office to show himself, again getting no response. After another minute, and with the wail of police sirens approaching Rayburn Towers, the police officer rushed farther inside before stopping only a few feet from the woman. Her chair was pushed up against the desk, keeping her from falling out of it. Blood had dripped from her ear onto her shoulders. Her eyes were closed.

The next sounds came from police in the lobby just outside the office, and EMTs were heard close behind.

32

Looking for connections

Lloyd Patterson was told only that something serious was happening at the Pradle Literary Agency but not given one clue what all that meant. Minutes earlier, he had been inside the Carlyle Hotel lobby, talking with Catherine and Davis, then all hell broke loose. Catherine noticed that Davis, who briefly stepped away from their conversation to answer his phone, seemed in distress. Lloyd watched as she approached Davis then followed him outside, where a car was waiting to take him somewhere. Seeing Catherine left alone as the car sped from the hotel, Lloyd went to her.

"Catherine."

Her hands were cupped in a prayer-like position under her face and she was trembling.

"Catherine, what in the name of God is going on?" He took hold of her shoulders. "Where's Davis going? Why did he leave so fast? Why are you crying?"

After walking her inside and finding a table where she could sit down, he asked the waiter to hurry with a glass of water for her. She was shaking and had lost color in her face, prompting him to suspect that she might pass out. After drinking a few sips of water, she looked up and faced Lloyd, who stood waiting for her response.

"Davis got a call from Sandra and immediately took off to be with her. I heard him say something about Charlotte being in trouble and then saying in a raised voice that he would be there in a few minutes."

As she was about to mention that she'd heard Davis tell Sandra that someone with Charlotte was demanding to meet with him, Catherine stopped talking and began sobbing.

What he'd heard before Catherine stopped talking angered Lloyd. He suspected that Sandra wanted a meeting to tell Davis that she was leaving Pradle. Perhaps, he suspected, she was going to reveal her plan to open her own agency, one of the first to be in full compliance with the Authors Guild's new Code of Conduct. The packaging of the writer with a screenwriter and an actor and director for TV or movies would be handled by Sandra's new agency, and writers would share equally in any profits in her fully owned literary agency.

If Sandra succeeded in signing up even a small portion of the fifteen thousand members of the Authors Guild, she could monopolize the literary agency business. Lloyd's plan to stop Sandra centered on him luring Davis Quigley away from Pradle—and from her. If he succeeded, it could discourage other writers from falling under her influence. If she failed, it would tend to end the Authors Guild uprising and allow business to resume as usual. Sandra Pierce had to be stopped!

Seeing that Catherine was still shaken, Lloyd decided to take her back to her room where she could rest and gather herself. He then left for his meeting with the other conference session speakers at the InterContinental Hotel. They had been told to meet in the Decadence Restaurant on the sixty-ninth floor.

The conference coordinator set up the luncheon to familiarize everyone with the schedule of breakout sessions, roundtables, and workshops.

Lloyd arrived a few minutes after the others were already seated at their tables and took his place at an empty spot by the head table. Upon noticing him, the coordinator left his place and came over and greeted Lloyd.

"Of course you've heard all about the big trouble over at Pradle," he began.

Lloyd was startled but responded that he'd been told very little.

"There was breaking news on CNN just minutes ago that someone broke into their office and that police and ambulances were seen up and down Wilshire Boulevard, all going to Rayburn Towers," he said.

"Was there more reporting than that?" Lloyd asked. "I mean, was anyone hurt? Do they know who did this?… and why?"

The coordinator looked around and saw that he was being waved back to the head table to give the welcome speech to those attending the conference.

"No, no, nothing more than what I just told you," he hurriedly responded. "But since it's his agency and Arthur Pradle is scheduled to speak at the banquet, I, uh… that is, we hope that you can be prepared to step in and take his place if…"

Lloyd's only response was a nod, indicating that they could count on him if it came to that.

33

A strange request

CHARLES KOLB HAD BEEN INVOLVED with writers' conferences for more than ten years and remembered many unplanned incidents that had popped up and threatened the success of almost every one of them. The experience he'd gained during those tension-filled episodes made him confident that in his role with the Pacific Coast Mystery Writers Conference, he would somehow find a way to manage this one. Perhaps no changes in the awards banquet would be necessary.

So far, there was only speculation that Arthur Pradle wouldn't be available to accept the Amos Nettleton Award at the closing banquet. There had been some break-in at his agency, and multiple emergency personnel were called to the location. If neither Pradle nor any of his employees had been injured, then substitutions might not be necessary.

"On the other hand," Kolb told his staff during a hurried conference call, "if whatever was happening there required Pradle to back out of accepting the award at the banquet, then the choice of Lloyd Patterson was the obvious solution. After all, the award was designed to go to the agent who represented the most authors with bestsellers during the year, and the Hurd Patterson Agency did come in as a close second." Best of all, Kolb had already secured Patterson's agreement to step in if necessary.

While Charles Kolb was busy confidently assuring everyone that nothing could derail the success of the conference, he read a text message that had been sent from Registrations while he was speaking at the session instructors' breakfast.

"A Mr. Harvey from Pradle Literary Agency wants to know if the authors of *Hounds of Hope* and *Dictated Choices* will be available for book signings today. He also wants to contact the authors and requested their hotel location. Both requests were denied, and Mr. Harvey remarked that it doesn't matter and left."

Those requests occurred frequently at writers conferences. New authors often wanted one-on-one time with well-known authors, publishers, and agents. To achieve such valuable arrangements, they sometimes went to great lengths, often fabricating a connection with the desired author.

That ruse might have had a chance since it mentioned Pradle Literary Agency. But giving it more consideration, Kolb just laughed. After texting Registration and learning that the mystery person had left the premises upon being denied the information, Kolb decided there was nothing more to be done and dismissed it as another good try.

34

Not incognito anymore

ARTHUR PRADLE SPENT THE FIRST morning after arriving at the InterContinental Hotel in much-needed leisure. His schedule for the day was almost completely free, with no meetings and no one to worry about. His role at the Pacific Mystery Writers Conference was limited to making one speech at the closing banquet. Even that was just to say thank you to the Writers' Conference for honoring him. Arthur was happy that the conference had selected him for their Amos Nettleton Award and planned to say that he was proud to accept it on behalf of the authors his agency represented. After all, they were who had earned the award for him.

When he sat at his laptop to write his acceptance speech, he thought about mentioning what it meant to be associated with such distinguished writers. The first writer he wanted to acknowledge was Davis Quigley and his bestseller, *Dictated Choices*. He planned to include comments about Franz Graber and his book about the kidnapping of the Lindbergh baby and subsequent trial of Bruno Richard Hauptmann, *Death of a Friend*.

He would end his speech with high praise for his "associate" at Pradle Literary Agency, Sandra Pierce. He smiled after noticing that he'd referred to her as his associate. That wouldn't sit well with Sandra. It was true that she'd discovered each of the agency's best-selling authors who'd written the novels that earned him the award. There were seven other authors that she discovered who fell just short of making the list this year. But Sandra's success was showing signs of feeding her ambition and causing her to make decisions that could probably hurt her in the long run. They would definitely hurt the entire literary agency business if she succeeded. Referring to her without acknowledging her position as a partner at Pradle just might dampen the influence she would require to persuade writers to fire their agents and recklessly fall in with someone who could was maneuvering with an effort that could still fail.

The breakfast that he'd ordered from room service was acceptable, but the coffee was actually excellent. When the empty tray was picked up, Arthur asked the bellhop if he might hurry back with another small pot. He was surprised by how quickly he heard a knock at his hotel room door.

Instead of seeing the bellhop standing outside his door, however, he was surprised to find a muscular man dressed in dark pants and a black T-shirt.

"Mr. Pradle?" the man asked.

Arthur wanted to enjoy the anonymity that accompanied his stay at the InterContinental. He was surprised that the stranger asked for him by name. His room number was known only by Charlotte Olson, who made the reservation. Other than her, only Richard Drake, the political operative who'd worked with Will Jennings and whose hotel room was a few doors down the hall, knew that information.

Earlier, Drake and Arthur had ridden an elevator to their floor, and Drake mentioned that he was at the conference to find an editor or agent for his new mystery. He quickly described why he wrote his manuscript, telling Arthur that he'd based this one on the contentious strife between this country's conservatives and liberals, as demonstrated recently during the television shows where Will Jennings and Catherine Lane attracted record ratings. He hoped to rewrite the story into a mystery, he said, by having one of his Lane- or Jennings-type fictional characters shot and killed during their final television discussion. He wondered if Arthur might make a quick read of his outline and offer his thoughts. Arthur laughed when Drake mentioned the murder, and said that he agreed to give the outline an hour or so of his free time while he was at the hotel.

No one else, not even Sandra Pierce, knew much about his schedule except that he was expected to arrive in time to receive the award at the closing banquet.

"Mr. Pradle?" the man repeated.

Once again, Arthur didn't respond and continued staring at the visitor, wondering if he knew him somehow.

The silence was interrupted by the buzz from Arthur's cell phone, which he'd left next to his laptop. Ignoring the awkward situation at the door, Arthur turned to answer the phone.

"Arthur." Sandra's voice revealed surprising anxiety. "Have you heard…?"

Suddenly, the phone was snatched away. Arthur turned and discovered that the man he'd just seen at his door had followed him inside.

The man threw the cell phone onto the bed and grabbed Arthur under his shoulders. He lifted him off the floor while pushing him against the wall.

"What do you want?" Arthur gasped. "Are you looking for money?"

The man laughed and let Arthur slide down the wall onto the floor.

"Listen very carefully," he began. "Do as I say, and this will all end soon."

"End soon? What's that supposed to mean?"

His answer was a hard punch to the side of his head.

"Just listen. Then do!"

Bewildered and confused, Arthur looked up and saw rage in the eyes of his attacker. He nodded to indicate he understood that last instruction.

35

Finding Arthur Pradle

ALMOST IMMEDIATELY AFTER THE police and EMTs arrived inside Pradle Literary Agency, Officer Tuttle hurriedly escorted Sandra from the scene all the way down to the Wilshire Street level.

"I know you're probably following procedures"—she squirmed as she tried to free herself—"but I work here. They are my employees. I want... I need to know."

Still in shock, Sandra found it almost impossible to speak without shouting. When tears began, accompanied by uncontrolled sobbing, she felt a sudden weakness that threatened her balance. Just as she almost fell, Davis rushed up from the busy street and caught her.

"Sandra! What is happening?""

She recognized his voice as she looked up now in his arms. "Davis! Oh, we were too late. Charlotte and Kirsch... They're..." Again, her voice failed to function through her anguished sobbing as Davis consoled her.

Davis's arms tightened around Sandra, drawing her closer. Officer Tuttle looked somber, standing there with his eyes downcast, giving little hope about the status of those inside.

"What happened? Who did this?" Davis repeated demanding to know more.

"The detectives are on-site already," replied Tuttle. "Hopefully, we should know something soon."

"Arthur!" Sandra suddenly shouted as she broke free from Davis. "Does Arthur even know what's happening?" Her questions received only silence. After reaching for her cell phone, she clicked on his number. The phone rang four times without being answered, but on the next ring, which she feared was sending her call to Messages, she heard his voice.

"Arthur?" she shouted. "Have you heard…?"

She listened as muffled sounds came from Arthur's phone, indicating there was some kind of havoc underway there. She heard Arthur ask why he was being attacked, and a bit later, a different voice said it would soon be over.

"Officer!" Sandra shouted. "Someone's attacking Arthur Pradle! Someone's attacking—"

Davis grabbed for the cell phone in Sandra's outstretched hand, but Officer Tuttle got to it first. He placed the phone to his ear and listened. Within seconds, he turned back to them saying that the call got cut off. "Where is he?"

"The only thing I can imagine is that he may have a room at the InterContinental Hotel, where one of our writers will be presented an award later," Sandra said.

The officer tapped on the radio mic clipped to his uniform shirt and called in, telling the precinct about the ongoing attack of one Arthur Pradle at the InterContinental Hotel.

Tuttle returned his attention to Sandra and Davis. "Do either of you know which room Pradle might have there where all of this is happening? Do you know your friend's room number?"

Sandra stole a quick look at Davis, but neither knew the answer.

"Now what?" she cried. "How are the police going to help Arthur without knowing where he is?"

Officer Tuttle told her to stay calm. "They'll have that information by the time they arrive. The precinct will call ahead to the hotel and inform them of the need to know Mr. Pradle's room number. The hotel will undoubtedly send their own security personnel to the room. Like I just told you, stay calm."

Sandra turned to Davis. "Let's go there. Okay?"

Davis shrugged. "Yes, its okay, but I don't have wheels. We'll have to take your car."

Sandra's disappointment was obvious. "I got here with Jeanne McHale, who dropped me off and then drove away after Officer Tuttle told her she was blocking an entrance that might be needed by police or the fire department."

Officer Tuttle was already nearing the squad car that he'd left parked in front of Masons Restaurant. "Hurry up!" he yelled back to them. "I'm on my way to the InterContinental Hotel. The detectives may need you to ID Arthur there."

36

A call comes to Davis

WITH FLASHERS AND SIREN ALERTING traffic to get out of his way, Officer Tuttle figured it would take only a few minutes to travel down Wilshire Boulevard and arrive at the InterContinental Hotel. After hearing Davis tell Sandra about Charlotte's call to him just before she was attacked, the officer asked if she'd mentioned what the intruder wanted.

"He seemed to know me or something. He told Charlotte that he knew about someone named Catherine and that he had information I needed to know."

"So, who is this Catherine?" the officer asked.

"I have no idea who or what he was referring to," Davis responded. "Unless…" He stopped talking when he realized the only Catherine he knew, was someone who would have nothing in common with the attacker.

Two police cars had already arrived and blocked the entrance to the InterContinental Hotel. Officer Tuttle pulled in behind them.

"I'm going inside, but you two stay here!" he ordered before rushing through the revolving door.

"I can't just sit here," Sandra said after a few minutes of anxious waiting. "I have to know how Arthur is and what's going on."

Davis listened but said nothing, apparently lost in thought even while the mystery of what was happening with Sandra's boss was ongoing. *How could this strange intruder know anything about me? Who is he? And why did he mention a person named Catherine? Am I supposed to know her? Surely its not the Catherine I know...*

"Davis, are you with me?" Sandra opened the car door. "Let's just go as close as the lobby."

Davis pulled her back inside the squad car, reminding her that whatever was happening, there were policemen with guns and an attacker who probably had his own gun. Like Officer Tuttle had instructed, they needed to stay in the squad car.

Sandra recalled seeing Officer Tuttle draw his revolver as he went through the entrance. "I know you're right." She sighed. "But this not knowing is killing me! All we do know is that this kook first barges into our offices and does whatever to..." Panic grabbed hold as her thoughts settled on Charlotte Olson. "Then we find out that later, he's somehow found Arthur over a mile away from our office building and may have done the same thing to him. And he wants you for some reason and lures you with some cryptic comment about someone named Catherine!"

Police sirens came screaming from both directions along Wilshire Boulevard. Sandra and Davis watched as the entire block in both directions was cleared. At the intersections, squad cars stopped, and police rushed into position to halt all vehicles and pedestrians within a block of the hotel.

Suddenly, Davis's cell phone buzzed. "Yes, I'm Davis Quigley," he answered. "What? You're who? You're someone who was just with Arthur Pradle? Where is he? Where are you now?"

The look on Davis's face revealed both surprise and anxiety. Sandra said nothing but squeezed closer to provide any comfort that she could.

Davis's breathing increased each fraction of a second that he stayed talking with the caller.

"But why? Why do you need to see me? What's our connection with each other?"

Davis was silent as he listened to the caller giving his reason for contacting him.

"Yes… Catherine Lane?… Yes again," Sandra heard Davis respond.

Gradually, his attitude was changing from anger and curiosity to alarm.

"You want me to bring her to the Pritzker Parking Garage? Why? Where's that?" Davis repeated each instruction as it was given. "Okay. It's by the Los Angeles County Museum of Art. Uh-huh, it's just a few blocks down Wilshire Boulevard. Got it! But what then?"

Again, Davis stayed silent. After a few moments, he clicked off his cell phone and turned toward Sandra.

"Did you just hang up on him?" She sounded confused and surprised.

Davis sighed. "No. He finished telling me what his demands are and then hung up before I could say that I would or wouldn't follow his instructions."

37

Hurry up and hide!

After Lloyd Patterson walked her to her suite then left to attend the speakers' briefing, Catherine Lane was alone with her worries over Davis and whatever was happening at his agent's office. Earlier, Davis told her that someone had gone inside the Pradle office and demanded to speak with him. It sounded like a struggle had ensued. Her need to be with Davis, or at least speak with him, prompted her to pull out her cell phone. Just before touching the Davis Q. contact on her phone, Catherine realized that any distraction like answering his phone might cause more harm than good. Was he hiding or perhaps talking with whoever... She needed more information.

Catherine tapped the CNN app on her phone screen, and a breaking news headline appeared, showing police cars and ambulances outside the entrance to the Rayburn Towers Office Building. Catherine knew that the Pradle Literary Agency had offices on the building's fourth floor. Her heart sank as she watched the screen. Two ambulances sat empty with their doors open and no medical personnel evident.

The CNN reporter said something and Catherine hurried to turn up the volume. All she caught was that an attack had been reported at the agency, and there were multiple casualties. Thinking that she would go crazy just speculating on what was happening or whether Davis was heading into danger by going there, she took the elevator down to The Carlyle Hotel lobby. A group of people in the lounge were gathered around and watching the news on television.

"Yes, ma'am?" the bartender asked as Catherine took a seat close to a group of people conversing about the news.

"Oh, I just want something to calm me down," she said. "Maybe a glass of Sauvignon Blanc?"

"I suspect I can do that." He smiled. "Let me pour you a glass of Whitehaven, a New Zealand brand. It's one of our most-ordered wines."

"You mentioned you wanted to be calmed down," the bartender said after serving her the wine. "That news about the troubles at that office building, is that what's on your mind?"

Catherine motioned toward the television. "I have friends who work there. I'm so worried, but I've seen nothing more than that there's been an attack."

"Well, I can't tell you any more than what's being reported by Fox News. I'm sure they'll have updates, and maybe soon we can all learn more." He turned to serve another customer.

Catherine decided that texting Davis probably wouldn't be as problematic as she'd earlier worried. Taking a few sips of her wine, she took out her cell phone, only to be surprised as it buzzed with an incoming call—from Davis!

"Are you somewhere safe?" Davis asked.

She told him where she was and how worried she'd been about him and what had happened at his agency's office.

"It's all still happening," he told her. "Only worse." Davis talked fast and sounded out of breath.

A minute earlier, just hearing his voice had eased away most of the worry that had caused her feeling ill. But hearing that it was all still happening brought those feelings to return in abundance.

"You say it's worse now?" Catherine asked. "I don't know all of what's happened, but worse? How could it be worse than the attack on people working there?"

"Catherine, listen to me," Davis said. "Charlotte and Kirsch were attacked in their office, and the same man who attacked them then rushed down Wilshire Boulevard to the InterContinental Hotel and attacked Arthur Pradle."

Catherine talked over Davis and asked him to slow down. "You said that Charlotte and Kirsch and Arthur Pradle were attacked? By whom?"

"I just got off the phone with that man, that attacker," Davis said. "I don't have much time to fill you in on everything, but I do know that I want you to get in touch with Lloyd Patterson and stay together with him, and then both of you must go somewhere where you'll be safe, with doors that lock. Double lock."

"Davis," Catherine was near tears. "What do you mean that you don't have much time? Are you in danger? Have you actually just talked to that man? Why should I be with Lloyd Patterson and not you right now?"

"Please, Catherine. Please do what I asked. I'll call you just as soon as I can…" Davis said as he ended the call.

38

A plan

After Davis's call from a man saying he'd just left Arthur Pradle and insisted on meeting with him in the Pritzker Parking Garage by the art museum within the hour, Davis called the police and contacted Officer Tuttle.

"No way," the policeman told him. "None of us yet know who this crazed ass is or what he wants or why he's done what he's done. This is work for trained law enforcement, and even then, it could be life-threatening," he said before repeating his instructions for Davis to return.

"Well, we know enough to believe he's going to be somewhere in that parking garage. If you can get some cops there in time for when he sees me and comes out of hiding, I think he can be captured."

"I repeat—" was all that Davis heard before shutting off his cell phone.

In the Uber on his way to the Pritzker Parking Garage, Davis saw a large billboard advertising the Los Angeles County Art Museum. He told the driver to drop him off at the museum instead of the parking garage and quickly devised a plan for waiting there to be contacted again. He thought it might be safer to be among a crowd, like in the museum, and wait. Surely, the man would call again, and he could lie and say that Catherine was close by, but first, he needed to know what the man wanted to do with them.

After exiting the Uber, Davis caught up with a small group of people who had stepped from a tourist bus and followed them to the Grand Entrance to the museum.

39

A nationwide ABP

How do you spell your last name?" the officer behind the desk asked. "I'm required to accurately identify anyone wishing to report a missing person."

Miranda sighed, impatient with the paperwork that seemed more important than the urgent situation. "Esquivel," she said hurriedly before realizing the officer appeared not to have heard her. "Let me repeat that for you. E-S-Q-U-I-V-E-L. Esquivel!"

"First name?" the officer asked without looking up.

"My name is Miranda Esquivel, and I live on Mead Avenue," she said, sounding anxious while placing two photos on the desk. "The man in that photo has been missing from his apartment since last week, and he's under court orders to report to me at least twice a day."

The officer looked up and stopped writing. "Court orders?"

"Yes, that's right!" Miranda said. "I'm deputized by the court to monitor his daily activities and coordinate that information with his appointed therapist. But as of a week ago, Mr. Harvey has gone missing…"

Her explanation brought a more ready attitude from the policeman. "I see." He picked up one of the photographs Miranda had brought with her. "Is this the one who is missing, or are they both…?"

"Yes. His name is Brady Harvey, and his condominium is on Weaver Street. He's suffering from a mental disorder and requires precise prescription dosage and regular psychiatric care," she informed the officer.

"You say he requires medicine and has psychiatric problems? Is he considered dangerous?"

Miranda started to respond but paused. "I should let his therapist decide how to answer your questions." She finally reached into her purse, retrieved the business card of Beverly Beckett Conforti, and handed it to him.

"And the other photo? Why did you bring that? Is she also a missing person?"

Miranda noted his sarcasm. "I don't really know much about her. But Brady has her pictures everywhere in his apartment, and with some, he seems to show anger, like drawing an *X* over the person the woman is with."

"And I suppose you think that our missing person may be looking to harm the lady in the photo?"

"He may, or maybe he's a danger to the lady's husband?" Her answer showed that she was concerned about not only where Brady was but also why he was now missing.

"Okay, I'll get this information into the system, where police have ways of keeping an eye out and hopefully finding him… or her!"

After leaving the police station, Miranda stopped by St. Mary's Church and offered a prayer for Brady and whoever he seemed bent on hurting. She also prayed about her concern that perhaps she shouldn't have reported his absence. She knew about his propensity to overreact and even become violent. She prayed that wouldn't happen and that he would be found and taken back to his condo.

On her drive home, Miranda noticed a police car in her apartment's parking lot. She pulled up to it, lowered her window, and asked the officer what the trouble was.

"We're looking for one of the residents, a Mrs. Esquivel."

When she told him that was her name, she was told that a detective was also there and wished to speak with her. As they talked, Miranda saw someone approaching her car.

After greeting her, the detective said there was big trouble out in Los Angeles and that his shift sergeant recognized the woman in the photo Miranda had taken to the police station.

"She's been identified as that author who's been on the television news shows, a Mrs. Catherine Lane. We wondered if the man you reported missing might have mentioned her."

"No, he never said what her name was, but it might be the same person," Miranda said. "You said there was some kind of trouble in Los Angeles?"

The detective told her that they'd already contacted Catherine Lane's publisher, who informed them that she was with her agent in LA.

Upon hearing Los Angeles, Miranda recalled seeing scribbled notes that Brady had left on his kitchen table. He had underlined LAX and something that looked like CDL. The scribbles hadn't concerned her, since Brady often jotted down things he might have just read or seen on TV. She told the detective about those notes.

He returned to the squad car where he called in the information and ordered the missing person report be sent to the police in Los Angeles along with the information Miranda had given him about Brady's mental problems.

"Ask them to put out an APB on one Brady Harvey," he added.

40

Finally...

YOU DON'T LISTEN WELL, do you?"

While Davis had expected a call, he was shocked by the brevity of the message. How did the caller know he hadn't completely followed the instructions to wait inside the Pritzker garage? Did he know that Davis didn't bring Catherine with him? Where was the man calling from? Could he see him? All of those questions arose the instant Davis answered his cell phone and heard the man's six words.

"I don't know what you mean," Davis began. "I'm here just as you wanted me to be. Where are you?"

A half moment of silence elapsed. "You're not at the Pritzker garage. You're standing on the entrance pavilion at the museum. And you don't have Catherine with you."

Knowing that his call to Officer Tuttle should have alerted the police to his plans for meeting the man wanted for the attacks at the Pradle Literary office and the InterContinental Hotel, he decided to ignore the threats and instead to take the initiative.

"Look, you can see that I've come and that I do want to meet you, just as you asked," he began. "But the rest of what you demanded requires that I first have at least some idea of what this is all about. Do we even know each other? Have we met or been together somewhere? And why do you insist on bringing Catherine into any of this?"

"Catherine is what this is all about," the man responded. "She's rightfully mine, and you and the others make your claims to her without even knowing who she really is."

Davis was confused. "Rightfully yours?"

Again, there was prolonged silence. Finally, the caller told Davis to walk away from the museum and wait on the corner of Wilshire Boulevard at Fairfax Avenue.

"When I'm sure you're alone, I'll go there and tell you more."

While that offered more than Davis had expected, he considered the danger it presented. After the caller hung up, Davis quickly called Officer Tuttle's phone number, which showed on his cell phone's recent-caller screen.

"This is police work now," Tuttle said, almost shouting. "We've been tracing your cell phone since you and I last talked, and we not only know where you are but also have undercover cops all around you. Do not, I repeat, do *not* leave the pavilion. If he's already seen you like he just told you, then he'll probably just approach the entrance, and before he can get close to you, we'll take him down."

Before Davis could respond, a man in a Dodgers jacket walked up to him and asked for a light for his cigarette.

"Do what you're being told to do," the man said softly as he handed Davis a book of matches to be used in their ruse. "I'll be over by the entrance, and we have a full squad of cops just waiting for your friend to make a move."

Almost fifteen minutes passed without anything happening. The undercover cop in the Dodgers jacket left, and a woman wearing shorts and an army jacket took his place. Davis saw two men take seats on a bench halfway between Wilshire Boulevard and the spot where he stood waiting. he suspected that the caller may had been alerted by any of those actions and perhaps changed his mind. He wondered if the man would call him again.

Suddenly, all hell was breaking loose a half block down on Wilshire Boulevard. Davis saw a man being chased by two men in uniform away from Fairfax Avenue and into the heavy traffic on Wilshire. The man looked back at his pursuers just as a pickup truck swerved to avoid a bus that had pulled away from the curb. Neither the driver nor the man in his path could avoid the horrific outcome.

Part 2

41

Santa Monica

T HE COOL BREEZES BLOWING in from the ocean had already chased away the morning fog and given Santa Monica the promise of "just another day at the beach," as Ursula Walkwitz described it when she invited Cora Charles to choose their lunch spot.

"Yes, it really is such a nice day, isn't it?" Cora replied. "But they're warning of some storms heading our way." She paused before telling Ursula that she was too busy preparing for her next podcast to meet for lunch.

"Cora Charles, I'm ashamed of you" came the angry reply. "You've been so tied up with that business you run on your website and with those podcasts that you've turned into more of a recluse than anyone I know."

Ursula's admonition struck home and caused Cora to reconsider the lunch plans. "I must agree with you. I guess I've been too tied down lately. If we're going to do this, I would prefer finding a small restaurant along Montana Avenue."

"That sounds nice," Ursula agreed. "Maybe you're thinking of doing some shopping afterward. Right?"

"You must have been a sleuth in an earlier life," Cora teased. "Of course, you only guessed correctly because you also like checking out the designer clothes at the luxury boutiques along Montana Avenue. We might enjoy spending the whole afternoon there together after lunch."

"Right on" was all that was left to say as they agreed to meet at Carol Gee's restaurant in two hours once Ursula googled to be sure they were open on Sundays.

Cora used the remainder of her morning to check on her Writers Words website. She was surprised to find it much busier than usual. As she read through the messages, a frequent discussion topic was a murder at the InterContinental Hotel. Cora remembered that the West Coast Mystery Writers annual meeting was going on there and skimmed the messages to see if the murder victim had been identified.

Seeing the name Arthur Pradle alarmed her. She'd met him earlier somewhere and had read recently that he planned to split his literary agency in half and would spend most of his time in New York. It was all interesting, but the extra time she'd already spent reading the website made her rush to prepare for the lunch with Ursula. Cora knew how upset Ursula would be if she wasn't already there when she arrived causing her to wait alone at their table. Cora hurriedly called for an Uber then prepared for her lunch date.

When her cell phone buzzed with incoming calls, rather than answering them, Cora put the phone on Silence. She had just enough time to use the bathroom before rushing outside to the waiting Uber driver. Upon arriving at Carol Gee's, Cora was troubled by a sneaky suspicion that in her haste to leave, she might have left her front door unlocked.

She soon spotted Ursula. "You've heard about the troubles they're going through at the InterContinental, haven't you?"

"Yes, I have indeed." She sounded miffed. "I saw all the police cars and that kind of activity all up and down Wilshire Boulevard and then saw that even more of whatever's going on there was also happening over on Fairfax. I suppose that's your reason for being late?" Her question implied that whatever Cora used as an excuse wouldn't be good enough.

Cora smiled. Once something got under Ursula's skin, it usually took more than one glass of merlot to rid her of the irritation. "I actually know less than you've been able to learn about that," Cora said. "I didn't have the television on all morning, and the only way I saw any news of this was when I checked my website, never expecting that anything there would take up so much of my time."

Cora's added explanation seemed to do the trick in calming Ursula.

"When I saw that news on Fox this morning, my first thoughts were about you since I know that the mystery writers group they mentioned is involved in the same business you're in," Ursula said. "Of course, knowing that someone was murdered today that close to where we live, no more than a half-hour walk away from us down Wilshire Boulevard, well, that's just too close for comfort, don't you think?"

Cora sipped her drink. Ursula made all the danger seem so much closer.

Shopping followed their lunch, and Cora said goodbye to Ursula outside of Maxine's on Montana, the exclusive clothier advertised as the place where "the women who make the movies" found everything from beachwear to business attire. Ursula had additional shopping ideas, but Cora explained that their time together had already exceeded her schedule, and she had an appointment with an author arriving in from somewhere in Connecticut. The meeting was a must or bust for her. She promised to call Ursula afterward and said she was anxious to hear what her friend finally decided to purchase.

The Uber was late picking Cora up for the ride home. The driver said he was slowed by the traffic along Wilshire Boulevard that quickly grew because of some police activity. Many others were on their way to the beach that inspired the western view from Cora's home. As she departed from the Uber vehicle, Cora wondered whether she might find time after the lesson to enjoy her usual walk in the sand.

The client for the one-on-one lesson had said his name was Corwin Wellington and that he needed her guidance in preparing a biography that a major publisher had encouraged him to write. He promised to give Cora full payment for the lesson as soon as they met and completed it.

Cora liked how that sounded. He'd already acknowledged that his request for an individualized lesson called for a larger payment, and he had no objection. He said he learned of her service through a friend but chose not to identify that person until the biography was published. Cora replied to his email and considered it a confirmed appointment.

All right, Mr. Wellington. Your lesson is now set for 4:00 p.m., and I expect you to be ready with the outline of your book and to be at my condominium building by that time. I have notified security personnel of your intended visit time, and you can ring me inside the entrance upon arrival, which I suggest be fifteen minutes before we begin. See you then.
Sincerely, Cora Charles

Cora was happy to discover that she had to use her front-door code to enter her condominium, proving that she hadn't forgotten to lock the front door as she'd suspected. Her good habits continued, even when she was in a rush or in those moments when her memory lapsed. After freshening up, she turned on her laptop and opened the program she always used to conduct personal training sessions for new writers.

All that remained was for her to watch for Mr. Corwin Wellington to follow her instructions to clear security and appear at her front door.

It was close to four thirty, yet Mr. Wellington had neither shown up nor phoned to cancel. Cora was upset not only because of the lost money but also because of the added insult of receiving no explanation for his failure to appear. She emailed him while waiting, and all the messages appeared to have been delivered but got no response. She was about to give up on this Wellington client when she heard a noise in her kitchen.

"What a day," she said aloud. "That damn mouse is back, and this time, when I catch him, it'll be curtains." As she sneaked closer, she caught sight of a shadow, one too large to belong to a mouse...

42

Officer Tuttle

R OMAN TUTTLE REALIZED HE'D gotten the plum job of working in the Detectives Bureau only because he turned out to be the police officer who'd talked with Davis Quigley following the murders at Rayburn Towers Office Building. He smiled as he remembered how one coincidence led to another, and all of them resulted in him being the person that Davis Quigley contacted after being called by the man now suspected of the murders.

"So, I suppose that you think you're smart enough to figure this whole thing out," teased Officer Karen Fund, his usual partner when assigned to patrol duty. "I admit it. I'm jealous."

"And well you should be," Tuttle said. "I'm the guy who was at the right place at the wrong time and figured out what to do when Quigley called about being contacted by the killer. The lieutenant apparently took note of that and decided to put me in street clothes."

His partner would have none of that bragging. "Look, I already said that I'm jealous. You know, if I hadn't been busting my butt and escorting bad men to lockup after they were convicted in traffic court at the moment when all those things happened, fate could have treated me as well as you're being treated."

"Yeah, I know, I know." Tuttle laughed. "You're always the one who stops to pick up a quarter on the street when the wind blows the dollar bill away before you even get there. But for now, at least, why don't we get to the reason you're calling me."

"Yeah, why don't we just do that?" She sounded irritated. "I've been assigned to the Virtual Patrols unit. You know, the place where we scan CCTV camera footage that gets streamed to us from those gas stations and other businesses along Wilshire Boulevard."

"Okay."

"Right," she said. "I was just wondering if maybe that killer we're searching for all over the city maybe walked away from that stolen car he left parked by the art museum and found some other car to steal farther down that route."

Tuttle remained silent after listening to her idea about Brady's possible getaway route.

"Still there, Roman?"

"Karen, listen, I think that's not only a possibility but perhaps the most likely way he got away," Tuttle said. "I have access here to the FBI's Next Generation Identification System. Maybe…"

She waited before responding. "And you think that's something that might work with what I just told you about the CCTV scans?"

"Yes, I do!" He was thrilled with the brainstorm that information prompted. "If we insert Brady's photo into the software containing the template you're now using with those gas station camera scans, we might actually see him stealing that car you just mentioned or at least find him walking down Wilshire Boulevard."

In less than two hours, their combined theories had produced the biggest piece of information yet in the hunt for Brady Harvey. Roman Tuttle was with Karen Fund at his side when he notified

Lieutenant Fitzgerald of their discovery. Brady Harvey had simply walked away from the scene of the accident where some low-life purse snatcher was chased into the traffic and was struck and killed. Brady was later seen on camera footage at four locations, walking toward the downtown shopping district in Santa Monica.

43

LAPD

I'VE OFTEN HEARD THAT BAD THINGS people do always come to a sad end," Chief Detective Fitzgerald said.

Detectives and officers assigned to the Brady Harvey case were meeting to go over evidence, witness statements, and other data regarding the episode that began with the murders at Rayburn Towers.

"But just when it all seemed that this was how his crimes were coming to their sad endings, it turned out to be just the opposite, didn't it?"

"Not sure I follow you there, Lieutenant," Officer Tuttle answered. Fitzgerald had been looking at Tuttle while he was speaking.

The detective sighed and wrote on the chalkboard.

1. **Rayburn Towers.** "We get notified by Officer Tuttle that he's inside an office at Rayburn Towers on Wilshire Boulevard, where two people have been murdered." The lieutenant glanced at Officer Tuttle, who gave him a nod.

2. **InterContinental Hotel.** "We get another call and now have three murders. All this after we radio two squads to provide support at Rayburn Towers, and we hear that another murder scene is active at the InterContinental Hotel, where the Pacific Mystery Writers Conference is going on."

"Yes, that's where the person from the Rayburn building was killed by a person or persons unknown," Tuttle added.

Detective Fitzgerald paused with a question that had bugged him ever since taking over the investigation. He asked Officer Tuttle why he'd thought it was appropriate to bring along those two writers who worked at Pradle's office when he was called to assist police at the InterContinental Hotel.

"Simple reason was that the woman, Sandra Pierce, said she knew Arthur Pradle. I figured she might be needed for identification purposes."

"Okay. Going forward now," Fitzgerald said, indicating that Tuttle's answer was satisfactory. "One of the passengers who rode with Ms. Pierce in Officer Tuttle's taxi slash squad car received a phone threat from a suspect later thought to be one Brady Harvey, subject of a just-released APB out of Greenwich, Connecticut, who demanded to meet him at the Pritzker Parking Garage. The passenger then calls police and informs Officer Tuttle, and the parking garage is subsequently surrounded by police units."

Chief Detective Fitzgerald halted his presentation long enough to refill his coffee cup. After taking a sip to ensure it was still hot, he set the cup down on the conference table and looked closely at each team member.

"The conclusion of the first part of this investigation was perhaps the most disappointing one I've experienced in my career on the force. Despite having all of the entrances at the parking garage covered by experienced police officers and then thoroughly searched for a period lasting longer than an hour—inside cars, under cars, staircases, elevators—no one, nada, had a fuggin' clue about who or where this Brady bastard was discovered. The *only* thing that did end there was efforts by police who were responding to a report from Officer Tuttle saying that our murder suspect was inside that garage! The man who was killed in the accident turned out to be a purse snatcher trying to escape from the art museum's security personnel."

After once again sipping from his cup, Fitzgerald spoke solemnly. "Brady Harvey is a killer. Brady Harvey is dangerous. Brady Harvey is a recently released mental patient currently wanted in Connecticut for violations of home-confinement rules. And the only thing we know so far is that **Brady Harvey** is on the loose… in our very own city!"

* * *

Sandra was relieved to see the name McHale Media on her phone screen. "Where have you been? Where are you now? Are you okay?" Sandra's questions came so fast that Jeanne McHale had almost no opportunity to respond.

"I'm just leaving the West Bureau Homicide Unit on Vermont Avenue and need you. Really need you," Jeanne said.

"Wait. What? You're where? Why?" Sandra's questions fired swiftly.

"The detectives came and got me when I called to report that my car had been stolen from a parking space around the corner from Rayburn," she said.

"Your car? The one you drove us over to the Rayburn office building in?"

"Yes, that's right. You remember. Right after we drove up and you got out, a police officer shooed me away from parking because other police were on the way there. Remember?"

"Yes, I remember," Sandra said. "But you're now over on Vermont Avenue with the homicide detectives?"

"I am." Jeanne sounded hurried and anxious. "Come now, will you? I have no car, and… I just… I just need you right now."

Sandra was confused by everything that was happening but focused on her friend. "I'll come right away," she assured Jeanne. "But why didn't you call me? And just where is your car now?"

Jeanne sighed. "The police found my car parked on Fairfax near the art museum and had it towed to their crime lab somewhere."

44

Ruth Harvey

R EVEREND CORWIN WELLINGTON WAS surprised to find someone sitting inside a black Chrysler that was parked two houses down from the Harvey home on Conyers Farm Drive. The man inside seemed interested in seeing who Wellington might be as he passed and turned in to the driveway at Ruth Harvey's residence.

After entering the house, Corwin peeked outside to see if the car had left. "How long has that been going on?" he asked after guiding Ruth closer to the front-door window, providing her with a look at the mystery car.

"Ever since," she responded while embracing her visitor.

They held hands as they walked into the kitchen, away from the front windows. "You mean, after what happened in Los Angeles?"

"Oh no. The police have been watching this whole area after the Greenwich police put out an APB around the time Brady went missing from his condominium. They seem to just drive around the block then return and park over there, usually around Mrs. Dallas's home."

"Do they go away and park somewhere else or...?"

Ruth looked annoyed. "I don't really care where they are or go." Her tone indicated her desire to talk about something else. "What have you been told?"

The pastor opened the refrigerator and removed a Pepsi for himself while Ruth sat down at the kitchen table. "To put this in the gentlest way possible," he began, "no one seems the least bit surprised to have learned that our boy Brady is now on the Most Wanted List."

Ruth brought a Kleenex to her face. "He's not a killer. You know that," she said defiantly. "He's done bad things before, and that was all caused by that illness he suffers from. But he never hurt anyone. Not really hurt anyone."

Corwin moved close enough to comfort her. "I know, I know." He cleared his throat. "He's a good person. God knows that."

"What's going to happen now if they catch him somewhere?" she asked. "I'm just afraid that if they don't let him get any of that medicine he needs so bad, that—"

"Right now, that concern isn't going to be at the top of any police priority," he answered. "They first want to capture him and keep him from finding that person he thinks owes him in some way."

Ruth looked surprised. "You mean Catherine?"

Wellington nodded. Then he escorted Ruth out of the kitchen and into her large living room, where they sat next to each other on the curved white leather sofa that seemed to float in the center of the room. Ruth faced him, and he could tell she had something serious to discuss.

"I've received a request from a woman, a Sandra Pierce. She said she's a literary agent and hopes I'll allow one of her authors to come here to interview me and perhaps others who know Brady."

Corwin was suddenly more interested in what she was saying. "I wonder why she would want to interview you. I hope she doesn't suspect that you know where Brady is right now."

Corwin moved closer and hugged Ruth. "Aw, forget I just said that. No, I don't suspect that she thinks that at all." He didn't want to give Ruth more to be concerned about.

"Then just what other reason would she have?" Ruth asked.

"We won't learn that answer unless you agree to her request," he said. "Why do you think she might want someone to write about all this?"

"The only thing I've seen in the newspapers or on television is just one-sided garbage about Brady maybe being crazy," Ruth said. "They've got hold of his police records and are playing it up to say that he's a terrible danger to our community and ought to be killed or captured by the police before anything around here can ever return to normal."

Corwin hugged Ruth closer before suggesting that Sandra Pierce might be able to get Brady's story told in a much more favorable way. "I'm not sure that's something she would consider, but if people could learn how much Brady suffered following the 9/11 tragedy that killed his father, then he might stand a better chance of surviving after they catch him."

*　*　*

After he learned of the murders at Sandra Pierce's office in Los Angeles, Franz Graber was happy to hear from Sandra that she was unharmed but surprised that she was already involved with business activities at Pradle Literary Agency.

"I can't tell you much about anything going on here since all this happened," she said. "But with everything still up in the air, I think it's a safe bet to say that this Brady Harvey has at a minimum made himself potentially the best-known author in the United States of America."

Franz wondered how she could even think about something so unimportant, especially right after her office manager had been killed inside the Pradle office. "Mind you, I'm not criticizing," he said. "Just wondering if maybe you're doing something now to distract you from what you're going through."

"Oh, I'm sure you're probably right about that," she said. "But for now, why don't you just allow me to return to the purpose of my call?"

45

The podcast

THE BOOK WORLD WAS SHOCKED when a crazed man, Brady Harvey, flew across the country, hoping to find his lifelong love and wanting to kill the man he thought was trying to steal her from him." Will Jennings spoke to his largely conservative listeners on his weekly podcast, The Will to be Right.

"My guest today is Richard Drake, who runs Richard Drake Associates. He and I have worked together often in recent years," Jennings told his listeners. "Richard Drake has provided research and valuable consulting contributions to my syndicated column, Just Jennings, as well as for many of my best-selling books. But the recent news about those West Coast murders of writers and publishers has involved him in a much more direct way. Isn't that so, Richard?"

"That's right," Drake agreed, adding, "much more in a direct way!"

Jennings laughed as he acknowledged the understatement. "Richard was with one of those who was killed just minutes before the murder occurred."

"I had prepared an outline for a novel and given it to Arthur Pradle, hoping to get it published. By strange coincidence, I met briefly with Mr. Pradle in the hotel where he was staying only an hour or so before he was confronted by Mr. Harvey."

"Arthur Pradle? He was the CEO of an agency that represented novelists and screenwriters and was among those who were attacked by Harvey, wasn't he?"

"Yes, he was, as were two of his employees over at Pradle Literary Agency in the Rayburn Towers building. Harvey first went to that location, seeking Catherine Lane and hopefully Davis Quigley, who he thought was stealing her from him."

"That information has since been well covered by TV and radio news," Jennings reminded his listeners.

Drake continued. "I went to Los Angeles, hoping to interest an agent or publisher in a manuscript I wrote that was a fictionalized version of the television programs that you and Catherine had appeared on a few months earlier."

Jennings groaned. "Wasn't all of that covered so thoroughly and so often already? Why would you need to write more about it and make it novel-length?" His tone indicated he was bored by the idea.

Richard Drake smiled, indicating that he'd anticipated such an objection. "Those two programs drew a large national audience and were interesting in so many ways. But they also inspired me as I watched them."

Jennings raised an eyebrow. "Inspired?"

"Yes, and what I mean by that is that I found myself wondering what it might be like if this all happened in a novel, one in the historical fiction genre. One of the two characters who were patterned after each of you, perhaps the Catherine Lane character, becomes enraged at something you might have brilliantly said that causes her argument to look foolish."

Jennings laughed. "That wouldn't be something for a novel," he mused. "Much more appropriately found in the nonfiction section at the bookstores."

"So in my fiction version, what if that character becomes angry enough to reach into her purse, pulling out a handgun and…"

Listening to his guest, Jennings leaned forward. "Don't leave us hanging," he demanded.

"Well, in my novel, she shoots her opponent dead—on *live* television."

"And *that* was the manuscript you handed Arthur Pradle shortly before something much like that actually happened to him?"

Richard Drake felt a tinge of undeserved guilt listening to that observation, although it seemed to be offered in a humorous way. "Yes, I did hand that manuscript to Arthur Pradle, less than an hour before his killer found him."

"Okay, okay. None of what I've said or of what you've said intends any disrespect for the dead. But before we move on, we should tell the listeners that you have written about your historical fiction manuscript on your blog, A Nose for News, which can also be reached through a link at this podcast. Just what have you decided on for the title to your novel?"

Richard sat up a bit straighter. "My book's title is *His and His Alone!*"

"That does not appear to be in any way related to the outline of your story." Jennings sounded puzzled.

"That's because you haven't yet heard what my story is actually about. A few months ago, I wrote a cover story for *Vanity Fair* that delved into the life of Catherine Dallas Lane. Her novel, *Hounds of Hope*, which she completed while still a student at Wellesley, became a bestseller and, combined with her appearances on television shows, made her an instant celebrity. The *Vanity Fair* story went much deeper, going back to her high school days in

Greenwich, Connecticut, and the experiences she shared with her boyfriend, Brady Harvey."

"Whoa!" Jennings interrupted. "Your *Vanity Fair* story included information about Brady Harvey? The same person now on the run after killing people, including the same Arthur Pradle whom you just told us you were meeting with minutes before he was murdered?"

"Yes. Brady and Catherine grew up as neighbors in Greenwich, Connecticut," Drake said.

"You are either extremely lucky or maybe just the most clairvoyant novel writer I've ever known." Jennings sounded amazed.

"Unfortunately, Brady's father was a passenger on one of the flights that flew into the Towers on 9/11, and it really crushed Brady," Drake said. "He suffered an emotional breakdown that progressively went deeper into depression, and never fully recovered. He was an only child and loved his father, trusting him and looking to him exclusively for answers to questions in his young life. To Brady, it seemed so unfair, so unexplainable. His dad was taken from this life, the one he and Brady had shared so closely. There were no answers for any of this that were able to console Brady. His mother tried but could provide only a little of the logic that Brady sought. Trying to help her son move on from the loss of his father, she took him for long rides in the countryside."

"'We all loved your father,' she told him. 'But we have to see that all those things that James meant to us while he was alive have now ended, and we must go on with only the memories he left for us.' She told Brady that love was really a gift one received or gave to another and that some gifts were more special than others because they meant so much—for both the giver and the recipient."

"In another effort to help her son accept the death of his father, Ruth referred again to the gift of love. "The gift you gave your father was with him when his life came to an end, which means that he will have it forever. It can't be lost or replaced or stolen from him... ever."

"How did you learn all of that, how Brady reacted to the 9/11 plane crash, to his loneliness and the other personal feelings that you wrote about in your *Vanity Fair* story? Did you ever interview him?"

"No, I didn't ever have the opportunity to talk with Brady Harvey," Drake replied. "But I did find it helpful to interview many others who were in his life. As I wrote in the magazine story that focused on the rising popularity of Catherine, Brady Harvey's life was an important influence on her during that time. I included names of many of the persons I found and talked with. Some were his neighbors in Greenwich, some were fellow students in high school. Others were police involved with the fights he started at parties and at school or during his confinement periods."

"So in your article, you tell readers that he loved and needed young Catherine Dallas but also that she loved and needed him," Jennings said, urging Richard to move swiftly toward the finish line. "How did you reach that conclusion?"

"He had only one close friend, and that was his neighbor, Catherine, while they were in school together. For four years while he was slipping deeper into his emotional breakdown, she was the only one he trusted as much as he did with his father. They excelled in their school studies, Catherine in composition and Brady in mathematics. They were very good-looking teenagers but not yet permitted to date until they turned sixteen. That led to them sneaking out and meeting in their large backyards on summer nights. During the winter months, they snuck over to be with each other inside their homes when their parents were away and experimented with their understanding of what life offered at that period of time or perhaps, for them, in the future."

"In the *Vanity Fair* article, you wrote about this in such a moving and beautiful way," Jennings added. "This is what many critics said was an error."

"Error?"

"Yes. They pointed out that earlier in your story, you told about his mental illness and how it made him become a danger to others in Catherine's life. You managed to make him much more sympathetic than people are used to feeling about someone who'd been charged with attempted murder and other such crimes."

Drake remained quiet to avoid appearing argumentative.

Jennings apparently saw that his reference to critics of the *Vanity Fair* article upset his guest and didn't press him for an answer. Instead, he asked if Drake thought such criticisms were unfair.

The smile reappeared on Drake's face, and his posture became more erect as he sat forward and looked straight into Jennings's eyes.

"I don't believe it's an author's privilege to define fairness. I can argue that what I wrote about Harvey was true and accurate. He did what I wrote that he did. His purpose was much too focused on his own personal wants but did spring from within his heart, a heart that had been broken after the death of his father, whom he loved. And when he found a love that he believed was coming from someone who needed him in her life, he discovered feelings that were more precious than the ones he lost on September eleventh. Whatever Catherine subsequently chose to do or be in her life, or even whom she chose to become romantically involved with, his feelings were set and kept him convinced that the love they once shared meant that he could never abandon her."

Will Jennings didn't accept that explanation. "Do you still have such feelings about Brady Harvey today, even after all of what has since led to the crimes he is now being accused of?"

"In many ways, I still do. I don't want to make him sympathetic, nor am I making excuses for him. Maybe making him better understood," Drake said. "Brady Harvey set out for Los Angeles to stop once and for all the relationship Catherine has with Davis Quigley, hoping to kill him, which of course I don't condone. He might have thought that murdering Charlotte Olson and Arthur Pradle was necessary to keep them from alerting the police, who would stop him before he could achieve his goal. Ms. Olson's friend, who was found deceased there, wasn't someone he killed but someone who was subsequently discovered to have suffered a massive heart attack."

"Wasn't Harvey earlier involved in the accident that killed Catherine's husband, Pemberton Lane?" Jennings asked.

"Perhaps" was all that his guest would add.

Will Jennings turned toward Richard Drake and thanked him for being such an informative guest, again mentioning his novel, *His and His Alone,* and reminded listeners to listen to Drake's blog, A Nose for News.

46

Police interviews

MR. HARVEY DID NOT INTEND TO let anything stop him in his effort to separate Davis Quigley from being with Catherine Lane, even if that meant killing others just to get whatever information he needed to do that," Richard Drake said.

"That can be the only reason he broke into our office and killed Charlotte and caused the death of our building's doorman," Sandra said. "You mentioned that you were with Arthur, discussing a book proposal, only a few moments before someone killed him. Is that why you called today?"

"Yes, that's the reason," he said. "Look, I know that you're going through a very tough time right now with the loss of your business partner and being with the person the police now think was, or is, still the target of the suspect. So I'll take as little of your precious time as possible."

"You said I was with the target of the suspect?" Sandra asked.

"I was referring to the author who wrote *Dictated Choices*, Davis Quigley."

Sandra saw that she was receiving a call from someone at the Los Angeles Homicide Bureau and immediately put her caller on hold. When she clicked back to the call, she explained that the police were busy searching for the killer, who had escaped, and wanted her to contact Davis Quigley and Catherine Lane and then go to their detective bureau on Vermont Street ASAP. "I'm sorry, but for now, I'll just have to ask for your understanding and get you to leave your phone number or any preferred way you may have to be reached."

The next voice that came on was a young woman saying that she was the office secretary, Amy Wang. She asked for the information that Sandra Pierce had just requested but was surprised to discover that the caller was no longer waiting on hold.

*　*　*

Officer Tuttle greeted Sandra at the front desk and escorted her into a room used by the police when interviewing witnesses. Sandra apologized for being unable to contact either Catherine or Davis and said she left messages for them on their cell phones.

"Oh?" The policeman seemed confused. "I have to apologize for asking you to contact them. We've already talked with them and made other arrangements for any subsequent interviews."

Sandra watched as Officer Tuttle called the desk sergeant and asked her to notify Chief Detective Fitzgerald that Sandra Pierce was "aboard and available" whenever he was free. He then explained to Sandra that Fitzgerald had decided to ask Catherine Lane and Davis Quigley to remain in hiding until Brady was captured or more could be learned about why Harvey wanted to kill them.

That surprised Sandra. "Do the police feel that Brady wants to kill Catherine? I've been filled in on why Davis is in danger, but Catherine too?"

Before Tuttle could respond, the door opened, and Lieutenant Fitzgerald entered. After the introductions, Sandra again asked whether Catherine might be considered a target and in danger. The look the chief detective gave Officer Tuttle led Sandra to suspect that information was supposed to be kept private.

After Fitzgerald settled into his chair opposite Sandra, he listened to Officer Tuttle finish telling her why the police wanted to talk with her. He ignored Sandra's earlier question.

"Catherine Lane was willing to come in and help us understand as much as we can about what motivated Harvey to travel from Connecticut to California last week with the intention of killing the man he thought was stealing the woman he'd loved with all his heart for most of his life," Tuttle said. "Harvey wrote those words in his book, *Algorithms and Blues*, and Catherine was a major character in that novel. Because of that, we requested that she tell us her impressions of what was written."

While the detective opened his file, Sandra stole a look at Officer Tuttle, who seemed sorry that he'd mentioned Catherine being a target. Sandra merely shrugged to let him know she understood.

"It seems that it was only a first-love type of feeling for her, and I believe for Brady also, when it all began. Perhaps a bit stronger than what's called puppy love, but it was only a bond of trust that they each had at first." Fitzgerald read from a typed outline of the interview notes.

Sandra still wondered why the police wanted to interview her. "I can appreciate the need to know about any relationship that either Davis or Catherine had with Brady Harvey," she said. "But really, I know very little about how Davis feels about Catherine Lane and even less about her feelings for him."

"And Brady Harvey? Do you know anything about him, such as any of his friends or family or business connections on the West Coast, in or near Los Angeles?"

Sandra shook her head. "I don't think I ever heard the name Brady Harvey before any of this trouble began."

Fitzgerald maintained a stern look, leaving no clue about whether he believed what Sandra said. After their silent staring contest, he rose, telling Officer Tuttle to escort Sandra out of the building and to be sure she wasn't being followed.

When Officer Tuttle returned he found Lieutenant Fitzgerald listening to the summary of his team's interview with Catherine.

"In his book, Algorithms and Blues, *Brady wrote about how that bond of trust between them was formed and how she stepped in after learning how his father's death had such an emotional effect on him. He wrote that she also had many concerns that he was able to address and provide her with a feeling of not exploring those life changes alone."*

During the interview with us, Catherine acknowledged that part as accurate but then hurriedly tried to explain that for her, it never amounted to anything she would use the word love *to describe. While interviewing Catherine, I then asked what words she would use instead, and she spoke clearly enough to be heard by the microphone I used to accurately record her while I continued writing in this notebook.*

"We were fourteen or fifteen years old, so I would describe our relationship as being best friends." She sighed, sounding a bit frustrated by the question. "Reading his novel, I realize now that Brady considered that time to be the beginning of a love that would keep growing and perhaps become eternal. It worked wonderfully until we got further into our teenage years, when that bond of friendship needed some updating."

"Updating?"

The detective's summary noted that Catherine paused. It appeared that was because she realized that she was again becoming defensive and revealing more about herself than she'd planned for what she thought was supposed to be just her impressions and memories of Brady's novel. She seemed to want to add only a bit to her description of how she knew their relationship ended, but she let slip the time when, as high school seniors, they had roles in the musical Grease.

"We both had roles, and it was performed within a few weeks of our final exams. Later, we graduated, and then some of the kids in the cast decided to have one last party together before leaving Greenwich for college. The party was organized by someone whose older brother was in the stage crew for a movie that was made in New Canaan a few years prior called The Ice Storm *and who by then owned a small motel in the city. It seemed to be a great way to celebrate our last times together. We took a train to New Canaan, as we also planned some serious partying and wanted no part of driving cars afterward."*

"Is that the time where Brady wrote about being arrested?" the detective asked.

"That's right. He was accused of pushing my co-star in that musical, Wyatt Deveaux, off the train just as it slowed when we were arriving in New Canaan. Wyatt was hurt and taken to the hospital. He accused Brady, who was then questioned but later released. Brady later showed up at the hotel where we had the party and got into a horrible fight with someone I met there and was again arrested. He made everything much worse when he fought with the police. It was then that I decided that he and I were through."

"That pretty much agrees with what he wrote," Detective Cobb said. "But he seemed to think that the only reason you and he were apart for so long afterward was due to him being detained in a mental hospital and unable to be with you while you were at Wellesley. He wrote that when he finally got the opportunity

to travel away from Greenwich, he went to see you but learned then that you had married the father of your roommate."

The interview was taking more time than either Catherine or Detective Cobb and his associate expected, and he decided to hurry it along.

"We really appreciate your cooperation and being with us as we discuss the novel written by Harvey and have only a minute or so left, but I have just a short question that I hope you can enlighten us on," he said. "I know this novel wasn't published and available to the public until very recently, but can you explain the title of it?"

Catherine appeared surprised that the time passed so fast and that the interview was almost over. She said the novel left so many questions unanswered and pointed out that very few were actually discussed during the interview.

"I can only guess at that," she said. "But Brady did manage to develop two patents, employing algorithms involved in artificial intelligence uses. During the time he was researching these studies, he was restricted by the court from any activity outside of the City of Greenwich. I've been told he went days without leaving his home, spending all his time on the research with his music as the only distraction. The dictionary defines an algorithm *as a specific procedure for solving a well-defined computational problem. He was a big fan of rhythm and blues music, and his favorite group was The Head and Heart. I suspect that the title of his novel was derived from those areas in his thoughts and considered appropriate as a way to explain both his feelings and himself."*

47

Algorithms and Blues

D AVIS HAD MANY QUESTIONS stirring in his mind when he was alone after accompanying Catherine to meet with the detectives. When they later talked about it, she told him she was surprised that the police had so many questions about things in Brady's self-published novel, *Algorithms and Blues*. Although he knew that Catherine was probably the focus of Brady's story, it brought back so many disturbing memories to her, Davis suggested that she tell the detective she preferred not to go through all of that. He hadn't yet read the book. However, the scuttlebutt on Twitter and Facebook indicated that the self-published novel would make her cringe. *Learning that she's already read it and was still anxious about discussing it with the police caused Davis to wonder how that make any sense. And most important, why didn't she tell him anything about what was in this book before she discussed the details with the detective?*

Struggling to find anything that might address his questions, Davis wanted a stiff drink and some alone time. He knew that combining the two was one fucking stupid way to make some really bad decisions. Instead, he returned Sandra's call.

"Davis? Oh, thank you for calling me now, right in the middle of seeing all that bullshit that's spewing on the internet." Sandra's tone was subdued.

"I'm not sure what you're talking about," Davis fibbed, knowing that he wanted neither bullshit nor sympathy. "Just before we ended our last conversation, you said something was important for me to know."

Sandra hesitated. "I received a telephone call a few days ago from a movie studio who said they're under contract with Netflix to produce three new movies. One is a drama, another a mystery, and the third, a thriller. They said that your novel, *Dictated Choices*, has their interest, and they want to know if you might consider selling the movie rights. They have a scriptwriter on staff who's hoping to meet with you. We didn't discuss money or really anything except deciding whether this would be something you might be interested in pursuing."

The news came out of nowhere, and considering how the last few days had come at him like a fire alarm waking him from a deep sleep, Davis had no ready answer. He remained silent while he sorted through what it would mean to have *Dictated Choices* made into a movie. Davis was sure that the courtroom scenes would prove interesting, as would the outcome of the life of his protagonist fighting to save her young client from the perils he faced after being sentenced. *Who would the movie company select to play the characters? How would such a movie affect sales of his novel? Would he retain any voice related to the production or the cast or—*

"Davis?" Sandra's voice startled him.

"Yes, I'm still here," he assured her. "You wondered if I wanted to look into their offer."

"No," she quickly answered. "There's no offer, just a feeler. They're hoping to learn if making a movie about your novel would have your interest. If our answer is yes, then I believe they'll arrange a meeting, and things can move forward."

"This is indeed interesting," Davis said. "But with my world spinning with all kinds of strange happenings right now, all I can say is let's think about it. Maybe have an answer ready by the end of the week, okay?"

Sandra said that would be a reasonable time frame for the studio to get an answer. But just before they hung up, Davis remembered that she'd indicated there was something more that she wanted to tell him. He hoped it wasn't anything more about Catherine that was in Harvey's book.

"Yes, it was about Harvey's self-published book. I can get a copy to you today, and we can have a conversation about it when you're ready."

Penny Lane

GOOD EVENING TO ALL RIGHT-THINKING people of the world! And welcome again to the Augustine Skinner Show from the Hallowed Hall of Reason! Stay tuned and hold on tight, because on this day, there's something happening that's sure to shake the world free from the lying liberals and the literature they publish that punishes our sacred truths."

Conservative radio's leading talk show aired on over four hundred radio stations throughout the world and often had something special to interest or excite the listeners. When little was happening in American politics, the host could make even that seem like can't-miss programming. During the week leading up to the program, the network teased that the show would feature the stepdaughter of Catherine Lane, the author of *Hounds of Hope* and "All That's Left to Know," as Augustine referred to her articles in *Vanity Fair*. Since she was currently in the news because of the search for Brady Harvey, Skinner made that connection the headline in his program advertisements.

"Penny Lane, welcome!" The radio host seemed as excited as ever to be welcoming the tall redhead to the program. "We should have been playing that great Beatles song as you entered right now. You know, the one that you were named after."

His guest sat with raised eyebrows, and with a brief shake of her head, she let it be known that the comparison had offended her. "Thank you, Mr. Skinner. I feel honored to be here this evening. However, if you only knew how often that mistake is made about my name, I'm sure you would refrain from repeating such hogwash."

"What? Hogwash, you called it?" Skinner was clearly feeling insulted. "What are you, someone the lefties found buried in the fiction section at a broken-down, deeply mortgaged bookstore?"

The young woman squirmed upon hearing Skinner's angry response. "No, I'm sorry to have started out the way I did. To begin this all over the right way, let me just say that I'm the Penny Lane who is the daughter of Pemberton Lane, who married my college roommate, Catherine Dallas, making her my stepmother. The Penny Lane that you referred to as the one in the Beatles song wasn't even a live person. That Penny Lane was a street in Liverpool. Paul McCartney wrote a song using that name in his lyrics. I like the song and the lyrics, but I'm a real person! And confusing me with that nice song set me off. Again, I apologize."

Augustine Skinner appeared to be at a loss for words. "Well, okay, then," he continued in a less confident tone. "Let's just agree that you're real and some street in Liverpool, England, is real but never has been related in any way to you." Some throat-clearing followed.

"The book that's in all the news because the author is a suspect related to the killings out there in… *Lost… Angeles,* is suddenly making noises that are usually unheard of from a self-published novel and is selling like those proverbial hotcakes we've enjoyed supping on at times. It's titled *Algorithms and Blues,* written by one

Brady Harvey. Yes, *that* Brady Harvey who is wanted in California for murders and is presently on the run. There's so much to say about the book, the author, and the young woman who cost him so much in his life that I think I'll let you pick which parts of it to begin our conversation… after we return following this word from MyPillow."

During the next ninety seconds, Penny sat nervously, watching the radio host going over some notes and mumbling the word "hogwash" over and over to himself.

"We're back! Okay, Penny-Lane-who-is-not-a-Beatles-song, why not begin by telling our listeners all about how you met this fella Brady Harvey."

Penny smiled and looked eager to get on with the interview. "Yes. I met Brady shortly after he came to Wellesley, looking to find Catherine Dallas. He told me that he grew up with her in Connecticut, and they lost track of each other after completing high school together. She went away to college while he lied saying that he was fiddling with various things closer to home. Eventually, he told me more fibs saying that he went on to become a writer and editor with *Harper's Magazine*, which wasn't even close to being anything true. He said he was hoping to interview Catherine about her novel, *Hounds of Hope*, and during his search for her, he learned that Catherine and I had been roommates at Wellesley. Eventually, one story led to another and he and I met up again a few times. After a couple of lunch dates, I became interested in him enough to open up and share my true feelings about Catherine."

"True feelings? Did these lunch dates lead to anything more that you can share?"

"I began to suspect that he was just someone who was jilted by her," she explained. "Catherine never even mentioned his name. He told me how close they had been until she became so popular in high school that she thought she was hot shit. He and

Catherine broke up, but when she needed him for something, he just put aside the hurt she caused and always went back to her."

"So…?" The radio host was showing some impatience.

"So I decided to share how the same thing happened between Catherine and me. We were just as close as Brady claimed he had been with her. We did things too, many that I didn't discuss in any detail with Brady but that I'm sure fed his certainty about being right about her after all."

"Oh, come on now," Skinner insisted. "You're here to talk about those things that are in his novel now. Tell us at least what she did that ended your being able to trust her with just about anything."

Penny's eyes widened while she considered how to respond. "Well, it all really ended between us when I discovered that she and my father were sleeping together."

"You're talking about the man Catherine married?"

"I'm talking about the man she deceived into marrying her!"

Augustine Skinner's surprise was evident. All he could say was three words. "Please. Go on."

"My father liked Catherine and helped her get *Hounds of Hope* published. He knew things. He knew people. And all Catherine knew was limited to being a talented author. Together, they were finding success, but she wanted much more."

"So, she wanted more. How did that worthy ambition cause you to think so badly of her?"

"It was the lie she used in her scheme."

"She schemed? She lied?"

"She told my father she was pregnant!"

Augustine Skinner appeared caught off guard by what he'd just heard. Still, he let out a loud laugh. "Of course she schemed and lied. She sounds like she must be a liberal Democrat!"

The Hallowed Hall of Reason radio program closed with something as close to poetry as he could manage, along with a challenge from Augustine Samuel Skinner about the events that had taken place only two days ago in the city he always referred to as *Lost* Angeles.

*"Day two has begun, and Brady is still free with a gun, and all the police know for now is that he's proved too hard to find even though he has already lost his mind. How much longer, Miss Liberal Lost Angels Mayor? He has murdered people all along Wilshire Boulevard and probably some others too. We're wondering, Ms. Progressive Mayor, just what you'll do before he decides to do even more of what he wants to do. Take note of this. Election Day comes soon. Maybe for you and your cadre of unqualified woke appointments, it'll become known as your very own final day to celebrate. One that will be remembered for being your **high noon!***

49

Catherine is called

H ELLO.”
The caller said only that one word, hello, yet it bored itself inside her mind and throughout every nerve path in her entire body. Instantly, Catherine Dallas Lane felt suddenly weak. She recognized the voice. It was him. She hadn't taken calls from him in many, many months yet still knew his voice all too well. *But now what?*

"Brady?" Her voice revealed surprise that he would be calling her. "We haven't spoken for so long that I hardly..." She stopped to take a breath. From somewhere in hiding, with all of California out looking for him, he was calling her, and all he had to say was hello? She wondered if she should continue talking. Was he calling to say they should meet somewhere? Did he want or need anything from her? The silence continued as Catherine's mind raced through all the possibilities that caused Brady to still want her enough that he was driven to do what he has been accused of.

Finally, after almost two full minutes of nervous nothing, he resumed talking. "I just listened to something on the news that they said was from a radio program where Penny Lane said some things."

"Penny?" she asked. "Is that the reason you're calling me now?"

"In a way, yes, it's part of that reason," he said. "I may have to hang up without warning, so please, just listen to me now. Please!"

Catherine heard the same hesitation in his voice that seemed to be there the few times they spoke after she went away to Wellesley… and he went away to a mental hospital. He always doubted her. He always suspected her motives, her truthfulness, even how she felt about their relationship. She heard the same cautious, desperate, hidden doubts that were always present when he spoke after she left their neighborhood in Greenwich. She was surprised to find herself worried about him now. *Where did that old empathy rush come from?* She whispered that she would listen to whatever it was that he wanted to say.

"Catherine, I think that I'm going to die. Maybe in the next minute." He paused. "Or at least sometime very soon."

She felt a sudden urge to comfort Brady. The murders, the terrible things he'd just done—and had done—no longer fit into the moment. Without having a reason she wanted only for Brady not to feel so alone. He needed to find forgiveness and accept that her concern for him was true. It was strange that she felt incapable of using words as a substitute for not being with him. There was no logic in her reaction. But it still lived undeniably inside of her and burned to come out and be known. She sensed that same need existed in his mind too.

"Catherine, before everything ends for us, I need you to know that no one can ever give to you what I have already given. That writer that I read about in *People Magazine* and saw on TV, the one they say is your lover, must prove that he's worthy of you, more worthy than what I have proven to be. I need to at least find a way to meet with him, to talk with him. And yes, to test him."

Catherine was confused and overwhelmed. Brady's words shocked her. *This is the reason for his call? He wants to use me to find Davis?* Those things he'd just said about dying soon… He said everything would end soon for *us*. He said *us*, not just himself. Was it meant to be the threat it definitely sounded like? The warmth that was in her heart just moments before turned into an icy fear that froze her in place. She felt crippled and lost the strength to even move her arms or legs. Before she could think of what to do next, who to turn to or call, she heard a click. Their call had been disconnected.

50

A meeting with the mayor

CHIEF DETECTIVE FITZGERALD DISAGREED that the time had come to call in the FBI. "The crimes were committed in our city, on our streets, and in our office buildings and hotels," he said at the meeting called by the mayor. "We have the ability to find this fugitive and take him into custody."

"So how do you explain that this much time has elapsed since he murdered two people and is still free?" the mayor asked. "Wasn't he surrounded by your police within an hour after he killed the man at the InterContinental Hotel and yet was still able to escape?"

The lieutenant agreed that was accurate but tried to explain how that didn't reflect as poorly on the LA police force as she seemed to imply. "Let's go over how all that came to be," he began. "Harvey somehow managed to fly into LA and set out to locate the man he was so angry about, a writer by the name of Davis Quigley, all without raising any attention. He knew that Quigley's agent was someone working at Pradle Literary Agency, located in the Rayburn Towers Office Building on Wilshire Boulevard."

"Yes, yes, we already know that," the mayor interrupted. "So he tries to learn where Quigley might be, and in his efforts to get that information, he murders the office manager and does other things that result in the death of Rayburn's doorman. So, fill us in on why he went to the InterContinental Hotel and murdered someone there."

Fitzgerald restrained himself from showing any sign of his growing disrespect for the mayor while she spoke. It seemed she was setting up the police for the criticism she had been getting for failing to find and capture the killer. He knew now that he had to take away some of the heat she was feeling following complaints by the press and others.

"His crimes at Rayburn Towers were discovered by Officer Tuttle, whose assistance in tracking the killer led us to the other murder victim at the InterContinental. While we were investigating that murder scene, Officer Tuttle learned that the killer made phone contact with Davis Quigley, telling him to be at the Pritzker Parking Garage within an hour. Having that information, we immediately dispatched four squads to be at positions at all entries and exits there."

"But he wasn't there, and now he's on the loose," the mayor said. "How did he escape from all of those things the police were doing to capture him?"

The lieutenant stood back from where the mayor was seated, but his stern expression didn't change. "There was an incident that occurred on Fairfax Avenue on the corner of Wilshire just outside of the Pritzker Parking Garage, where a man who was being chased was struck by a vehicle. We all believed that man was Brady Harvey and hurried to that location."

The mayor rolled her eyes. "It wasn't your suspect who was struck, was it?"

"No, ma'am. Harvey wasn't the man who was killed there. We discovered later that Brady stole a car that was parked close by

Rayburn Towers. He found it after murdering Charlotte Olson and used it to drive to the InterContinental Hotel. Then, after he murdered Mr. Pradle there, he drove away and parked on Fairfax, where he could view the location he told Mr. Quigley to meet him at. We have surmised that the accident caused him to change the plan to meet Quigley, and he exited the stolen car and walked away unobserved."

Lieutenant Fitzgerald's report included some items the mayor was unaware of. He knew she would probably use that information at her next press conference, and that would go a long way toward conveying that she was fully informed and in charge.

"Thank you, Lieutenant. And now, before we end this briefing, I just want to know if there is anything further I should be aware of."

Fitzgerald placed his chair back where it was before. "We just learned in the moments before I left the Bureau to come here that Catherine Lane received a phone threat from someone she's convinced was Brady Harvey."

The mayor, who had stood up as if preparing to leave, looked again at her police lieutenant. "Brady Harvey?" She looked surprised. "You should have opened this meeting with that information. Do you know anything more? Are you tracing that phone call? Just what *are* you doing?"

Fitzgerald shrugged. Even if that call really did come from Brady Harvey, it wasn't likely to benefit their search since he would have immediately canceled the location and/or GPS setting or just turned his phone off.

When he returned to the Homicide Bureau, the lieutenant called together the detective team working on finding Brady Harvey and updated them on the meeting at the mayor's office. "She's catching some grief from the press and even from that right-wing conservative radio guy who warned that our lack of success in capturing Harvey could cost the mayor at election time. I gave her everything that we've got so far, including the latest on that threatening phone call made to Catherine." The lieutenant then asked if there was any update on that call.

"Catherine told me that after calling 911, she then called and spoke to Davis Quigley, warning him that she thinks Brady has them both in his sights now," Officer Tuttle replied.

Fitzgerald then pointed out that the basic principles they'd all learned during their training were the steps that needed to be followed.

"He was last suspected to be in a stolen vehicle that he abandoned during the incident across from the art museum. So let's go back to that. Brady is either hiding inside Los Angeles, or he has fled somehow. If he fled, let's figure out how," Fitz said.

"We have his photo and identification information already furnished to all transportation possibilities. Buses, trains, airports, etcetera," Tuttle said.

"Right," Fitz acknowledged. "But stay on top of everything there. Don't assume that each of these checkpoints remains as alert and in compliance as we need them to be. This fella is a smart-enough cookie to maybe figure some way around our system."

"We also are working with Greenwich police, and they're talking with everyone there who is known to be someone he might have contact with," another detective reported. "They're keeping surveillance on his residence, his mother's residence, even his therapist's office. He won't be anywhere near any of them without us knowing about it."

Fitzgerald allowed a smile. His team had been taking all the proper investigative steps. "So, what this tells us is that it's most unlikely that Brady Harvey is anywhere outside of right here in Los Angeles, where he's finding somewhere to sleep, eat, and avoid being captured. Now then, let's see how anyone can do all of these things—for as long as he's been doing these things—right under our very noses!"

51

Answers hiding in the shade

After Catherine called the police to report that Brady had contacted her, she immediately phoned Davis to alert him. "He told me that everything must come to an end." Her voice was still weak as she told Davis that she thought Brady was threatening to murder not only Davis and her but also himself.

So Brady was somewhere close enough to make himself believe he could do any of those things—calling Catherine, meeting with Davis, killing them, and committing suicide, all before being discovered by police. That caused Davis more concern for Catherine but also for himself.

"You said that he made those threats then hung up?" Davis wondered how that made any sense. "Why would he risk contacting you that way? Surely, he must realize that police have certain methods of tracking cell phones."

"I asked Officer Tuttle about that very thing," Catherine said. "He told me they couldn't track cell phones that had shut off their location settings or that had been turned off. That makes it almost impossible for the police to find him."

"Okay, that answers the question I had about why Brady bothered to make the threats after contacting you then hanging up before hearing your response. But still, how did he know where you are and how to contact you?"

Catherine waited to respond. *Should she tell Davis about those times that Brady and she called each other after she left to attend Wellesley and before getting married Pemberton Lane?* Those were questions she'd sought answers to herself after falling in love with Davis. *Does he really need to know everything that happened back then between Brady and her?*

"Catherine? Are you there?"

Hearing his voice, she quickly returned to the present. "Oh yes, I hear you." She still debated the necessity of telling Davis everything. "I should have mentioned that Brady had my cell phone number ever since high school. But after I left him facing all the trouble he got himself in, I just wouldn't answer his calls and rarely responded to any messages. I wish now that I hadn't reacted so impulsively this time when I answered this last call without seeing that it was from him."

None of what Davis had just heard from Catherine made sense. But then, not much of anything that had happened since Sunday morning at Rayburn Towers made sense. He was sure that eventually his questions would be answered but just now it was more urgent that he protect Catherine and himself—and then stop Brady Harvey from remaining in their lives.

52

A bad book needs a good author

I WAS HAPPY WHEN I RECEIVED your text message wanting me to come so soon after what just happened Sunday," Franz Graber told Sandra. "I've been worried about you and planned on waiting a while longer before calling and seeing if there was some way for me to help."

Sandra had rushed over to greet Franz when Amy Wang led him into their temporary office on the third floor. "Are you telling me that I need an excuse to invite you to come back from your university position to where your other career, that of a successful author, had its very beginning?"

Each smiled, knowing their background had once included more than an agent-author relationship.

"It's been too long," Franz said as they took seats by her desk. He looked around at the small space that Sandra had leased on a lower floor at Rayburn Towers. Police were still investigating the crime scene in what had been her office just two days ago. "It's smaller, but still, I think it was kind of a miracle that it was available," he said. "Will you keep the Pradle name in your agency now that Arthur's died?"

Her slight frown and head shake showed her sadness. "I will tell you this much," she said. "Arthur was as responsible for my success as anyone could possibly have been, and he also provided us with a wonderful name that continues to draw respect throughout the literary agency world."

Franz did not expect her reaction but wanted to avoid bringing up what she'd gone through on Sunday. He'd decided to focus on what needed to be done to get beyond the senseless tragedy.

"The royalties for *Death of a Friend* are making my return to university life so pleasant." He hoped to show his appreciation for her contribution to its success.

"Yes, we're all quite happy by how well the reading public showed such interest in your retelling of the Lindbergh-baby kidnapping-and-murder trial," Sandra said. "And it was that success that prompted me to think of your storytelling abilities when I considered trying to purchase the rights to Harvey's novel, *Algorithms and Blues*."

"Hey! Congrats on all of that. But what are you saying? That you were thinking of me when... What?"

Sandra grew more excited. "You see, Brady's novel was self-published, and while it has surprised everyone with how well it sold as an indie-published book, it deserves to be out there now once it finds an established publisher and gets introduced to a much larger audience."

Franz nodded, but his eyes revealed confusion. "Okay. But you're talking to me, an author. Not someone skilled in getting it published and marketed in a professional way. What do you see as my role?"

Sandra's smile assured her friend that not only did she have a plan but also that he was being chosen to help it succeed.

"In many ways, Brady is a brilliant man," she began. "But his story becomes a bigger seller only because his pursuit of our Davis Quigley caused these deaths and 'killer on the run' news. Brady Harvey is breaking news everywhere now, making his name known nationally, and however it comes to an end, it's already become his biography. What he lacked in writing skills when he wrote his story is what you've proven to have in abundance. I want you to rewrite *Algorithms and Blues*, capturing the nuances, the hurts, and the logic he used for his sometimes heinous results."

"Are you suggesting that I would be identified as a co-author?"

"Oh no," she quickly responded. "In no time, critics would piece things together and realize that Brady's novel was self-published through efforts of his estate."

"Then…?"

"What your rewrite would keep on the cover would be the title, *Algorithms and Blues*, and his name. Then, in the same size font, it would read, 'A Biography by Franz Graber, author of *Death of a Friend*.'"

53

Brady's book

DAVIS WAS SURPRISED BY HOW fast Sandra kept her promise of getting Brady Harvey's novel delivered to him. After getting her email, he arranged with Officer Tuttle for the book to be picked up at her office at Rayburn Towers and taken to where he was staying. While he was on detail with the detective bureau, Tuttle wouldn't be in uniform and thus would cause no concern to others living in a condominium near the one where Davis was in hiding. Identified as the target of the "mad killer," Davis had been advised to keep out of sight and told he should avoid anything but cell phone contact with others, especially Catherine. She remained in her Carlyle Hotel suite that Lloyd Patterson had originally reserved for the two of them before Brady Harvey entered their lives.

Secretly, Davis kept away from Catherine as a precautionary tactic and stayed in a luxury condominium on Ocean Avenue in Santa Monica. It belonged to Charles Clayton, Lloyd's oldest friend from college days, who was vacationing in Europe, thus making his condominium available. The ocean-view property provided maximum security for its wealthy residents, as well as a scenic view of the ocean and beaches.

With nowhere to go that wouldn't expose him to danger while Brady Harvey was still on the loose, Davis found the book a must-read that helped pass the time while he remained in hiding. Only Officer Tuttle knew where he would be staying until eventually, Brady Harvey's whereabouts became known. Almost immediately after breakfast, Davis opened the novel and discovered that Brady had invented an imagined version of his father, James.

Instead of James being a passenger on one of the planes that crashed into the Twin Towers on September 11, Brady wrote that his father had divorced his mother soon after Brady was about to begin high school. Davis knew almost nothing about Brady except that he was obsessed with a love for Catherine. Davis decided to read the entire novel and hoped to learn why Brady wanted to murder him.

All that was said was that my father was going to leave Connecticut forever by next Saturday. I'll stay and live with Mother in the same home here in Greenwich where we've been living as a family. I felt desperate as I answered Catherine's question about why I was so glum.

So my dad waited until I was thirteen and not even in high school to tell me about the sudden divorce plans that had to have been quietly decided upon months ago. It came as a complete shock, and my parents didn't offer any reason for the divorce. Why? Was it something I did that hurt my father? Have my parents concluded that I'm unlikely to ever achieve what they expect from me?"

Catherine looked puzzled. "Do you think that any of this is because of what he saw us doing last week after dark in our pool house?"

I paused to give that possibility some thought. "No, I really think he was more concerned about making sure Mother wouldn't find out anything about that. After he watched you go back to your house, he took me back inside ours and said that he thought that what we were doing should wait a bit longer to happen, at least until after high school. He warned me that Mother was already concerned about us being such close friends and that she'd asked her friend Reverend Wellington for advice. It was his suggestion that persuaded Mother to get me into therapy."

Davis stopped reading long enough to jot down the name Reverend Wellington. He was someone Davis hadn't heard mentioned before. On his scratch pad, Davis noted that Brady often switched between referring to himself in third person—using his name, Brady—and first person, using the pronoun "I," sometimes switching back and forth in the same paragraph. Davis knew that Brady did not have any type of editing assistance for his self-published novel which became more and more obvious as he read further.

Davis went back to reading *Algorithms and Blues*.

Sharing Brady's secrets and concerns had been his dad's role. During the many times his father had to be away on business, Brady had no other person that he trusted as either a guide or companion. Neither he nor his dad had kept secrets from each other—or so he had thought.

Ever since his dad's news dump that led so fast to his desertion of the family, Brady had trusted no one. The only exception was his next-door neighbor, Catherine Dallas. Like him, Catherine was an only child and had just graduated from eighth grade at the all-girls Greenwich Academy. That summer, they drew close, as she seemed to need him too.

Their parents were friends, and when Mrs. Dallas learned that Brady's mother had him seeing a therapist, she allowed her daughter to spend more time with Brady during the summer months before they began high school in the fall. While he would attend Brunswick, an all-boys school, and Catherine would go to Greenwich Academy, the schools were across the street from each other. Students at both schools would often share classes and extracurricular activities.

During the summer, the two of them spent hours together, sometimes in the Dallas's' backyard swimming pool or walking into town for a horse neck sandwich, a favorite of theirs at Porters Restaurant. During these times, they talked about their private thoughts and concerns. Catherine shared her worries that high school was going to be so different from middle school. She was popular and had many friends but seemed confused about knowing just why that was so. She was worried that some older boy in Brunswick Upper might want to be her boyfriend. Her parents warned her that those concerns could wait until she was in college.

Brady told her he expected the summer months to provide only brief opportunities for him to shake off his despair and the questions regarding his future. He wondered why he didn't fit in with kids his age better than he had so far. He was different in their eyes and didn't understand what caused his classmates to ostracize him.

Brady opened up to Catherine about his lack of self-confidence. He was one of the smaller boys in eighth grade, and that really bothered him. His mother explained it was due to his grades always being so much better than those of the other kids. He studied hard and was a fast learner. Three years ago, his school recommended that he skip the fifth grade and advance to sixth grade in middle school when the new term began. His parents agreed. He remembered how it seemed to make his father even prouder of him, but the move also resulted in him being a year younger than most of his new classmates. Brady continued to score the highest grades on his exams, but that produced jealousy that separated him from the friendships he sought. He worried about not fitting in.

By sharing their concerns, Brady and Catherine formed a bond. I began escaping from those feelings of failure that in my mind were earned by whatever I had unknowingly done to cause my parents' divorce. In their place, I could focus on Catherine's worries and maybe do something that would help her.

Davis set the novel down again, going over how Brady had written about the starting points in his life. He invented a reason for his dad's exit that deprived him of guidance and close companionship. Brady also found it convenient to point to the bonding period between him and Catherine, tying it to his lies about his parents' divorce.

Earlier, Davis had seen on television that a severe storm was expected to hit the area sometime during the late morning. The sky had already darkened. After boiling some water to make another cup of instant coffee, Davis returned to the novel, where he found chapters of similar made-up stories that seemed little more than excuses for Brady's social failures in high school. Davis hurried through them with little interest, instead looking for more about Catherine until he came upon the chapters about the school musical, *Grease*.

Wasn't it Catherine who understood me before even I realized what my dad meant to my very existence until he deserted me? She knew that I loved him and always looked only for his counsel to explain what was going on in my strange world. I thought that he loved me as much as I loved him and that he had to see how dependent on him I had become. He had no excuse. Heck, there was no reason for him to divorce Mother and move out. Very simply said, he betrayed me. He decided that his feelings for someone, probably a customer of his in faraway London, was important enough for him to make that decision. He said that life brings changes, and for now, it was better for Mother and me if he made that move. All it told me was that I wasn't as important anymore.

That summer after we graduated from middle school, Catherine called and asked if I wanted to come over and be with her by their pool. To my surprise, we did things that were completely new to both of us. It was the first time she ever showed any interest in me like that. She told me that she heard her parents talking and learned about the divorce and that I was so sad afterward that it affected my emotional health. That didn't scare her, and she spent that summer mostly just hanging around with me and talking about our lives, both then and in the future. I also learned about things that frightened her. We each worried about how life was changing, what high school would really be like when we began there after summer ended. She worried that she might meet the wrong people, maybe kids who were older in the upper classes. Often, these worries caused her to begin crying. She kept saying that she wasn't ready for those things that older kids seemed to want from her. Then we hugged, and I told her not to ever worry because I would never leave her where she could be hurt.

The things she was worried about that summer actually happened later after she settled into life in high school. She was always one of the best-looking girls in middle school, but almost as soon as she entered high school, her body started making huge changes. She grew a bit taller than she had been, and the rest of her soon started developing at a much faster pace. By our sophomore year, Catherine had become one of the most popular girls at Greenwich Academy. She was invited to parties, boy-girl parties. When the boys at Brunswick Upper School, where I attended, took notice of her, she seemed to lose any thought of me. Her parents wouldn't allow her to go out on dates, but with her family's swimming pool in their backyard, there were always plenty of boys who dropped by for a visit. One of them started messing with her when no one else was around, and she grew fond of him, very fond. He was in senior year and was popular enough to have developed a reputation, and you know what that means.

When we began our third year in high school, her parents became alarmed at how her popularity was affecting her studies. Other than her extracurricular activities like when she was in drama or a writer on her school newspaper, she was restricted to coming straight home after classes. The only time she could be with anyone else was when she invited me over from next door. Her parents liked my mother and trusted me. It was during these times that Catherine and I shared many private moments, discussing how our lives seemed to have new things happening almost every day. She knew that I was still being treated for those emotional problems that I wasn't able to shake free of after my parents divorced. She wondered if therapy might be something she could benefit from.

One day soon after our third year began, she asked if she could trust me with a big secret. I thought she was going to tell me that she also had some kind of emotional problem. I eagerly assured her that she could trust me with any information that she needed to share. Then she held my hand even more tightly and said that she'd made plans to visit her boyfriend, Bryan Hines, who had graduated from Brunswick last June and was attending college. She said that he was getting too serious and she decided to break up with him but felt she should do that in person. She needed me to cover for her. She made up a story, telling her parents that she was helping me surprise my mother on her birthday by taking her and Catherine out for dinner downtown. That way, she figured her parents wouldn't check with Mom, as it was supposed to be a surprise. She told me that she needed *this time away from home to really convince Bryan that it was the best thing for both of them to just end things.*

All I knew was that she intended to meet Bryan when he came back to Greenwich for some reason, so I was more than happy to take part in her scheme. But that was the only part of her plan that she shared with me. I wanted to be sure that I would be close by if something happened where she might need me, so I followed her when she left her house to be with him, taking care not to be seen. She met him at the Greenwich train station, and I saw them walk a few blocks to Bistro V, the restaurant with outdoor tables. They were busily engaged in conversation, which permitted me to sit unobserved at a nearby table within earshot. I heard only parts of what they were saying, but when he mentioned they still had an hour before catching the train and going back to New York City together, they kissed.

I was shocked when I saw them kiss, the way she seemed to want that and made no effort to push him away. But I was more surprised when I heard bits of what she had to say next about how exciting it was going to be for her, staying with him in his university dorm apartment. My gosh! Catherine was the same age as me, sixteen. What was she thinking? Was she planning on running away with Bryan? Did she plan to get on that train that I heard him mention and just flee from her family? From me? I knew then that I had to do something to stop her from leaving Greenwich to be with him. But what? After they finished eating, he left her alone to go to the men's room and then pay the check. I saw my chance.

I called her cell phone number and made up a story about how her mother and my mother had spent the afternoon together at a Woman's Club meeting, and one thing led to another, and her mother knew it certainly was not my mother's birthday, and any story about a surprise celebration was pure bull and was no longer believable. I acted as if I was still at home and didn't let on what I'd found out about her scheme with Bryan. I suggested that at the very least, she should come back home from wherever she was and help me come up with some new reason for her going out that evening since that whopper about a surprise birthday dinner for Mother wouldn't work and that both mothers knew I was home alone.

My call seemed to completely surprise Catherine. Whatever her plans with Bryan were all about, they had no chance now. She was crying when she said that this was all my fault and now her parents would really crack down on any free time she might have expected to enjoy. I couldn't understand how any of this could be blamed on me, but I knew better than to argue with her. Not in her current condition anyway.

By the time I got home, I learned that Catherine was able to turn things around so completely that it got her not only excused from being in trouble but also in a way that was even better for her. She called her mother after she left Bryan at the train station and was on the drive back home. She made up a story about how it was my idea to use the fake birthday surprise for Mother as a way for me to be with her on a date in downtown Greenwich. She said I knew that she wouldn't otherwise go out with me and felt sorry for me. She said she was doing this as a gesture of sympathy because she thought it might help me in getting past the depression that was still dominating me.

Mrs. Dallas had no idea what her daughter was trying to tell her, as the whole episode about the surprise birthday flop for Mother was just something I'd created to trick Catherine into not going with Bryan back to his university in New York. But she did say that her daughter deserved praise for caring about another's feelings and suggested that she call me and invite me out for a soda somewhere.

Yes. That soda date was the last time Catherine even smiled my way, but it convinced me that she appreciated my efforts to *be there when I thought she needed me. I now knew what true love really was all about. It's when someone loves another so much that he will do anything, or at least imagine anything, to save her. And every time I enjoy a vanilla ice cream cone in my future, the memory of her showing how much she appreciated me that evening will relive those warm thoughts of the closest I have ever been, so far, to actually knowing love.*

The following year, the senior class at both schools combined to perform the musical Grease, and the last person in the world fit to play Danny Zuko was Wyatt Deveaux. He got selected to share top billing and sang and won Catherine's love on stage while I was stuck playing Sonny (what a dud he was!). Grease is a stupid choice for a senior class musical. The only good role is Sandy, which Catherine played so well. I felt so cheated not getting the role I wanted to play. I performed a lot better than that conceited prick Wyatt, but Miss Norman picked him over me for the choice role. Too bad what happened later when we were on our way to celebrate our performances at the after-party in New Canaan and Wyatt fell off the train before we arrived at the train station. Yeah, too bad! Just a coincidence that the accident happened minutes after I overheard him bragging that he wanted to get Catherine drunk at the party and finish what he couldn't do on stage with her.

Even though she never knew it, there have been other times I had to figure out how to save her.

Wasn't it I who came to her rescue after she got pregnant and fooled that older man into marrying her? That bastard was old enough to be her father yet somehow still believed he was the one who got her pregnant.

Davis was surprised by that part and also by the last paragraph in the chapter, which referenced a news clipping that for some reason Brady decided to include.

News-Notes: Catherine Dallas performed in the senior class musical Grease and won great reviews playing the lead female role. Later, the students attended a party thrown for the cast and members of the orchestra who were also involved with the play. There were reports of wild sex games, underage drinking, and consumption of illegal drugs at that party. The police were called and broke it up and made a few arrests. However, because of their ages, no record exists of who was arrested or of anything illegal being discovered.

Davis then skipped a few pages until seeing that Brady wrote more about the cast party. He mentioned that he was involved in the incident on the train they all took into New Canaan for the party.

After being questioned and then released by the police, I arrived late and went looking for Catherine. I caught her, shall we say, locked in love with someone who looked to be in his mid-twenties and earlier told people that he had been an extra in a movie called The Ice Storm *that completed filming there a few years ago. I arrived a couple of hours after the party began and got into a brutal fight with the movie star extra and beat the shit out of him. Cops were called, and then I was taken into custody. Nothing ever made it into the papers about me and the others in the cast party because of our ages.*

Davis saw that from then on, Brady referred to himself in third person.

Yeah, things like that get taken care of quietly, real quietly in that small little city that all those billionaires call home. Well, he didn't exactly get off. They said that he was either a wacko before he started that brawl or he suffered some kind of mental breakdown during it, but he did enough damage and injured enough people at that party that he was detained overnight with the local police and, after his appearance at the next morning's court hearing, was ordered to spend some time in a mental hospital ward.

The last chapter in *Algorithms and Blues* caused Davis the most alarm. Brady wrote about what he'd found in an obituary for Pemberton Lane who was Catherine's deceased husband. They showed the date that he died from an accident. The article said he died from drowning. Brady then told the reader to check the date of Catherine's husband's accident. He closed the chapter by writing that he'd managed to be unaccounted for a few days earlier but was subsequently identified by police investigating the drowning as the only witness to the accident that killed Pemberton Lane.

54

Maybe a hiding place

THE STORM THAT ARRIVED WHILE Davis was engaged in reading Brady's novel alarmed him. The thunder booms grew more frequent, and flashes of lightning streaked across the darkened sky. Davis took a few minutes away from the book to stand by the large windows in the living room, considering how nature paid so little attention to the lives and concerns of him or Catherine or even the man who intended to kill them.

After reading Brady's book, Davis wondered if it was even possible to understand a motive. There was just too much in Brady's story that was new to Davis—not only about himself but also about Catherine—that needed explaining. Some of what Davis read, he already knew, and most of it made no real difference in how he felt about Catherine or Brady Harvey. The problem was that Harvey's account of his relationship with Catherine had many aspects that served only one purpose—to show his unbridled love for her. Sometimes he told half-truths, and other times, he wrote unadulterated fabrications.

His father, James Harvey, did in fact perish on 9/11. Catherine had told Davis that on one of the few times she even mentioned her neighbor. The only reason for Brady to tell that whopper of a lie about a divorce was to explain his father's absence. He wasn't looking for sympathy. He was explaining that the love he once had for his father was no longer competing with the truer love he had come to have for Catherine.

Other people or places mentioned in *Algorithms and Blues* provided clues about him and his life. They might be useful in helping Davis understand Brady. He hoped he might be able to anticipate Brady's activities and perhaps help in his capture. *Who is this Reverend Corwin Wellington? Why did he seem to have a closer relationship with Ruth, Brady's mother, than her husband, James, enjoyed?* Brady's mention of him was brief but nonetheless raised some questions.

Another name that intrigued Davis while reading Brady's novel was of someone Brady found on the website Writers Words. He wrote about liking Cora Charles and trusting her to read and publish his manuscript. The way that she treated Brady later led him to conclude that she was probably scamming people like him who wanted to become published authors.

Davis thought about calling Catherine to see how well she was adjusting to the "witness protection" treatment. She might also provide background on the two persons mentioned in Brady's book who raised questions for Davis. But calling her and talking about Brady and his novel didn't seem like anything that would help calm Catherine. Instead, Davis decided to google that information. If his effort failed, he might then later call Catherine.

Reverend Corwin Wellington was the first name Davis typed into the search bar. Other than listing him as pastor of an evangelical church in Greenwich, Connecticut, there was little information about him. Wellington also was active in the church's study group, which was looking for ways to attract more African

Americans. Davis found no quotes or background information, such as where he received his education or positions he held in other evangelical churches.

Just before clicking off the page, he noticed a group of small photos, some of which referred to Wellington's most recent meeting with his study group in Atlanta. The photo patch contained six tiny photo squares with names, and one of them included Ruth Harvey. Using two fingers to enlarge the photo, Davis saw that Ruth stood alongside Reverend Wellington after they returned from attending seminars in Atlanta. There was no further mention of either of them.

The next name that Davis entered in his search engine was Cora Charles. Immediately, he found a link to the Writers Word website and clicked on it. Below the greeting, the site listed a menu that included current podcasts, seminar information, and Zoom sessions.

Davis looked at a photo of an attractive woman in her mid-fifties who was conducting a class for authors in what appeared to be her living room. Those attending the class sat on a sofa or chairs. When he looked further at the website, he saw that Cora had included not only her email address but also her mailing address as well as a street address for people attending in-person lessons. Davis's research was halted by a boom of thunder followed by lightning so close it seemed inside his very room.

When he caught his breath and returned to the website, he looked again at the address posted for Cora Charles—Ocean Avenue in Santa Monica, California!

55

Contacting Catherine

BRADY HARVEY'S NOVEL SEEMED to be wedged so tight inside his mind that Davis was unable to find alternative distractions. He found it difficult to dismiss the book's mentions of Catherine and Brady in high school, in the musical, and at the after-party events. Just as troubling were the parts about Penny Lane and her father who competed for Catherine's love, and about the pregnancy that Brady said deceived Pemberton Lane, who, Brady wrote, *foolishly thought he could be the father* and thus married her.

Less than a year has passed since Davis and Catherine had fallen in love. But now, reading about her past, made him doubt his ability to find a second chance with love. Davis knew better than to compare Catherine with Ellie. His mind screamed that such thoughts could lead only to giving up on the woman he now found so precious.

He remembered learning from someone, probably mentioned inside a poem, the axiom, *"One who is loved can never be replaced, nor should that purpose ever be sought."*

After allowing the memory of those words to settle inside his mind, Davis decided he needed to hear Catherine's explanation. He needed to get rid of any doubts, and he had to talk to her about them. Before calling, Davis convinced himself that he wouldn't make her feel that he was confronting her or challenging the reality of their own love. He hoped he wouldn't hear any excuses or worse, a mea culpa.

Catherine was excited that Davis chose to break the rule about having no contact with each other. They each asked about how they were handling the threat that was coming from Brady. After briefly discussing the stormy weather, Davis told Catherine about reading Brady's novel. He asked whether she had more to add to what Brady had written about Reverend Corwin Wellington and where he fit into the life of Brady's mother, Ruth.

"There was neighborhood gossip that surely they must have had something more than the practice of religion to discuss when they were alone so often." She laughed. "But as far as anything Brady might have thought about their relationship, it wasn't a concern that he ever talked about during our growing-up years in Greenwich."

Davis decided not to ask about the incident in the Dallas's' pool house or the time Brady's father caught them fooling around there. He did ask how she felt about Brady's description of her popularity with the boys in high school.

"Well, his whole description of many of those incidents left me feeling uncomfortable," she said. "In some ways, it was like going down memory lane, reading about how my life took so many turns during my high school years. I must admit, though, that I felt flattered by Brady's description of my physical appearance and the way it encouraged attention from my classmates and all. Still, that was something that I couldn't even begin to understand."

"Yes, he covered that part very well," Davis acknowledged. "But all of that led up to your senior class musical performance in *Grease*."

"I'm not sure what you're referring to." She sounded suspicious of where the conversation was headed.

Davis recognized that he might be making Catherine uncomfortable. "I'm just asking about the cast party that occurred later and when Brady got into those troubles that perhaps led to significant changes in his life."

After an awkward silence, Davis apologized if his questions had failed to include his concern and support for her.

"But still, you have so many questions now after reading Brady's novel, right?"

"Catherine." Davis's tone was calm and supportive. "My questions are ones that should only be asked when we're together, not when we're talking miles apart on the phone."

"I definitely agree with that. Right now, I want to be in your arms, Davis, more than anything I've ever wanted."

That brought a loving nudge inside of Davis. "Until they capture Brady, it's not something we can do. The police want to keep us safe. We have to trust that this will all work out the way we want it to." After she told him that she loved him, he said he loved her too. They kiss-kissed before saying goodbye.

56

Located on camera

P ATROL OFFICER KAREN FUND WAS thrilled that her assignment
to monitor CCTV camera footage, which originally seemed
like a boring way to spend her afternoon, ended up being an
integral part of the LAPD's efforts to find Brady Harvey. Working
together, Acting Detective Roman Tuttle and Officer Fund used
the FBI Next Generation Identification System software and
entered the data available for Brady Harvey, along with photos
of him from Greenwich police. Already, they'd had a dozen
camera sightings of Brady walking down Wilshire Boulevard
away from Fairfax Avenue toward Santa Monica.

"At approximately 2 p.m., he's seen standing by the Pacific
Amusement Park at Santa Monica Pier," Officer Fund told
Detective Tuttle. She had called to tell him that she had just
been tasked with checking on a missing person from that area.

"A missing person? From that same area?"

Fund waited a moment before answering him. "Yes, that's
right. The person missing is a resident in that luxury building
in the 1200 block along Ocean Avenue. I doubt very much that

she is in the slightest way related to our search for Brady Harvey. Those wealthy people leave nothing to chance when they hire security for themselves and their homes."

Tuttle started to sound excited. "I'm looking at the map of all the Oceanside condominiums and apartments close to the Santa Monica Pier. That address of the missing person, did you say it was in the 1200 block along Ocean Avenue? That's less than a few blocks away from where the camera footage last showed Harvey!"

That came as a huge surprise to Officer Fund, who was then talking to Tuttle from her squad car as she approached that area. She confirmed her location, and he told her to call it in and ask for additional police cars to be sent there ASAP.

"What did you say was the name of the missing person?"

Officer Fund looked at the instructions that she'd received earlier. "It says her name is Ursula, U-r-s-u-l-a. No. No, wait! That's the name of the person who reported her as missing. The woman who's missing is… Cora Charles. C-h-a-r-l-e-s!"

* * *

The conversation with Davis made Catherine realize that others who read *Algorithms and Blues* might have a similar reaction. "Damn you, Brady Harvey!" she shouted. Her life was being summarized through the lies and exaggerations of someone who'd never shown the ability to understand the difference between what was real and what was imaginary. Catherine knew that Davis loved her as much as she loved him, and those doubts he'd just mentioned must never serve Brady's goal of separating them.

Catherine needed to talk with Davis before another moment passed. She knew he was right about how it would be best if they were together—in each other's arms and looking into each other's eyes.

She considered what would be involved to not wait any longer and perhaps order an Uber to take her to him. *But where is Davis now? How can I find him without either calling him first or telling him to meet me somewhere?* That didn't seem likely to happen anyway. He'd just said that the police were keeping them safe by keeping them apart. She knew better than to ask Lloyd Patterson to give her the address of his friend's condominium in Santa Monica. That would surely end with her being urged to remain where she was and subsequently monitored more closely.

She hoped to find a bar or restaurant near the Pier on Ocean Avenue. There she could call Davis and tell him where she was and that she would be waiting for him. She hoped he would slip away from his condo and come to her. After googling the map of such places in Santa Monica, she found just what they needed. She called for the Uber, and when it arrived, she snuck out of her suite at The Carlyle Hotel and left without being observed. When the driver asked for her destination, she told him to take her to Bruno's Italian Restaurant, about one block from the Santa Monica Pier on Ocean Avenue.

57

Killer in the neighborhood

AFTER HE TALKED TO CATHERINE, Davis returned to the notes he jotted down while reading *Algorithms and Blues*. His questions regarding the identity of Rev. Corwin Wellington weren't resolved, as the only thing she remembered about him was there was some neighborhood gossip but nothing that upset Brady enough for him to discuss it with her. Catherine and her family didn't attend Wellington's church, and neither did Brady. James, his father, wasn't a churchgoer. Ruth, however, was not only a member there but also a very active one. She often traveled out of state with the reverend to attend functions or seminars with him.

What really caught Davis's attention was the information about Cora Charles that he'd discovered on the Writers Words website. She was the woman Brady mentioned as a potential publisher for his novel. Davis opened the book to those pages and wondered whether the Santa Monica address was anywhere near his current location. The condominium where he was staying, belonged to Lloyd's friend and was within walking distance of the Santa Monica Amusement Park Pier. Cora Charles made no mention of that feature when showing her address, but still, both addresses were on Ocean Avenue. Davis decided to call Officer Tuttle and point out the connection. He also wanted to tell Tuttle that he noticed that both the Los Angeles County Museum of Art and the Pritzker Parking Garage were close to Wilshire Boulevard, a direct route into Santa Monica.

Tuttle was busy when he took the call from Davis and stopped him from speculating on Brady's whereabouts.

"Davis, I'm sorry," Tuttle interrupted. "We've just learned more information, and we now think that Harvey is right there close to where you are staying." Speaking fast, Tuttle sounded tense and excited. "I've sent police squad cars to secure your building and surrounding area and will assign a patrol officer to go immediately to your condo and stay there with you. Do *not* go out of your condominium. Stay inside with the policeman until we either capture Brady or send out an all-clear.

Chief Detective Fitzgerald was swiftly updated with the news that they might have located Brady Harvey, at least the general area where he was hiding. "If Brady is anywhere inside the same building where the missing person's condominium is, then I have a question." He paused and looked directly at Roman Tuttle. "They do have their own security inside the entrance lobby, right?"

Tuttle confirmed that was accurate and added that he had already spoken to the building management. He'd learned that Cora Charles was seen by their lobby camera returning to her condo at 2:20 p.m. and that she was alone.

"So she was alone, and now someone has reported her as a missing person?"

Roman Tuttle's facial expression swiftly turned from confident to being confused. If she came in and never seen leaving afterward, then that could only mean that she was still in her condominium.

"I'll send Officer Fund over to check and see if maybe she's just asleep or perhaps fallen and can't get up or something like that," Tuttle responded.

"Yes, that's what should be done now," Fitzgerald said. "Let's double-check with the person who called in the missing person report, Ursula, and find out if anyone was living with or perhaps visited Cora Charles earlier."

"I'm on it," Tuttle said, "and I'll have that information to you within the next half hour."

Fitzgerald looked like he still wasn't satisfied with how Acting Detective Tuttle was performing. "Make it happen *faster!*"

58

Officer Fund's findings

KAREN FUND WAS THE POLICE officer closest to Cora Charles's address on Ocean Avenue when Tuttle put out the call for a patrol car to head there and get answers regarding any visitors.

"I'm parked right on the condo's entry drive," she answered Tuttle. "Should I wait here for backup, or how long should I expect to stay here?" She hoped to be with the crew searching the area for Harvey.

"Not sure yet about how long," he answered. "After you finish up there, I'll need you to head over to where Davis Quigley is staying. I'll get that address to you, but see if anyone where you are now can inform us if that missing person, Cora Charles, might have had any visitors earlier today."

"Roger that," she answered. "By the way, if no one opens the door, how can we know if she's okay or asleep or…?"

Tuttle was quiet for a few seconds. His mind was busy, considering how to search for Brady Harvey in that neighborhood. "See if any neighbor has access to her condo. If not, I'll send over one of the patrol squads to help you get inside to make your checkups. No search warrant is needed for this action."

Core Charles' neighbor was obliging and, by prior arrangement, had the code to unlock her front door. She stayed in the hall as Officer Fund called out for Cora or anyone else there to make themselves known. The only light in the condominium came from outside and was barely more help than the officer's flashlight. She shined the flashlight left and right as she slowly walked through the rooms but found no one. Then, as she looked to her left while entering the kitchen, she stumbled on something and fell.

What the neighbor heard next was Officer Fund using her mic to call for assistance. She thought she heard the words "appears to be deceased."

Karen Fund's career in the LAPD had been limited to being a patrol cop until the all-out effort to find the man suspected of the earlier murders in Los Angeles led to her partner, Officer Roman Tuttle, being selected for the detail with the Detective Division. While she worked the assignment desk and checked footage from cameras in gas stations or attached to street lights along Wilshire Boulevard, her detail merged with the needs of the search teams that Officer Tuttle was involved in. Then everything happened fast, and she was the officer who discovered the body of Cora Charles. Until then, Officer Fund had never seen a corpse.

On this day, her police academy training kicked in. First, she checked for signs of life in the person she tripped over then reported the incident to police headquarters. She stayed close by and ensured that no one entered the crime scene. When the ambulance personnel arrived, she briefly looked through the remaining rooms in the condominium for any evidence.

Her inspection unearthed a huge clue or, as she called it in her report, a piece of evidence. A laptop on a desk in the room just outside the kitchen was on and still had a message on the screen instructing someone about what was required for his four o'clock appointment that day. The person named was Corwin Wellington.

59

A bit of confusion

A S THEY DROVE ALONG WILSHIRE BOULEVARD, Catherine asked the Uber driver what he could tell her about Bruno's, the restaurant where she hoped to tell Davis to meet her. She planned on calling him once she arrived and telling him that since she'd managed to get out on her own, she expected that he, too, could slip away to join her.

"I love that restaurant," the driver said. "It's a real favorite in these parts, and it's so close to Santa Monica Pier that afterward, you and anyone with you can enjoy a terrific walk down the length of the pier."

Catherine could almost feel his excitement. "I'm going to call someone and have him meet me there. If we decide later to have a cocktail, is there a place you recommend?"

Right then, her cell phone alerted her to a call. The Uber driver guessed it might be the person she planned meeting there. "Looks like he must have known about your idea to meet up, yes?"

She worried instead that Lloyd Patterson was aware of her absence from her suite at the Carlyle Hotel. Would he go looking for her or just notify the police if she failed to answer her phone? Catherine reached inside her pocket and tapped the answer circle on her cell phone.

"Hello, Catherine."

* * *

The detectives who hurried to Cora Charles's condominium—now a crime scene where she was apparently murdered—had already completed the initial phase of their investigation when they received word that Fitzgerald had called for a hurry-up meeting with all members of the team. They left the condo guarded by a police officer and hurried to the bureau headquarters on Vermont Street.

When Fitzgerald opened the meeting, all seven detectives assigned to the case were present and seated across from each other at the long table they used for briefing and planning sessions.

Fitzgerald had previously told Tuttle that since it was him that gathered most of the current information related to the case, he would be called on to open the meeting with reports from the camera footage showing Brady Harvey near the Santa Monica Pier. He should also report what police had learned since then.

"My patrol partner, Officer Karen Fund, was already at the location of the condominium on Ocean Avenue when the decision was made to enter that property and determine if the reason no one was responding there was due to an illness or accident or whatever," he began. "She was able to use the front door code to Cora Charles's condo, and shortly after entering, she discovered the body. The woman had a kitchen towel over her head and an electric appliance cord secured tightly around her neck. The coroner's preliminary finding is that Cora Charles was suffocated to death."

"Do we have any guesses how the person who killed her gained access?" Detective Armstrong asked.

Tuttle smiled. "Within the last hour, we were able to identify a person who had an appointment with Ms. Charles by the name of Corwin Wellington."

The Chief Detective took over. "This man was shown on the victim's laptop to have an appointment to be at her address at 4:00 p.m. The entrance-lobby camera showed him in the hallway to Cora Charles's condominium where it seems he was able to go inside without using the entering the code in the handle."

"So this Wellington guy was admitted into her condominium and then maybe decided to murder her for some reason, making him our prime suspect, right?" Armstrong asked. Not waiting for an answer, he added, "We know of no prior approval for Wellington to be on the premises and we know from Officer Fund that he wasn't present when police gained access and found the victim. Is that also correct?"

Fitzgerald looked at Tuttle, who had moved away from the table after yielding to him earlier. "I've been concerned about the safety of Davis Quigley, who remains number one on Brady Harvey's hit list. Because of that, I stayed in contact with Quigley after the murders on Wilshire Boulevard and knew he was being kept in hiding in a condominium that, coincidentally, is also on Ocean Avenue. When I called to make him aware of this, I also told him about the murder of Cora Charles."

"What, pray tell, made you think that giving this information to Davis Quigley was going to make him any safer than otherwise? And how is all of that going to help us find this suspect, either of them?" Armstrong mocked.

Roman Tuttle knew better than to argue with the senior detective. Nonetheless, he was being shown up for his lack of experience as a detective and couldn't help smiling when he answered Armstrong.

"Davis Quigley knew many things about Corwin Wellington, which he said he learned by reading *Algorithms and Blues*. Corwin Wellington is a close personal friend of Ruth Harvey, Brady's mother. I called Greenwich police, and they ran a squad to Wellington's home address in that city where they found him and verified his alibi regarding the times shown on the lobby and hall cameras. They emailed us his photo, which proved he wasn't the person using that name who had an appointment with Ms. Charles."

By then, Lieutenant Fitzgerald was smiling. His rookie inspector was indeed able to handle Detective Armstrong.

"So, where does any of this crap help us not only find the person who murdered Cora Charles but in any way answer a thing about Brady Harvey?" Armstrong persisted.

"Well, the photo of the man using the Wellington name for the appointment on Writers words website turned out to match our photos of Brady Harvey. Since we have multiple squads looking through every nook and cranny in the entire area that surrounds the businesses and buildings along Ocean Avenue, I'm feeling much more confident than I have been since that bastard came to Los Angeles," Fitzgerald said concluding their meeting.

60

Surrounded!

H ELLO."
Once again, he spoke only that one word. It did not, how-
ever, cause the same level of fright as it had the previous time.
Catherine was already aware that Brady had escaped from the
Los Angeles police by abandoning the car he'd stolen from
Jeanne McHale. He had simply walked away.

"Brady?" she asked.

"I can't take more than ninety seconds to say what I need for
you to do right now," Brady said in a rushed response. "Trust
me. I know that you're passing by the pier in what's probably an
Uber car. Don't even be concerned with how I know this. Where
is he driving you?"

Catherine was shocked that Brady already knew of her whereabouts. She looked ahead and behind and on each side of the
car. *Where can Brady be? He sees me now?* Frightened but wanting
him to keep talking so that she could have the driver call 911,
Catherine took her phone away from her mouth and whispered
that she needed the police—right away! The driver turned back

and saw the desperate fear in her eyes and pulled to the curb. They were a block from Bruno's.

"Please, Brady! Please just leave me alone."

"Okay, you've stopped. I'll meet you and that prick writer friend of yours inside the park in ten minutes. Get him here, and do not—*do not*—call the police. If you just do this, all will become clear then. If you choose not to do this, I'll be forced to bring it to a finish… for all of us."

Again, he left no opportunity for Catherine to answer. The phone call ended.

Although he pulled over and stopped, the Uber driver apparently didn't feel he could call the police without knowing more. "Ma'am, what kind of trouble are you in?"

Catherine was frustrated. Somehow, Brady knew where she was, so rather than responding to the driver she called 911 herself.

"That man the police are searching for, the murderer, Brady Harvey? He's trying to kill me, I think. Where? Ocean Avenue. Somewhere by the pier. He's watching me now. I'm in an Uber. He must be close to us. What? No, I don't see him. We're parked close to Bruno's restaurant. Please hurry!"

The driver was listening to the call and had figured out how Brady knew where they were. "He's tracking your location on your cell phone," he said. "Throw that fucking phone out of this car right now! I'm heading as far away as I can as fast as I can! Throw the phone out now or else. I don't want that phone anywhere near me!"

Catherine's mind raced. She understood now how Brady knew where she was. But she needed her phone so she could warn Davis. Brady demanded that she and Davis get to some park "or else." He didn't say which park or where it was located. He just said for her to do that within ten minutes. *But how? Where?*

Her driver was clearly as frightened as she was. "I'm sorry, lady, but I can't wait any longer. I'm leaving and want you to leave with me, but that damn phone has to be thrown away, and I mean *now!*" He stepped out of the car and held the door open and screamed for her to get out.

"Right here?" she cried. "Can't you at least take me to the safety of the restaurant?"

The driver looked around and apparently realized they were sitting targets. He jumped back behind the wheel and pulled away from the curb. He tapped 911 on his phone and told the operator to send police to Bruno's Restaurant on Ocean Avenue. "The wanted man, the killer, is after us!"

When they reached the restaurant, the driver stopped. "Lady, I don't think you'll be safe here. Just please throw out your phone, and let's get away."

Before Catherine could act, she heard sirens.

A squad car pulled in front of their Uber car, and another came close by on their side of the street, blocking it in. A policeman in the squad car in front jumped out with his gun drawn and commanded everyone in the car to come out with their hands over their heads. A third police car pulled up and stopped in the middle of the street, blocking traffic.

61

Death waits for no one!

C HIEF FITZGERALD SAW EVERYTHING happening on Ocean Avenue. He was watching video from the cameras on the uniforms of police at the scene. "All units," he commanded, "surround the 1600 block on Ocean Avenue and block all traffic."

Acting Detective Roman Tuttle, who had just called Davis instructing him to stay inside, stood near Fitzgerald where they both watched and listened to everything as it appeared on multiple wall-mounted computer screens.

Davis could hear much of everything happening through Tuttle's phone. Confused and feeling helpless, when he heard Tuttle inform his chief that the woman that police had just ordered to exit the car was Catherine Lane but the man with her wasn't Harvey, Davis panicked. All he could think about was that he had to be there to protect Catherine. It was all happening close by. He didn't need a car to get to her. He could run to the 1600 block of Ocean Avenue. His safety be damned!

"The whole scene on Ocean Avenue is simply crazy growing into crazier," Tuttle told Officer Karen Fund who was in her position. "And now this guy, Davis Quigley, seems hell-bent on making everything **craziest!**"

"I know. Have you been able to spot him anywhere around the scene?"

Tuttle eagerly looked at the computer screens when he saw someone who looked like… "Yes. Yes!" Tuttle shouted. "There he is. He's busting his butt to get through the crowd that's gathered across the street."

Fitzgerald glared at Tuttle. "There *who* is?" he demanded. "And who the fuck are you sharing all this information with?"

Tuttle said he was on the phone with Officer Fund, who'd just notified him that when she went to provide protection for Quigley at his condo, she'd discovered him gone. "He left, and then I saw over your shoulder there on the screen that he was in that crowd across the street from where the police have Catherine Lane's car blocked."

Fitzgerald looked at the screen to see what Tuttle was talking about and saw Davis waving to Catherine across the street. She was being rushed from the Uber car to sit inside the squad car in front of it. The officer drove her away from the growing crowd of onlookers then abruptly stopped and turned in to the entrance to Tongva Park.

Seconds earlier, Officer Fund had called Tuttle to report that cameras around Tongva Park showed Brady Harvey was there and appeared to be hiding in the crowd, watching the Ocean Avenue police activity.

Davis grew more anxious when he couldn't get through the crowd and catch up with Catherine before she was driven away. He saw the squad car turn onto Ocean Avenue and was surprised when it suddenly stopped in front of the entrance to Tongva Park.

Finally getting through the crowd, Davis ran full speed toward the squad car with Catherine inside and saw other police units rushing to Tongva Park. Some of them appeared to surround the park while others drove inside of it. When Davis reached Catherine, he heard her shout for the officer who was in the front seat to let him get into the car with her.

They kissed and embraced then heard someone on the police radio inform the officer that another squad car was on the way there to take Catherine to safety. Almost immediately, Officer Karen Fund arrived.

Following the instructions from Officer Fund to jump into her vehicle, Davis and Catherine were quickly whisked away from Tongva Park.

"We have captured photos of Brady in camera footage the police looked at from stores and intersections and street corners along Ocean Avenue," she told them as she drove past the Santa Monica Pier and Amusement Park. "Chief of Detectives Fitzgerald saw you there and ordered me to take you away while police there go after Brady. We think he's keeping out of sight somewhere inside the park."

Catherine placed her head on Davis's chest. "Everything is happening. You know that he just called me again, right?"

Davis hugged Catherine tighter, hoping to calm her trembling body. She was right about how everything was moving all at once. She was fearful of all the activity, and he realized he knew little more than she did. "Where are we going?" he asked Officer Fund.

Before she could respond, they arrived at the condo where he was temporarily staying.

"Fitzgerald wants you both to remain safe and well-guarded until we put an end to this nightmare," she said as they walked through the lobby and took an elevator to the fourth floor. "The three of us are going to stay right here, together in Davis's place for the duration of the police search underway at Tongva Park. If we catch Brady tonight, that'll end the danger, then I'll take you back to The Carlyle Hotel," she said.

Catherine's mind raced through all kinds of thoughts, everything from the danger they were still in to the storm outside. She looked at Davis and asked what the plan was if Brady remained on the loose. "I have all of my clothes and toiletries and the like at the Carlyle Hotel and…"

Officer Fund led them to Davis's condo, first ensuring that no surprises waited inside. A few minutes passed before she returned and waved them inside.

Karen Fund had a bland look on her face hoping to make things seem a bit normal. She noticed a newspaper ad lying on the kitchen counter and, turning to Davis, suggested that perhaps the best thing for the three of them to do was what she suspected most of the rest of Santa Monica was doing—turning on the TV, and watching what was happening over at Tongva Park.

*　*　*

Back in Greenwich Ruth Harvey's blood pressure was shooting up as she watched live coverage on CNN of the events happening faraway in Santa Monica. Two days ago, she'd discovered that her son was suspected in three murders, and everything had gotten worse from there. She couldn't sleep and found it too difficult to even pray. The news persons kept saying that Brady had killed people and was considered dangerous to anyone who had the misfortune of getting in his way.

"They just don't know Brady," she told Corwin Wellington who was at her side and just as interested in what was on the TV. "Now they say that he's cornered in that crazy park and they're sure to get him. What's that's supposed to mean? Get him how? Are they not going to stop until they kill him?"

The doorbell rang, and they looked at each other. Neither of them was expecting a caller. Ruth finally answered the door while Corwin sat frozen in place on the sofa watching the television. Ruth looked through the peephole thinking it must be a neighbor or someone from the *Tribune* who wanted to see how she was handling all that was happening.

"Corwin, come quick! It's Brady's attorney, Lester Worth."

Reverend Wellington quickly joined them at the door, relieved that it wasn't anyone who would find his presence there suspicious enough to add to the growing gossip that he recently became aware of. As the men exchanged greetings, Ruth spied some sudden activity on her television and left them standing together by the front door.

"I just received a text from Sandra Pierce," Worth said. "You know, the woman who wants to buy the rights to Brady's novel."

"Huh? Oh yes, we've talked," Corwin said. "But you know what's going on right now, don't you? Why was that text important enough for you to run over and tell Ruth about it?"

"That's just it," the lawyer said. "Ms. Pierce is also watching the news very intensely. She's concerned that they'll soon capture Brady."

"Yes, it's beginning to look like that," Corwin said, implying that he was still waiting to hear what had really persuaded Brady's attorney to come over just now.

"Ms. Pierce asked me to fly to Los Angeles tonight so that when they take Brady into custody, I'll be there to advise him and make certain his right to remain silent is protected."

"You two are worried about that right now?" Wellington asked.

"It's the book, the biography rights to *Algorithms and Blues* that we've agreed to sell to her, that she wants protected by keeping Brady quiet when they interrogate him," the attorney explained.

Ruth heard much of their conversation, preventing her from focusing on TV coverage of the police pursuit of her son. She returned to join their discussion and asked the attorney what he suggested she do.

Lester Worth pulled out a hastily prepared legal document authorizing him to act on behalf of her and her mentally ill son and asked her to sign. It included verbiage stating that Ruth agreed to pay all the travel and other expenses for the attorney during his stay in Los Angeles.

62

Breaking News on the national network

REPORTER CARRIE FERGUS COULDN'T believe her good fortune in being sent to cover the search for suspected killer Brady Harvey. Although she had only recently begun her career there at KABC-TV as a low-level on-the-scene reporter, she always described her job to friends as "simply thrilling." None of the other times, however, would probably be as important as the one she was working on for the nightly news that evening.

"As you can see, David, it's raining now in Santa Monica, and nowhere can it be less wanted than right here on Ocean Avenue, where hundreds have crowded into this area watching police clear everyone out of Tongva Park while searching for the man whom police named as a mass murderer. Brady Harvey is the man suspected of having killed three persons on Sunday in two locations along Wilshire Boulevard. The police responded in hopes of capturing him, but he escaped. Later, it was determined that Brady simply walked along Wilshire Boulevard, away from the trap the police had set up."

She turned to her left, allowing the camera to show more police cars arriving at the park. "Harvey was seen on camera footage that police use to locate persons wanted for committing crimes," she continued. "He was discovered within the last hour walking along Ocean Avenue near Tongva Park right here in Santa Monica. When the cameras spotted him hiding in the crowd that had gathered to watch another police action taking place close by, it was subsequently discovered that Harvey moved from that group to hide inside the park. The police surrounded the park, and they're inside now, clearing it of visitors as they search for this man who is thought to be armed and definitely considered very dangerous."

Television cameras were set up all around the young reporter while helicopters buzzed overhead inside the park. Yellow police tape was secured around nearby tree trunks and park benches, effectively establishing that the entire park was considered a crime scene. Both Sky Map7 and Air7HD provided videos to the television studios, showing the cautious but aggressive actions being taken by police conducting the search.

The KABC-TV reporter left her position by the front entrance and followed a small crowd who were screaming that they'd just seen someone inside being chased through the water park toward one of the large structures known as Weather Field Number 1. The cameraman followed closely and quickly set up a position for the update. Rain and wind increased, and streaks of lightning pierced the darkness, providing an eerie background for all there as well as those watching in homes across not only California but also much of the country.

"David?" Carrie called out the name of the TV News Anchor, wanting to alert viewers to the reason for the excitement inside and outside Tongva Park. "David, I'm being told that we can see where the police have someone cornered inside the park, and they're yelling for him to surrender and come away from the structure… where he… Wait! We can see him now! Over there!" She pointed for the camera to show the large Weather Field Number 1 structure, where two policemen had chased the man inside.

As police moved closer to the structure, the camera clearly showed Brady bracing himself against the storm's wind by grasping and standing between two of the steel poles. Just then something very loud happened. A lightning bolt shot through the clouds, striking the poles. A crash of thunder deadened all sound in the surrounding area which resumed only after shouts were heard coming from the police in pursued of their target

"He's down!" the closest policeman yelled.

63

Shock and sadness

A S THE SCENE AROUND THE PARK grew increasingly tense, the reverend and the lawyer, keeping their eyes on Ruth Harvey while also on the TV, stopped talking at the doorway and rushed to watch the developing drama and to stand alongside of Brady's mother. Her eyes were glued to the television.

"My son… Oh please, God. My son. Oh no!" was all Ruth could say as she watched the police cautiously urging Brady to leave the Weather Field structure and surrender. "Will they shoot him? **Brady, please give up. They have guns!**"

Wellington stood next to Ruth and tried to comfort her with words from the scriptures. "He will surrender," the reverend said with confidence. "Look there. Brady's signaling to the police now. See?"

Then, with the heavy rain blurring the television picture, Ruth's eyes rose straight up towards the ceiling, praying for her son to let go of the steel poles and let the policemen help him to stay alive. "Please. *Please.* Please. ……" Suddenly, everything became as bright and clear as if it were occurring right there in her living room. Brady had listened to her or at least to her prayers. He moved around inside of the structure and motioned to police that he was surrendering. Then the thunder boomed and jolted everyone watching.

"He's down!"

Lester Worth heard it first and surprised himself when he repeated it although not really understanding what was happening there.

Corwin pulled Ruth closer as she screamed, **"No! No, no. Please, God..."**

Carrie Fergus appeared to need help to continue standing. "David", she tried to resume her reporting while clearly shaken, "Brady has been struck by that bolt of lightning, and he's lying between the steel poles in the Weather Field structure... and... he is showing no... no sign of life."

64

Santa Monica

THE GRIM SCENE OUTSIDE THE park continued as the KABC-TV reporter was wrapping up her on-the-scene interview with Chief Detective Fitzgerald.

"The coroner was present within a few minutes after the suspect was struck by lightning and has pronounced him dead. The body will be taken to the Los Angeles County Coroner's location, where additional information will determine the victim's identity and a complete examination of cause of death," Chief Fitzgerald responded to her questions.

Carrie Fergus added, "This has ended in perhaps the most tragic way possible. TV viewers throughout Santa Monica and many other cities that linked to our broadcast are feeling much safer knowing that it has ended."

Fitzgerald raised his eyebrows, indicating her summation was incomplete. "Brady Harvey was wanted for the murders that were committed on Sunday. He's also suspected now to have been involved in a murder that happened this afternoon in a condominium nearby on Ocean Avenue."

* * *

Davis felt confused by the extent of Catherine's grief. Along with Officer Fund, Catherine and he watched the final moments of the police search for Brady Harvey and the shocking way it concluded. Shortly afterward, Officer Fund left, telling Davis that Catherine was obviously unable to be of further assistance to the investigation after witnessing the death of her former neighbor. She suggested that both of them stay together in seclusion to avoid the press or others interested in interviewing them about Brady.

Once Officer Fund left them, Catherine's crying became more intense. Davis hugged her closer but she pulled away saying that she needed time to herself. He kissed her and said he understood saying that he would remain in the living room while she rested and perhaps got some sleep. When she went into to the bedroom, she closed the door.

Though her reaction wasn't something he understood, Davis now knew that she and Brady had indeed been close friends, at least in high school. Considering the shock that she had to have experienced watching the tragic end to Brady's life made it easier to realize her need to be alone.

Davis checked his cell phone and found numerous messages, many from friends concerned about him regarding the events that were televised nationwide. Cooper Logan was first to get a reply from him. Davis sent a text telling him how much he appreciated their friendship, especially at this point in his life. Coop and his family could expect Davis to return home soon. What Davis felt less sure about was whether Catherine would be with him when he returned.

Lloyd Patterson called Davis and explained that he'd first tried to reach Catherine. "I know that the two of you have just gone through something that would simply overwhelm most people. I was hoping that you might be able to speak with Catherine and tell her how relieved we all are at Hurd Patterson, knowing now that she, and you also, are safe."

"I'm sure she'll call you herself," Davis said. "Probably after she gets some sleep and takes some time to recover." Davis added that he appreciated the loan of Lloyd's friend's condominium as his safe place while Brady was still on the loose.

Sandra Pierce was next to get a reply.

"Oh, Davis." She sounded very happy that he'd decided to call her back so soon after the Brady Harvey threat ended. "I watched everything. I was so afraid for you and Catherine while it was happening but still much taken by the excitement of it all."

Davis wondered about her use of the word "excitement." It seemed to be a strange way of putting it. The editor side of her might wish to have it removed by her proofreader side, he silently mused. "Yes, it's good that it's been resolved. At least for me, that's the case. You know me, Sandra. I'm always looking for motives, and dammit anyway, I've never understood his reason for wanting to kill me and deciding that murdering Charlotte and Arthur and Cora Charles and causing Kirsch's death was any way to win back someone he decided was his and his alone."

Sandra agreed. "You're one who has asked that question, w-h-y, more than any author I've become acquainted with in my entire life," she said in a soothing voice. "But Davis, if you don't mind me asking, where did that reference about his and his alone come from?"

Davis was thrown by her question. "I… I just said it, I suspect, because it's the only way of fathoming Brady's conclusion about his and Catherine' lives since their high school days ended their times together Why do you ask?"

Sandra laughed and told Davis that Richard Drake was writing a biography of Brady and had used that title for his manuscript.

"Well, maybe that's where it came from," Davis considered. "I heard he was to be a guest on a podcast by that columnist Will Jennings, and perhaps that was in the tease. I was involved in way too much, as you already know, to have been able to listen in."

Sandra said she knew that Franz Graber was also going to write "a book about a book" that would compete with Drake's. "But this call isn't the time to drift into discussions about Brady's biography. When I texted you, the only thing on my mind was you and how you're doing. The rest can wait. Agree?"

65

The secrets in our souls

CATHERINE WAS AWAKENED BY sunlight shining too brightly for it to still be morning. As she lay all alone, she struggled to remember where she was, how she got here, and who brought her to this large cloud-soft king-size bed next to a floor-to-ceiling window with a view of the ocean. She was aware that she was emerging from sleep and seemed only to remember that there was danger and people causing her to worry. Or was that just one person? She began remembering that she was with someone and was crying but not for any reason that made sense. Why was she so frightened? Why was she so sad?

She turned over and discovered that she wasn't dressed in what she recalled wearing in her dream. There, she was dressed in much more than merely the black T-shirt and panties she now was wearing. In her dream, she was driving a police car, then suddenly, she was in some place, watching someone in a park, and he was waving that he needed to tell her something. He looked so desperate!

Catherine opened her eyes, wanting to free herself from the curious feeling of not being able to shake loose from these thoughts, these feelings. She had no answer for any of them as she stepped from the bed and walked out of the room.

Davis was standing nearby in the living room and hurried over to where she entered.

It's okay now. I'm safe now. The fog that gripped and tricked her mind slowly ebbed further away, replaced with seeing Davis. He pulled her into his arms. They stood holding onto each other without speaking. They knew, now, all that ever needed to be known.

* * *

Catherine was feeling much more herself than when she first awoke. She and Davis were now walking on the sandy beach within steps of the Santa Monica Pier. They were with each other. They stopped only when he spotted a sea shell that he picked up and impressed her with how far it sailed from his hand away into the ocean.

About the Author

Tom Wood became a reporter and byline journalist at four newspapers in suburban Chicago after retiring from the U.S. Postal service. *Alone Along Writers' Roads* is his first published novel.

Tom is available for select readings and locations. To inquire about a possible appearance email rightermi@gmail.com.